ALSO BY CINDY PON

Silver Phoenix

Fury of the Phoenix

Serpentine

Sacrifice

Want

RUSE

CINDY PON

SIMON PULSE

NEW YORK   LONDON   TORONTO   SYDNEY   NEW DELHI

SIMON PULSE

An imprint of Simon & Schuster Children's Publishing Division

1230 Avenue of the Americas, New York, New York 10020

First Simon Pulse hardcover edition March 2019

Text copyright © 2019 by Cindy Pon

Jacket illustration copyright © 2019 by Jason Chan (front panel) and

Thinkstock (back panel and flaps)

All rights reserved, including the right of reproduction in whole or in part in any form.

SIMON PULSE and colophon are registered trademarks of Simon & Schuster, Inc.

For information about special discounts for bulk purchases, please contact

Simon & Schuster Special Sales at 1-866-506-1949 or business@simonandschuster.com.

The Simon & Schuster Speakers Bureau can bring authors to your live event.

For more information or to book an event contact the Simon & Schuster

Speakers Bureau at 1-866-248-3049 or visit our website at www.simonspeakers.com.

Designed by Steve Scott

The text of this book was set in Adobe Garamond.

Manufactured in the United States of America

10 9 8 7 6 5 4 3 2 1

Library of Congress Cataloging-in-Publication Data

Names: Pon, Cindy, author.

Title: Ruse / Cindy Pon.

Description: First Simon Pulse hardcover edition. | New York : Simon Pulse, 2019. |

Sequel to: Want. | Summary: "Jason Zhou, his friends, and Daiyu play a treacherous cat and mouse game in the labyrinthine streets of Shanghai, determined on taking back what Jin had stolen"—Provided by publisher.

Identifiers: LCCN 2018041435 | ISBN 9781534419926 (hardcover)

Subjects: | CYAC: Pollution–Fiction. | Virus diseases–Fiction. | Survival–Fiction. | Shanghai (China)–Fiction. | China–Fiction. | Science fiction.

Classification: LCC PZ7.P77215 Rus 2019 | DDC [Fic]–dc23

LC record available at https://lccn.loc.gov/2018041435

ISBN 9781534419940 (eBook)

For my father, Steve Pon, who loved to tell a tall tale

CHAPTER ONE

THE BOMBING

LINGYI

Lingyi was their leader. And she was sending them headlong into danger—possibly even to their deaths.

She forced herself not to dwell on this, on every possible awful outcome. She needed to keep the surge of panic at bay. If Lingyi lost focus, her friends would pay for it.

It was a huge risk to blow up Jin Corp the same night they needed to save Zhou, but they couldn't use the fire alarm ploy twice. It was tonight or never. Still, it hadn't felt quite real before—a challenging game, a far-fetched fantasy. But there was a sense of finality tonight, when she had kissed Iris once before the group departed. They had all agreed to do this, had worked for months toward this end, but planning and doing were two very different things.

She feared for their lives.

Lingyi studied the nine video feeds pulled up on her wall screen. Three were from the body cams attached to Iris, Victor, and Arun, following their every movement. The other six were from Jin Corp, with one trained on the main entrance and lobby, one directed at the back door her friends would use, and another showing Zhou, who was slumped in a chair, unmoving. She toggled between various corridors and areas in Jin Corp with the other three feeds.

Lingyi paced the small area of her sitting room. Iris had always insisted they needed a bigger apartment, but Lingyi thought this was perfect. Cozy. She had chosen to orchestrate everything from her apartment tonight instead of their headquarters. Headquarters was too filled with the presence of her friends—echoes of them at every turn. She hadn't expected to feel the same hollow emptiness in her apartment.

Iris wasn't sprawled on their sofa, napping, with a hand tucked beneath her ear—her favorite pose. She was nearing the back entrance of Jin Corp, and from her body cam, Victor and Arun were right beside her. Lingyi tapped the screen that showed Zhou in that basement room littered with old machines. Flickering fluorescent light illuminated the space. She stared at Zhou, trying to detect any movement at all; the rise and fall of his chest, the jerk of a knee or shoulder, but saw nothing. There was no sound from Jin Corp's feeds, and she was terrified for him.

"You there, boss?" Victor's voice came in close and clear, as if he were standing beside her in the room.

Lingyi jumped. "Here. Everything looks good." She made her tone light, not letting the anxiety slip in. They needed her confidence and guidance so they could do their tasks quickly and right. "The building's quiet. Move fast. I won't have access to the security system until the fire alarm is triggered." If a security person happened to see them slip into the building, it'd only make things harder.

Iris used Daiyu's access code to try and enter the building. Lingyi held her breath, her heart in her throat. After a few seconds, the door clicked open and they each filed in, letting it close securely behind them.

"Arun," Lingyi said into her earpiece. "Zhou is in one of the rooms in the basement. Go down one level."

"Got it, boss," Arun replied.

They had gone over everything at headquarters earlier that day. But Lingyi couldn't help but call out the commands, directing each of them to their tasks. It gave her a false sense of control. "You have twenty minutes once the alarm goes off," Lingyi reiterated.

They knew, but Lingyi's palms dampened with sweat from saying it out loud. Arun headed down a dark stairwell, emerging onto a long corridor filled with blank doors. It was dimly lit; he began trying the knobs. He didn't expect to run into anyone down there.

The majority of the doors swung open, revealing empty rooms filled with machinery and other junk stored below the building. He used the motion detector for the rooms that were locked to try and locate Zhou. Lingyi's heart speeded up every time, but the detector never found him behind the locked doors.

Arun was cursing under his breath, and everyone could hear it. "I've already checked all the rooms on the right side. I need more time."

He picked up his pace, running from one door to the next, his cam bobbing with the motion.

"I'm coming up on the fire alarm," Iris replied. "The longer we hold off, the more likely we'll be discovered."

"Just five minutes." Arun was panting.

Five minutes to give security a chance to glance at any of the cameras that showed Arun, Vic, or Iris skulking around. Five minutes could give them all away. They'd already discussed and argued over this earlier in the afternoon. Iris was right.

"We don't have time," Vic said in a grim voice. "Stick with the plan." Lingyi knew Victor loved Zhou like a brother—it couldn't have been an easy thing to say.

"He's somewhere down there, Arun," Lingyi said, her chest constricting. Was she issuing Zhou's death sentence? "Iris, sound the alarm."

Iris's gloved hand pulled down on the red handle. A pulsing alarm immediately filled Lingyi's earpiece. A soothing female voice broadcasted over the building's sound system, "Attention. Please leave the building via your nearest exit. You have ten minutes."

Lingyi swung into her seat at her glass-top desk, accessing Jin Corp's main security system now that the alarm had been sounded. The building was in emergency mode. Even the security crew had left their areas. Lingyi watched as a few employees trickled out of the main entrance. At this time of night, they were mostly security and custodial staff.

Vic and Iris stayed out of sight as Arun continued to run down the basement corridor, trying doors. Lingyi checked on Zhou's feed. To her immense relief, he had woken, probably from the blaring noise of the alarm. He looked around, slowly rolling his shoulders, possibly trying to get out of his bindings. "Hang on, Zhou, Arun's on his way," she said, even though she knew he had no way of hearing her.

"I can't find him!" Arun shouted in frustration.

"Keep looking," Lingyi replied. "He's down there and awake!"

Arun began screaming Zhou's name over the sound of the insistent alarm. But Zhou's mouth was bound, and even as Arun shouted, Zhou gave no indication he could hear him.

Lingyi forced herself to turn her attention to the ground floor.

Vic and Iris were running down a wide corridor and stopped at an elevator. Seven minutes in, and the building already looked empty. There were a few stragglers hurrying toward their nearest exit. "The elevator is clear," she said, toggling between the security cameras.

"Thanks, boss," Iris and Vic replied at the same time.

They entered the empty car, and Victor punched the third- and fifth-floor buttons. He then adjusted the silver cuff link at his wrist. Vic had put on a sleek gray suit with a silver vest and blue tie knotted perfectly at his throat. Lingyi almost smiled, would have teased him under any other circumstances. Iris slipped out on the third floor, and Victor got off on the fifth and highest floor. There wasn't enough time to set a bomb on each floor with only two people, but they could strategically set two each on the third and fifth. The bombs would be powerful enough to destroy the inside of the building.

When Iris had argued that she should take the fifth floor, because she was faster than Victor, and the location was riskier, Vic had countered that he had a better handle on the tech, should anything go wrong. In the end, Lingyi made the final call, like she always did. Victor would take the higher floor. Lingyi suddenly realized she could feel her heart thumping hard against her chest, as she followed both Iris and Vic on their feeds.

Arun's panicked voice burst into their earpieces. "I still can't find Zhou. I've checked every room down here twice. We have to abort!"

Lingyi lifted her head to the wall screen, then jumped from her seat, fighting the sick feeling in her stomach. She touched the feed that had displayed the dingy basement room Zhou had been trapped in. It showed only an empty chair. "He's gone!" she shouted.

"What?" Arun stood stock-still in the middle of the basement corridor. "Where did he go? Is he still in the building?"

Lingyi pushed up her glasses with a shaking hand. "I don't know. But we can't abort now."

"First bomb is set," Iris said.

"First bomb is set," Victor replied not ten seconds later.

There were eight minutes left before people would be let back into the building.

They were halfway there with two bombs set. No turning back now.

Lingyi skidded back to her desk, toggling through all the cameras located within the basement of Jin Corp on her computer—more than two dozen. Most of them only showed empty, dark rooms. "Arun, you have to get out. I don't know where Zhou is."

He let out a long string of curses. "I won't just leave him!"

Lingyi ignored the sudden stinging pressure behind her eyes. *Zhou.* She flicked between the feeds again, seeing nothing. She loved him like a brother too. Now she was sealing his fate, abandoning him. "Arun. There's less than six minutes and the bombs are going to blow." Her voice cracked. "Go. Leave the building now!"

"Second bomb set," Iris said into their earpieces.

Arun was staring down on the floor, both hands clenched into fists. "Fuck!" he shouted, then began running toward the stairwell. She watched until his feed showed he was out in the alleyway again, behind Jin Corp.

Lingyi let out a long breath, even as she swiped at the corner of her eye, knocking her glasses askew. Readjusting them, she checked on

Iris's and Victor's progress. Iris was in another stairwell, headed down to the ground floor. Vic's feed showed him fiddling with his second bomb. The timer was counting down already, but one of the three lights that controlled it glowed red, while the other two were green.

Something was wrong.

"Victor," she said into her earpiece, trying to keep her voice even. "Leave it. Now."

He didn't budge. She watched in horror as he worked the wires with his long fingers. Victor wore a rectangular titanium ring on his right hand. Lingyi felt like she was floating out of herself for a moment, adrift. The clock showed less than three minutes before detonation.

Then she slammed back into her body and was screaming again, "Victor!"

"I heard you, boss," Victor replied in a calm tone; cool and collected. "But we're down two bombs without Zhou's help. They all have to blow for the maximum damage we need. I've almost got this." A hand reached up, out of view, and Lingyi saw the word MUTE light up in green on his feed.

"No!" Lingyi screamed.

"Boss," Iris's voice came in through the earpiece. "What's going on? Where's Vic?" She had stopped in a stairwell.

"Keep running, Iris," Lingyi ordered. "Clear the building!" She was trying to draw enough breath. "Now!"

The clock began counting down from one minute. Vic continued to work the wires patiently. Iris stood frozen in the stairwell, and then the first of her bombs went off, so loud Lingyi ripped out her earpiece. Iris's feed shook from the impact, and she was running again, bursting through the emergency exit door onto the ground floor.

Lingyi felt light-headed. Terror smothered her, like a monstrous beast sitting on her chest.

The ground shuddered beneath Victor. He flicked a switch on the bomb, and the light that had been red suddenly turned green. The digital clock started counting down from ten in red. Vic had been crouched over the bomb, but straightened now. He brushed off the sleeves of his suit jacket, then flashed her an *okay* sign with his hand. There was a burst of blinding white light from his feed two seconds later.

"Vic!" she screamed again.

His feed displayed only gray static.

Frantic, she toggled between all the screens, searching for him, knowing what she was doing made no sense. The cameras within Jin Corp showed only chaos, shaking walls and crumbling floors, machinery collapsing onto each other. Iris's feed was obscured with dust and smoke. Tears blurred Lingyi's vision. She grabbed the earpiece and put it back in her ear. Lingyi had to get Iris out.

"Head to the main entrance," Lingyi directed, her voice wavering and thick. She cleared her throat.

"Should I wait for Vic?" Iris asked, pausing at the sliding doors that led into the main entrance area.

"No," Lingyi managed to croak. "I lost his connection." She couldn't bring herself to say anything else.

Iris didn't speak, then pressed the button to open the curved golden doors, revealing the grand foyer. She ran to the front entrance, but the doors wouldn't open for her. She slammed her hand onto the square button, then pounded on the steel doors, but nothing worked.

Lingyi searched through Jin Corp's security system. "The building's in lockdown." She tried to override the command, then worked on manually opening the front entrance. Nothing worked. Lingyi checked who had initiated the lockdown. Jin. Not two minutes after the first bomb went off. "Nothing will open now, not without special access."

"How do I get special access?" Iris shouted above the rumbling noise.

"There are some emergency exits on the ground floor. Turn right. We might be able to use Daiyu's access code to open them." But Lingyi was only guessing. She couldn't face the notion that she might lose Iris, too.

Iris was trying to navigate through the smoke-filled haze in the corridor, when she exclaimed, "Zhou! Thank gods, Arun couldn't find you—"

"Daiyu got me." Lingyi heard Zhou's familiar voice crackle through her earpiece. "She knows the way out."

Lingyi held herself taut, because otherwise, she would collapse onto her desk from relief. Zhou was alive, and Daiyu would take them to safety. Iris was speaking to her, but none of the words were registering. Instead, Lingyi found herself searching through every camera still working in Jin Corp, looking for Victor's familiar shape. He was always slick, always a step ahead. If anyone could actually cheat death, it'd be Vic. She squinted at the corridors filled with smoke, searched the rooms sparking with live wire, writhing like electric serpents.

She checked Iris's feed but couldn't see anything except thick smoke, and the vague sense of someone moving in front of her. Suddenly, she heard Zhou screaming that they needed to go back. To find Vic. Lingyi wanted to say something but couldn't form the words. She heard Iris instead, her love, her heart, convincing him to keep heading toward the exit—telling Zhou that Victor was gone.

No.

Lingyi couldn't see. She wiped her nose with one sleeve, then blinked hard, flicking through the security cameras. There were fewer and fewer that still worked, and all of them showed chaos and ruin; gaping maws, fire, and smoke. She could hear voices speaking on Iris's feed, but Iris didn't say anything again. Then they were outside, clear of the crumbling building.

Lingyi drew a long breath that erupted into shaking sobs.

They were out.

Iris and Zhou were safe.

Iris's feed jostled as they ran away from Jin Corp. Lingyi felt as if she were floating outside her own body again, untethered. Then Iris spoke directly into her ear, summoning Lingyi back to herself. "He's not coming."

Lingyi tried to grasp what Iris meant. No, Vic wasn't coming. *Vic was dead.* Then she saw Zhou standing there beside a girl who looked vaguely familiar. "Let me speak with him," Lingyi said, her voice cracking.

Iris stalked toward Zhou and shoved her earpiece into Zhou's ear.

"Come home, Zhou," Lingyi managed to say.

"Is Arun all right?" he asked.

"I'm here, bro. Where *were* you?" Arun interjected from his earpiece. "I searched all through the basement."

"There are two levels," Lingyi heard the girl standing beside Zhou say in a quiet voice. Daiyu.

Arun had been on the wrong floor, because Lingyi hadn't studied the building plans thoroughly enough.

"I need some time," Zhou finally replied in a hoarse voice. "Victor's dead."

"Oh, Zhou." Lingyi broke into a sob. "I know. Go with Iris. Please."

A long pause. "I can't," he finally said.

Iris and Zhou argued, but Lingyi barely heard them.

Lingyi couldn't blame him. She had ordered Arun to abandon him—good as dead. "You're angry," she said. "Because we failed to find you. We left you there—"

"No," he cut her off. "I'm not angry. It was always the mission first. We all knew that."

She did know that. But Lingyi had been the one who had been forced to make all the tough decisions, had forced her friends to abide by the hard choices. And now Vic was dead; and his blood was on her hands. She'd failed them. She said more to Zhou, but it was as if someone else had taken over—someone blathering meaningless words.

Finally, the voices stopped in her earpiece.

Lingyi folded her arms onto the cold glass and rested her head down on them. Most of Jin Corp's cameras had winked out by now, displaying static. She closed her eyes and felt hot tears slide down her face.

The image of Victor giving her an *okay* sign flashed before her eyes, before he, too, had been consumed by gray static.

Lingyi lost track of time.

CHAPTER TWO

JANY

When Jin Feiming's airlimo arrived at Shanghai University graduate housing to pick Jany Tsai up, she gaped from the entrance of her old dormitory building. The invitation from the multibillionaire written in exquisite calligraphy had been shocking enough; now she felt like she was being whisked into a mysterious and unknowable world. Jany was so engrossed in trying to guess why Jin had summoned her, she missed taking in the sights of her short journey. The airlimo glided onto a private runway with Jin's Concord jet waiting, red carpet rolled out to greet her. She had only ever traveled through China by train.

The sleek plane was painted a jade green, with Jin's personal emblem on its side: the character of Jin emblazoned in glittering gold.

The man, Jany thought, was not subtle.

A gorgeous woman dressed in a deep purple qipao greeted her at the top of the stairs leading into the jet. Her black hair was coiled expertly at the nape of her neck. "Ms. Tsai"—she extended a hand to offer Jany a flute of sparkling champagne—"welcome! Mr. Jin is eager to meet you in Beijing."

The short flight was smooth and uneventful. The attendant asked twice if Jany needed anything, but she said no both times. When she deplaned, an airlimo that appeared to be an exact replica of the one that had transported her in Shanghai was ready to whisk her directly to Jin Corp Beijing.

They cruised over the capital, and Jany gazed down with a mixture of awe and horror. She'd never ridden in an airlimo before today, had never imagined she'd get a bird's-eye view of this ancient city. It stretched endlessly beneath her, gray concrete built upon more gray concrete, smothered in a blanket of brown haze. If she had thought Shanghai's air quality was bad, Beijing's was many times worse. Studies had shown that ten years had already been shaved off the life expectancies for those living in northern China. How soon before that was a reality for the entire country?

Her airlimo veered, flying along the edge of the Forbidden City. Jany had never visited Beijing—the trip was far and too expensive for her family, who lived in a small town in the Yunnan province. But she recognized the sprawling imperial grounds immediately, like recalling some deep, ancestral memory. The majestic buildings were set in neatly lined squares. It was clear that the Forbidden City was a no-fly zone, as the airlimo stayed outside its limits. Jany pressed her nose against the window, peering down at golden curved rooflines and all the white stone steps, so clean they seemed to gleam in the hazy light.

The extravagant trip did not impress her, as she was certain was Jin's intent. Instead, she felt overwhelmed by his blatant wealth and wary of his intentions. She had suspicions about why Jin wanted to meet, but they seemed improbable. Jany had no idea what to expect, and she didn't like it.

Not long after, her car glided onto the rooftop of a high-rise, its opaque golden windows reflecting the skyline surrounding them. A tall man in a black suit opened the airlimo door for her. "Welcome to Jin Corp Beijing, Ms. Tsai," he said in a gruff voice.

Jany nodded, gripping the worn straps of her backpack as she slid out of the car. The rooftop held at least a dozen airlimos and air-peds. She followed the taciturn man into an elevator with gold doors, etched with chrysanthemums. "Twenty-ninth floor," he said aloud.

In mere seconds, it seemed, the elevator dinged and the doors opened onto an opulent foyer tiled in white marble. A dark circular mahogany console was set in the middle. Another beautiful woman who was dressed in the same deep purple qipao as the attendant on the plane beamed at Jany as they approached. "Ms. Tsai, welcome to Jin Corp Beijing. Please step forward for your scan."

Jany blanched. Government institutions used retina scans for identification purposes, but why would Jin, whom she had no connection with? The suited man had disappeared behind a discreet side door. "I'd rather not. I have my student ID."

The woman smiled, flashing perfect white teeth. "ID cards are so easily replicated. For your safety as well as the company's, we must insist on verifying your identity."

"How would you even have a record of my retina scan?" Jany asked.

"I assure you that Jin Corp has it on record." She inclined her head in what should have been a gesture of acquiescence, but instead, Jany could feel the hairs on her arms rise. Jin was a private business, which meant it had paid someone for access to retina scans it wasn't supposed to have. This only magnified her unease.

"Jin was the one who wanted to meet with *me*," Jany replied. "Does he want to or not?" She spoke with more bravado than she felt. "I can leave now." She forced herself not to search wildly around the foyer for an exit. She probably couldn't even access the elevator.

The woman pressed two fingers to her ear and dipped her chin. "Yes, sir. I'll send her in." Jin had been watching the entire exchange. Jany knew Jin's reputation as a ruthless businessman, but she suddenly realized how out of her depth she was—she hadn't even told anyone about this meeting.

"Please make your way through the double doors." The woman stood, revealing the intricate embroidering details on her qipao, and swept a hand toward the opposite side of the foyer, where opaque glass doors had slid open. "Mr. Jin is waiting for you."

Jany turned and drew a long breath; there was no going back now. Her sneakers squeaked loudly against the marble floor, and she tried not to cringe. The glass doors opened into a wide hallway aglow with warm ambient lighting. Another woman, this one petite and curvaceous, waited for her. She was dressed in a deep blue suit. "Good afternoon, Ms. Tsai." The woman gave her a slight nod. "Please follow me."

They walked along the endless corridor across plush carpeting. Jany took in as much as she could, but other than walls adorned with exquisite scrolls of Chinese brush paintings, and a few closed doors, the journey offered little. Finally, the woman stopped at double doors inlaid with jade carvings—scenes of mountains, clouds, and pine trees—and stood beneath a domed contraption—a brain wave scanner. Her features were illuminated in blue neon as the scanner confirmed her identity. It stopped with a short whirling noise, and the double doors unlocked. The woman pushed one door back and nodded. Jany entered, gathering courage in knowing Jin was the one who'd asked her to come. She had the upper hand.

She stepped into a corner office with two banks of floor-to-ceiling windows overlooking Beijing. A long wooden table dominated the room, flanked by curve-backed chairs. But Jin himself was sitting on a leather sofa by the windows. He didn't bother to stand, or even to greet her. Jin simply raised an elegant hand and beckoned her over, like she was some obedient lapdog. Not knowing what else to do, Jany approached him.

"Ms. Tsai," he said, scrutinizing her face, then letting his dark eyes take in her worn sweatshirt and faded jeans. There was a hole in the toe of her right sneaker, and she wished more than anything she had worn her other pair of shoes instead, even if these were more comfortable. Jany was certain those sharp eyes missed nothing.

Then anger flared in her chest, because she had felt shame under his gaze. Shame that she was too poor to afford better clothes for this meeting. Jin treated her as lesser than him; like he was used to seeing everyone as his inferior.

"Mr. Jin," she replied, and stared at him unabashedly in turn. The man was trim and well dressed; his suit, shoes, and accessories probably cost more money than she'd ever seen. His thick black hair was perfectly coiffed, and his features were youthful, unlined. She knew Jin was in his midforties, but he glowed with a healthiness and assurance that only wealth could afford.

"Sit." He indicated a leather chair across from him. "I hope you had a smooth journey?" He smiled a smile that did not reach his eyes.

"Yes." Jany did not relax into the chair, but instead sat straight-backed, with her backpack still on.

Jin lifted an eyebrow, then waved a hand. The same woman who had led her here approached with a tray of tea. She poured in silence, then set plates of walnuts, dried dates, and candied pineapples on the table between them before disappearing again.

Jin took a sip of tea. "I'm familiar with your background, Ms. Tsai." His lips curved. "A student with excellent grades and test scores gaining entry into the prestigious Shanghai University's competitive graduate engineering program, continuing to receive top scores and grades"—he steepled his long fingers together—"but what interests me is what you have been doing *outside* the university, on your own."

Jany's scalp crawled. She had suspected Jin had called this meeting about her invention—but how had he known? Fewer than a handful of people were aware of this project she had been working on. "Oh?" she said, keeping her expression blank.

Jin leaned forward. "I understand your air filter is more effective, compact, and energy efficient than what is currently on the market. And likely much cheaper to build. An incredible achievement, Ms. Tsai."

Jany saw no point in denying the fact, but it was clear he didn't know the specifics. Her invention was no ordinary filter. "Why am I here?" she asked.

He refilled his teacup, and even though she was thirsty and hungry, she had nothing. Somehow, she felt if she partook in what was offered, he would gain even more of an upper hand in their meeting.

"You are spare with words and cut to the point." He laughed, and it sounded genuine. "I admire your intelligence and drive, your obviously strong work ethic. I'm always looking to support young inventors and entrepreneurs. . . ." He trailed off.

Jany's heart picked up speed. She had just filed a patent for her design and was ready to research the best way to fund-raise and gain investors, so she could bring her catalyst onto the market. If she could get help from Jin, with his money and reach, anything was possible. "I'm looking for the right investors."

Jin grinned, and it made him appear younger, but wolfish at the same time. He sat back and threw an arm casually across the top of the sofa, then cocked his head. "I'd like to buy your invention from you outright, Ms. Tsai. You do need the money." He uttered the last sentence as a statement. "I can offer you eight million yuan for your air filter. I take it off your hands, you pocket the money and finish your doctoral program." He paused. "Take care of your family."

She felt the blood drain from her face. What did Jin know about her family?

As if he were looking inside her head, Jin continued, "I know your mother has emphysema and your younger brother struggles with asthma—illnesses that can both turn serious without the right medical attention. Your family would benefit so much from this deal. Wouldn't it set your mind at ease?" Jin smiled that fake smile again.

Jany's shoulders tensed. Although Jin's words and tone were kind, she detected an underlying current, and it belied his apparent concern. "I'm not looking to sell."

"Ah." Jin drummed his fingers against the sofa top. "I think you're being rash. To get something like this off the ground might take years—never mind the funding necessary."

"What do you want to do with my invention?" she asked.

"Show us Jin Tower," he voice-commanded.

The wall of windows beside them darkened, went opaque, and then Shanghai's famous skyline came into view. Jany recognized Jin Tower immediately. At 188 floors, it was now the tallest building in the world, a silver shard jutting into the brown skyline.

"My vertical city." Jin tilted his chin toward the Shanghai views. "This is the first, and I plan to build many more throughout China, Taiwan, and the rest of the world. Clean air is a luxury your filters can provide for my vertical cities."

Of course. The filters Jin was using now were huge and cumbersome, requiring special cranes to lift them into his tower. Jany had observed them with interest during the building's construction. They were also massive energy sinks. "I wanted my invention to be used in hospitals, clinics, orphanages"—Jany gripped the armrests to keep her voice even—"for those who need them most."

Jin nodded understandingly. "Of course. I don't see why not."

She barely contained her snort, making a strange choking noise instead. She knew what Jin meant. He'd sell her invention to anyone who wanted it—at the right price. "No."

He leaned forward, capturing her with his sharp gaze. "I'm impressed by your negotiating skills. I'll double my offer: sixteen million yuan."

Jany swallowed hard. She couldn't help thinking of everything she could do with that amount of money—do for her family. She closed her eyes a moment and knew in her gut that Jin would not take no for an answer. She was trying to outsmart a man under criminal investigation for coercion and blackmail in Taiwan, trying to negotiate with someone who believed everyone could be bought for a price. She'd use that belief in her favor. "I . . . I don't know. That's a lot of money." There was no need to act shocked, because she was. "I need to think about it."

Jin smiled, and this one seemed genuine. He was pleased. "Of course. It's a big decision. But I think after a good night's rest, you'll realize it's the right one. You have a suite at the Four Seasons tonight, and everything's on me. Enjoy Beijing. We can talk again tomorrow."

He rose, and she stood awkwardly. The windows became translucent once more. She could see the Forbidden City from here. "I'm sure we'll come to an agreement, Ms. Tsai. My driver will take you to the hotel."

Jin lifted his palm in a gesture of dismissal. The jade doors had slid open noiselessly, and Jany exited the room, relieved that he didn't want a handshake.

▲▼▲

Jany rode to the Four Seasons Hotel in Jin's airlimo in a daze. The driver parked expertly at the front entrance, and she somehow stumbled out and found her way into the hotel's glittering lobby. Dazzling chandeliers cast a dreamlike glow over the rich patrons staying at the hotel, wearing jade and diamond jewelry and clutching designer purses worth more than her family had seen in a lifetime. The purified air smelled slightly perfumed with gardenia. She checked in with a man dressed in a black jacket at the marble reception desk; a massive landscape brush painting served as the reception area's backdrop.

The young man glanced behind her, as if looking for luggage, and smiled graciously. "Will you need help up to your suite, Ms. Tsai?"

Embarrassed, she shook her head. "I'll find my way."

She wandered down a wide corridor flanked by marble columns, then spotted what she was looking for. Slipping into the bathroom, she went into a private toilet more opulent than she'd ever seen and locked the wooden door securely behind her. Quickly, she scrolled through her Palm and booked a ticket for the first available high-speed train from Beijing to Shanghai. There was no way she'd stay to see Jin again the next day. It wasn't until she was settled on the crowded train, the air thick with everyone's breath and sweat, that Jany finally allowed herself to lean back in the seat and let out a long sigh. She'd be back at her dorm in five hours.

▲▼▲

Jany kept glancing over her shoulder on her way home from the train station. The crowds were thinner this late in the evening, and she felt exposed. Unable to decide if she should walk in the well-lit areas or slink through shadowed streets, she finally chose darkness. Having studied at Shanghai University for three years, Jany knew the area well and usually felt safe walking alone, even late at night.

But tonight felt different. She had stayed vigilant during the long train ride home and had not seen anything unusual in the crowded car. Yet ever since she'd exited the train station, she couldn't shake the feeling that she was being watched, being followed. As she slinked down a dark alleyway, she heard someone behind her. Fear settled in her stomach, and she walked faster, glancing over her shoulder. A tall figure strolled a short distance behind, taking brisk steps. He wore a dark cap, and the shadows clung to him. Jany thought she saw a flash of white teeth. Was he smiling at her? Or grimacing in anticipation?

The long, narrow street felt abandoned. No city noises reached them. She began running, and her shoe slipped through a shallow puddle. Jany slammed the heel of her hand against a wall so she wouldn't fall, and she heard a noise from the stranger. A low chuckle. She sprinted full speed now toward the end of the alleyway, which opened onto a main street with more foot traffic. She no longer heard the stranger behind her, but it seemed every thud of her foot was magnified—was he matching her step for step?

Finally, she burst from the side street, nearly slamming into a woman wheeling a wire basket stuffed full of vegetables. Without apologizing, Jany pushed past her and kept running, plowing through a group of men in business suits. One cursed at her, but she didn't pause until she skidded into a brightly lit McDonald's and ran down the stairs to the lower level. There was a back exit by the restroom, she knew, and she pushed through, emerging into another alleyway, this one reeking of rotten cabbage and urine. She kept running, looking back only once. No one was behind her.

When she reached her graduate housing fifteen minutes later, she was out of breath, her heart thumping hard against her rib cage. The tightness in her chest didn't ease even as the main building's door clicked shut behind her. She secured the flimsy lock to her dorm once inside and took stock of the cramped room. Her MacFold, probably her most prized possession, was sitting on the narrow wooden desk where she had left it. All her work on the catalyst existed only there and on a backup drive. She needed to secure her design.

Jany sat on her narrow bed, rubbing her temples. She knew one person who could help her. She reached for her Palm and typed out a message with trembling fingers, remembering the vivacious fourteen-year-old girl she had befriended so many summers ago. Jany and Lingyi had spent two summers together, when her father had let her stay at Lingyi's home in Taipei while she took courses at National Taiwan University. Despite the five-year age gap, they had so much fun exploring the city, and Lingyi's parents had trusted her as a chaperone. Jany felt too paranoid to even dictate the words.

Lingyi, I know it's been years since we've seen each other. I'm in trouble and need your help. Could you meet me in Shanghai as soon as possible? Tell no one.

She felt better as soon as she sent the message. It was clear she needed to take her MacFold and backup drive somewhere for safe-

keeping in the meantime. It was well past two a.m., but Jany set her alarm to be at the Bank of China when they opened at nine a.m. the next morning.

▲▼▲

Her alarm beeped insistently, startling Jany awake from a troubled sleep. It felt like her body had gotten no rest at all. She recalled nightmares of being chased, of fleeing faceless strangers all night. But she left her dorm with a renewed sense of determination. Jin's interest and insistence on buying her invention meant that what she had was really good, brilliant even. It could be a game changer. Had Jin actually sent someone to mug her last night? Or worse? She didn't know what to think.

Jany decided to walk to the Bund, where the Bank of China was located, instead of taking public transportation. Walking always helped to clear her head, and she felt she had a better chance of escaping if pursued on the streets again, rather than being trapped underground on the metro. Barely eight a.m. and the air already felt thick and humid, but August was always like this. She readjusted her face mask and glanced at the pedestrians jostling past her to their work or school, most with their faces hidden behind masks too.

She was just passing the brick facade of the Bund Tea Company on Dianchi Road when someone bumped her hard in the back, so she stumbled into a man dressed in a business suit. He glared at

her but didn't break his stride. As she tried to regain her footing, someone grabbed her messenger bag strap, wrenching her shoulder painfully. Fear surged through her body. Jany spun just in time to see a knife flash and plunge into the thick fabric of her bag. She had her heavy engineering book with her, and it saved her life. Her MacFold and drive were tucked behind the text. If she hadn't twisted around, she would have gotten that knife in her back.

The man tried again to wrest the messenger bag from her, but she gripped the strap in both hands, refusing to let go. His eyes were beady and sharklike above his black face mask. Letting go, he slashed at her and the blade cut through her denim jacket, drawing blood. She didn't feel the cut, only saw the red bloom on her sleeve. Shouting, she stomped the man hard on his foot, then kneed him in the groin—a move she had perfected on the streets of Shanghai against lechers who had wandering hands.

Commuters exclaimed in surprise but skirted around them. No one stopped to help as the thug doubled over in pain, gasping. Over his shoulder, Jany saw another man in a black mask, pushing people aside to reach her. The adrenaline hit her like an injection, snapping Jany from her shock. Jin was desperate and ruthless enough to try and murder her on a crowded sidewalk in broad daylight. Hell if she'd let herself be stabbed like some fool tourist on the streets of Shanghai.

Jany whirled and ran into the morning commute crowd, disappearing into a throng of early sightseers, at least forty strong,

all gathered on the pavement wearing orange caps. They shouted and shoved back as she fought her way through them, swallowing the sob that threatened to tear from her throat. Still, she kept both hands fisted over her messenger bag strap, refusing to let go.

Over my dead body, she thought. Then she realized just how dire her situation was, as her cut continued to bleed, saturating her sleeve. She ignored the sharp aching pain pulsing through her forearm.

She skidded into an empty side street, and then another, running until her lungs hurt. Jany never looked back, too afraid she'd find her killers right behind her. She didn't know she had been crying until the doors of the metro at Nanjing Dong Road slid closed behind her, and she swept a shaking hand across her wet cheek. Passengers stared at her blood-soaked sleeve, and she clutched her arm to her, trying not to give in to the sobs that threatened to rack her body.

CHAPTER THREE

LINGYI

The flight from Taipei to Shanghai took under an hour. Still, Lingyi was hoping she'd be able to sleep through it. She hated flying, but even worse, she'd had trouble sleeping ever since they had blown up Jin Corp six months ago. She had suffered from almost daily nightmares after, unable to recall anything from her dreams, only to be woken again and again with Iris's strong arms wound tight around her as she murmured reassurances, reeling Lingyi back to reality. Lingyi's heart would always be racing and her face wet from tears.

"Do you remember?" Iris would whisper, her lips brushing against Lingyi's throat.

And Lingyi would shake her head.

No, she never remembered.

There were no snippets, not even fragments of an image. What she was left with from those dreams were *feelings*: betrayal, loss, sorrow, regret.

But they would never speak the word that hung in the humid air between them. Because Lingyi was too afraid to face the onslaught of overwhelming emotions, to come to terms with his death; because Iris was too afraid to ask.

Victor.

They never said his name aloud.

The soothing tones of the flight attendant wishing them a pleasant flight had barely faded when the lights dimmed to a cool neon blue in first class. The majority of the passengers had already pulled the VR helmets over their eyes and ears, plugged into their entertainment of choice—from playing hero in their favorite game, to traveling to wherever their heart desired, to acting out more illicit fantasies. *You get what you pay for,* Lingyi's father had always said, and first-class passengers were granted whatever they wanted in virtual reality.

Lingyi had popped a sedative in desperation before the short flight, hoping the medication would knock her out, give her some peace of mind. But the gods were not kind. She drifted into an agitated waking dream instead, punctuated by the hacking cough of the passenger behind her and the sharp wailing of a baby to the side. Sleep would not claim her. Instead her mind kept wandering back to moments in time. . . .

I couldn't bear the thought of losing you, Lingyi.

Victor had kissed his gloved hand and gently caressed her cheek after, a gesture mostly lost on her group of friends because everyone had been so relieved she and Iris had survived the horrendous avian flu Jin had released. But Lingyi did not miss the tenderness in Victor's warm brown eyes, or how he had allowed himself to gaze at her, heart open and vulnerable; he loved her still.

She had known that, yet had avoided talking about it with him. They had dated several months and she had liked him, but Lingyi hadn't been in love. This became starkly clear when Iris had shown up one night in Lingyi's small apartment, invited by Vic himself. Iris with her platinum hair shorn short had given Lingyi the faintest of nods when Victor had introduced her, her slender eyes flicking briefly across Lingyi's face, before sliding away. She didn't say a word, instead pacing the small living room, reminding Lingyi of a caged cat, one that would be much happier roaming free outdoors.

Keeping a wide smile plastered on her face that entire night, Lingyi had spoken in forced and cheerful tones, like a songbird prodded to sing by having a stick thrust at her. She chirped on in bright and nervous notes until Iris suddenly stood still and looked Lingyi square in the eyes. "I like your skirt," Iris said in a low voice. "The colors."

Lingyi had been wearing a pouffy fuchsia skirt dappled with indigo chrysanthemums. She remembered that moment so clearly, because she had stopped talking midsentence, like a recording cut off. Then the slow rise of heat climbed from her neck to her cheeks. She was certain she glowed as bright red as a ripe summer tomato, and Iris didn't miss it with her sharp gaze. It was clear Iris was not saying, *That's a skirt* I'd *like to wear*; it was obvious that she was complimenting Lingyi in her quiet and aloof way.

Lingyi hadn't known if Victor had caught her blush as well, because in that moment, she had forgotten that he was even in the room.

Iris had been an enigma and a surprise; she came into Lingyi's life and had turned her entire world on its head.

▲▼▲

The plane lurched, jolting Lingyi awake. Not long after, it thudded onto the runway, bouncing hard enough that her teeth clacked together. She must have fallen asleep for a bit and had not suffered a nightmare, thanks to the sedative. Yet she felt more exhausted than before the flight began—emotionally drained. She never thought she'd return to China again, not when her last visit was filled with happy memories spent with her parents and younger brother, not when her father had told her in no uncertain terms to never return, because she should break all ties with him if she wanted to lead a quiet life in Taipei. Her father had fled back to China after it was revealed he was the infamous "little mouse" hacker from decades back. He didn't want his reputation to taint hers.

Lingyi rubbed her eyes, feeling the corner of her mouth twitch upward ruefully. That was before she and her friends decided to bomb Jin Corp—before everything changed forever. She was skilled enough in her hacking to escape any detection, and none of it could be traced back to her. She had been taught by the best, after all. But if her father had any inkling she had been involved, she suspected he'd feel proud, very proud, right before he sent her to live somewhere isolated on a tundra so she would keep out of trouble.

But he would never know. Just as he could never know his daughter had returned to China, against his direct wishes and her own better judgment. Lingyi had felt a knot of anxiety ever since she'd agreed to meet with Jany in Shanghai, and that tightness in her chest had never eased. But she had such fond memories of Jany's stay with them for two summers. Lingyi was the eldest in her family, but she had gotten an older sister in Jany for those few precious months. While her brother stayed home playing computer games, Lingyi got to explore Taipei in a way she never had as a fourteen-year-old, because Jany herself had been nineteen. They had lost touch in recent years, but Lingyi knew Jany had received a master's in engineering and was pursuing her doctorate. She remembered Jany as smart, funny, and kind. Lingyi could never leave her hanging if Jany needed her help, and had booked her ticket immediately for the next day after receiving Jany's message.

Lingyi grabbed her larger carry-on, then slung her leather messenger bag carrying her MacFold across her shoulder and deplaned with the stream of first-class passengers. They were guided by black velvet ropes to the cavernous immigration area, lit too bright under white fluorescent lights. She followed the signs written in simplified Chinese directing everyone to the VIP section for Chinese reentering the country. China had long refused to see Taiwan as its own country, but it still made her bristle, this power play for visiting Taiwanese. Exhausted, Lingyi swayed on her feet and gripped the metal railing. The sedative should be wearing off now—she had taken a tiny dose—but maybe she shouldn't have risked it. Lingyi didn't have to wait more than fifteen minutes before it was her turn in front of a bored-looking Chinese man studying her from behind his glass partition. He had a buzz cut and sharp cheekbones. Lingyi stood still as the floating bot hovering beside the immigration officer scanned her retina.

"Are you on drugs?" the man asked. "Your pupils are constricted."

She blinked. "I took a sedative . . . flying makes me nervous."

He made a noncommittal grunt, and Lingyi's pulse quickened.

"Reason for your visit, Ms. Chang?" the man asked, his gaze trained on the screen in front of him.

"For pleasure," Lingyi said. She had hacked into the Bureau of Consular Affairs and altered her passport account with a false identity. She didn't think her father would be trawling, but she couldn't risk him knowing she was in China. It was safer that no one knew.

The man finally looked her full in the face, took in her purple hair and pale blue maxi dress—she had tried to tone down her usually bright clothing choices for the trip. "How many days are you staying?"

She cleared her throat; her mouth had gone dry. "A week." Lingyi had no doubt her work for this false passport identity was solid, still she couldn't suppress her nerves. "I'm staying in the Waldorf Astoria on the Bund," she added. She hadn't chosen one of the most expensive hotels in Shanghai to impress the immigration officer; it was because if you were rich, you were subjected to less scrutiny. People trusted wealth.

The man tapped on the glowing keyboard set in his console, then nodded and waved her through without another word.

▲▼▲

The relative quiet of the VIP section of immigration turned muggy and noisy the moment Lingyi emerged into the airport proper, navigating her way through a crush of people and floating bots trying to sell her hotel stays and airped rentals. She fought her way out of the terminal, only to be met with a winding line of at least one hundred impatient people waiting for a taxi. She stood behind a heavyset man shouting into his Palm, feeling the sweat trickle down her back, before the oppressive August heat became too much.

The glass terminal curved above them, and aircars and limos zipped overhead, avoiding the congested traffic below. A covered escalator took people onto a landing where airlimos were gliding in to pick up their rich passengers. Being the daughter of one of the most successful building and cybersecurity entrepreneurs in the business meant that Lingyi had always grown up as *you*, a rich girl who was familiar with the luxuries that wealth provided. But at times, she still balked at its advantages. Her father had been born dirt poor and became a self-made millionaire, but he never hesitated to express his frustrations over the inequalities he saw in China, and then in Taiwan. In this moment, however, she was willing to spend the cash to get into a cool airlimo and arrive at Jany's two hours faster than suffering on the ground for a regular taxi.

When she climbed into the air-conditioned cabin of the silver airlimo and sank against the tan leather seat, Lingyi knew she had made the right choice, even given the outrageous three thousand Renminbi price for the ride. A barbot hummed over, and Lingyi requested an iced winter melon tea, which incredibly, the bot could provide. She sipped the sweet, refreshing beverage and felt her shoulders relax as the driver behind the black opaque divider guided them upward, whisking them through the air at a speed only possible in the open skies.

She gazed at the endless apartment buildings below in the Pudong District, stacked so close they looked like concrete dominoes. Curving highways wound around them, filled with cars, trucks, and motorbikes, crawling like insects as her airlimo flew overhead. Soon Shanghai's famous skyline opposite the Bund emerged from the thick blanket of brown smog, just beginning to glow in neons as dusk settled across the vast city. Jin Feiming's latest venture, Jin Tower, dominated among icons like the Pearl Tower and the Shanghai World Financial Center, looming over them, taking the title of tallest building in the world.

Jin Tower, the world's first "vertical city," was a sleek study in glass, a 188-floor high-rise much more ambitious than the 101 in Taipei, housing offices, residences, restaurants, grocery stores, and shopping centers, including garden levels—a city in itself—the idea being that a person would never have to leave. Its twisting shape was rumored to replicate a dragon emerging from the earth. Jin had broken ground on the project three years ago but put construction in overdrive in the last six months, since Jin Corp headquarters had been destroyed in Taipei. News sources claimed Jin was preparing for a grand opening this month in Shanghai like the world had never seen.

The high-rise was beautiful, but monstrous. Now that the Jin suits were currently off the market, Lingyi knew he was searching for a different way to profit from the filthy air that polluted the city—and much of the entire country. With a population near twenty-six million, the most sought-after things in Shanghai were prime real estate and good air. Jin guaranteed both for his buyers with the vertical city. As her airlimo followed the bend of the Huangpu River and swept past the magnificent high-rise, Lingyi felt the hairs on her arms lift, and she clenched her fists. The reaction was visceral; she didn't hate many people in life, but she hated Jin. Not only had he ordered

Arun's mom, Dr. Nataraj, to be murdered, Lingyi also blamed him for Victor's death.

Jany had instructed Lingyi to go to Yuyuan in the Old City of Shanghai and given her specific directions on how to get to her apartment on foot. I'd meet you at the airport myself, Jany had messaged. But I'm too afraid to leave my home. Please be sure you're not being followed. Lingyi remembered a Jany who would easily break into a smile, revealing a deep dimple in her right cheek, with a carefree and robust laugh. They had giggled over so many silly things over those two summers—like when Lingyi had stolen the cap off a person in Pikachu costume promoting a Pokémon buffet. She did not come across as someone prone to exaggeration or dramatics. Lingyi knew from that single exchange that Jany had somehow gotten herself into a very serious and dangerous situation. She was worried for her old friend.

Dusk cast the city in a dirty golden haze, and despite the setting sun, it was still unbearably hot, especially after the coolness within the airlimo. It was rush hour as men and women dressed in business suits stampeded out of buildings and made their way to the metro or hailed taxis. Again Lingyi was struck by the sheer number of people moving on the sidewalk, even as more people zoomed by in haphazard fashion on mopeds and bicycles, some on contraptions they must have built themselves, the back of their vehicles stacked high with boxes or other strange inventory. Because Jany had refused to share an actual address, Lingyi stopped often, searching for landmarks, only to be bumped or elbowed by someone rushing past without so much as a glance in her direction. She wiped the sweat from her brow with a handkerchief and coughed, trying to ignore the tightness in her chest—that feeling of unease. The thin face mask she wore did little to disguise the smog that permeated the city air, the pungent stench of fuel and exhaust. Shanghai's pollution was as bad as Taipei's, if not worse.

Finally, she found the colorful fruit market on a corner opposite a Family Mart as Jany had described. Lingyi paused, pretending to examine the large mangoes on display. She had tried to see if anyone had been following her, but there had been too many people on the sidewalks. She then slipped into Jany's street and stopped several doorways down, leaning against the wall. It was more like an alleyway, flanked by squat brown buildings, their facades marked by decades of grime and pollution. Laundry poles jutted out from every window above, with blankets and clothes hung out to dry. These three-story buildings were much older than the high-rises that surrounded them, and occupied by poorer folk, who could not afford the high-tech apartments and city views, but it was quieter here, secluded almost. Lingyi had left the hordes of people and endless honking cars behind, stepping into a different world, it seemed.

She glanced at the Vox strapped to her wrist and waited five long minutes. No one peered around the corner or followed her into the street. The only thing that noted her presence was a calico cat curled up on a concrete step. It blinked at her, then began grooming itself. The laundry shifted in the breeze overhead, dappling the ground below in strange shadows. Satisfied she hadn't been tailed, Lingyi stepped away from the wall. She passed an older woman with graying hair sitting outside her home as she washed vegetables in a red plastic tub. Lingyi pushed her glasses up, looking carefully at every door she passed. She was near the end of the street when she finally spotted what she was searching for—a red paper door god taped to a splintered wooden door painted a deep green. The frame was so old it appeared the door could topple out. Lingyi was taken aback. She knew Jany didn't come from wealth, but she was a respected doctoral student in the field, the last she'd heard, and Lingyi hadn't expected to find the young woman living in squalor.

Suddenly nervous, she lifted her hand and knocked on the door, three times, paused, then twice, paused again, then one last time, as Jany had requested. Leaning in, she could hear nothing but dead silence on the other side. Lingyi swiped a hand across her damp hairline. Was this the right place? She had been foolish enough to get this far and never even have picked up a weapon along the way—a pocketknife at least. Knives reminded her of Zhou, and with a sharp pang, Lingyi shoved the thought aside. They hadn't talked in months. Fighting her nerves, she was about to turn away when the door creaked open, revealing the dark shadow of a person peering from within. "Lingyi," a woman whispered, before she opened the door and dragged Lingyi inside.

Lingyi managed to suppress a scream of surprise. Her eyes took a moment to adjust to the dimly lit room she was in, but she recognized

Jany immediately. The young woman appeared haggard, with dark circles under her eyes. Her hair was pulled back in a messy ponytail, and she was dressed in a loose gray tee and black sweatpants.

"I'm so glad you made it," Jany said in a low voice, as if she feared there were people eavesdropping. She reached out and gripped Lingyi's fingers briefly. Without hesitation, Lingyi gave her friend a hug. Jany was stiff at first but then hugged her back, letting out a long sigh.

"Are you okay?" Lingyi asked. "What's going on?"

Jany leaned in closer, and Lingyi saw how pallid her coloring was, as if she hadn't been out in the sunlight for weeks. "Jin," she said, so softly this time that Lingyi had to read her lips to be certain. But the fear in Jany's face left Lingyi with little doubt.

"Jin," Lingyi repeated. "Shit."

▲ ▼ ▲

Jany was not like the quick-to-smile girl Lingyi remembered from years ago. She was a ghost of her former self, moving around the dingy area designated as a kitchen with the nervous motions of a timid mouse, as she brewed hot tea for them. Lingyi took in the run-down communal area she sat in that served as living room, dining room, and kitchen. The ceiling was so low that she was certain she could touch it if she stood on her tiptoes—and Lingyi was not tall. One narrow window set high above the kitchen sink let in scant light and appeared to have been boarded up from the outside. A single bulb flickered overhead. Besides the front door, there was one other narrow doorway leading into a darkened room. The bedroom, Lingyi assumed.

Jany sat down across from her on the only other stool at the splintered wooden table and set a chipped teacup down. Lingyi murmured thanks and lifted the steaming cup, smelling fragrant jasmine tea. The familiar scent steadied her. Jany took a sip, and it seemed to calm her as well.

"I'm sorry for all the secrecy," Jany said after a long pause, staring into her teacup. "Thank you for coming. I could think of nowhere else to turn for help."

"Of course I came—you're like a sister to me," Lingyi said in a gentle voice. "Tell me everything."

Jany flashed her a quick smile, her deep dimple appearing, then disappearing again like a magic trick. "You know I'm working on my doctorate in engineering. But I've been doing a side project on my own for years. I was just playing around, but I stumbled onto something I realized could be very useful—very lucrative." She paused, as if ashamed to admit it. "I want to help my family."

Lingyi nodded. She knew Jany had been smart enough to win scholarships for her graduate studies, but being a grad student garnered no salary, and her family was poor, much like Lingyi's dad's was. Lingyi suspected that was one reason he had taken her in those two summers—her father had seen something of himself in Jany.

"It could revolutionize air filtration," Jany went on. "It replaces the physical filter with a chemical catalyst that captures pollutants and converts them to harmless by-products. They're cheaper to build and can last for years." Jany's words picked up speed in her excitement. "They can be made to adapt to current filters in easily portable cartridges. Just imagine all the spaces that could benefit from this: schools, hospitals, orphanages—the possibilities are endless. I think they could clean outdoor air too, especially if laws were passed to curb Shanghai's pollution at the same time."

Lingyi shook her head in wonder. "That's tremendous, Jany."

The other woman crossed her arms in front of her and snorted. "Yes, so tremendous that Jin somehow caught wind of it."

Lingyi's scalp crawled. Of course Jin had found out.

Jany proceeded to tell Lingyi what had happened: her visit to meet Jin in Beijing, her refusal to sell him her design, and her near murder the morning after meeting him.

"He doesn't know the specifics—that I've created a new filtration system, not a new filter. At least he was in the dark about that." Jany's pale face flushed in anger. "But I realized then that he'd stop at nothing to steal this from me. And it's made me more determined than ever to keep it from him. I knew I needed to secure my data, and you were the only one I could think of. I wasn't sure if it was safe to get in contact with your father—"

"You're right. He's likely still under surveillance, if not by Jin himself, then by the Chinese government."

Jany's dark eyes widened. "Your father has ties to Jin?"

"Only in that he said no to Jin too. He had refused to take on a contract with Jin Corp, and a few months later, my dad's past life as a hacker in China was leaked." Lingyi cleared her throat. "I don't believe that was coincidence."

Jany let out a low whistle.

"I'm glad you've been cautious. Jin is dangerous, with unlimited resources, and you have something he wants."

"So what do we do?"

"First, we destroy your backup."

Jany gasped.

"Then we take your laptop completely offline, and I'll encrypt it so only you and I have access. We're going dark with all your data."

CHAPTER FOUR

It took the entire night and following day for Lingyi to secure Jany's data. She worked for hours without taking breaks, not knowing what time it was in the dingy, airless apartment. "It's finally done," Lingyi said, flexing her fingers, then throwing her arms overhead to stretch her sore shoulders. "I can take your MacFold to a bank and put it in a vault on Monday morning," she said. "But let me grab some food for us now." Suddenly, Lingyi's stomach growled loudly. She was starving. She convinced Jany that it would be safer if she stayed home, because Jin's informants were everywhere. Shanghai was a city that thrived at all hours, and it was easy for Lingyi to disappear into a crowd, be anonymous.

Lingyi headed out. It was past eight p.m., when the throngs were still thick in the popular tourist areas around Yuyuan. The classic Ming Dynasty garden was a main attraction for those visiting Shanghai and was surrounded by a busy tourist mart with even more stores and stands fanning out from the classical garden. With a felt hat on and a black mask covering the lower half of her face, Lingyi battled her way through the masses to pick up scallion pancakes and pan-fried dumplings, all scooped piping hot into paper bags.

She got lost in the sprawling mart, accidentally wending her way across the famous Jiuqu zigzag bridge as cambots hovered to take photos for tourists posing in front of gilded lanterns and classic Chinese buildings with beautifully tiled curving rooflines. Tour guides and vendors projected their voices through voxbots that zipped amid the shoppers, detailing the best deals on purses or candy or fresh-grilled squid. Near the end of her foray, Lingyi had gotten better at pushing her way through the crowds, literally fighting for space, but the ordeal left her exhausted and anxious by the time she was ready to return to Jany's derelict apartment.

And tonight, when there was cause for celebration that she had finished encrypting Jany's data, Lingyi felt even more on edge. She knew Jin; he wouldn't give up. She glanced over her shoulder, seeing a blur of faces, then walked faster. Even thinking the man's name felt like summoning the devil.

One young man was demonstrating holographic fireworks in the square in front of a popular xiaolongbao restaurant. "We Chinese invented fireworks," he said, flourishing his hands. "And now, many centuries later, we're reinventing them." He swung his arm in a dramatic arc, and silver and gold holographic fireworks exploded above the crowd, raining downward like dazzling raindrops. All the people gathered around him gasped in unison, their eyes lifted heavenward.

Lingyi stood at the edge of the gathering, feeling like a lurker on the fringe. But she'd always been drawn to the vibrancy of colors. She loved coding, it was in her blood; she dreamed in code. But that world was a life without hues. It was why she always dressed in bright colors, dyed and adorned her hair in neons, because the world of her work was so often a stark contrast of black and white.

Unable to resist, she lifted her hand and brushed her fingertips against the fireworks. A spray of turquoise showered down on them, trailed by deep red starbursts that formed into hearts. It suddenly made her miss Iris. They had been incommunicado for days. She knew Iris trusted her but would worry anyway. She tried to capture the glimmering heart shapes, but it was like swiping at phantoms.

"Impressive," a man near her said in a brusque voice. "But what good are fireworks when they don't make noise?"

His lanky friend laughed. "Yeah, what's the point if your ears aren't ringing? How're you supposed to scare the evil spirits away?"

The first man gave his friend a playful shove. "You sound like my grandma!"

Lingyi let the strange sensory moment wash over her: the jostling of bodies and the cacophony of voices, the colors blooming overhead, and the overwhelming feeling of being alone surrounded by this frenetic chaos. How did you ward off evil spirits in this day and age? And what if the devils that plagued you so often took on human shape? She had focused so hard on helping Jany, she didn't have time to feel afraid. But fear settled in her chest now, cold and hollow.

Lingyi swallowed a knot in her throat as a woman pulling a toddler by one hand bumped past her, headed for the ice cream stand serving giant scoops in dragon-shaped egg cakes. She knew she had this. She'd secured Jany's data, and they would find a way to keep her safe, perhaps alter Jany's identity and smuggle her out of China to Taiwan.

Lingyi would always look back on this moment with bitter regret, knowing in retrospect how wrong she'd been.

▲▼▲

Lingyi and Jany shared their dumplings and scallion pancakes, speaking in hushed tones, before falling into a companionable silence. Then Jany said, "I miss Taipei's night market food so much—I dream about it."

Lingyi grinned. "I would have brought stinky tofu for you if I thought I'd make it through customs."

Jany laughed that familiar boisterous laugh Lingyi remembered, making her laugh in turn. "I don't think the oyster omelets would have fared much better!" Jany replied, her cheek dimpling. "Remember when we lied about your age and snuck you into that nightclub, Vampire's Kiss?"

Lingyi truly laughed now. She had been fifteen and left their house with fake leather knee-high boots, a short skirt, and a flower tank top in a bag. They had picked up a deep purple lipstick—what Jany and she assumed goth girls would wear to a club with that name—and lined each other's eyes poorly in black. But when they actually made it inside the club, they were stunned and a little horrified to find a group of *mei*s and *you*s dressed as actual vampires, with sharp fangs, dribbling blood and speaking in strange accents.

They had hustled out of there pretty fast, especially after a couple approached, asking if they would participate in some neck biting.

After the reminiscing and laughter died down, Jany refilled their teapot with hot water, then poured more tea for them. They nursed their chipped cups, and Lingyi tried again, bringing up a topic of conversation that Jany had brushed aside earlier in the day.

"Won't you even consider it?" she asked. "It's too dangerous for you to stay here, Jany." Steam clouded Lingyi's glasses, so she took them off and set them on the wooden table. Jany's face was a soft blur before her. "You can stay with me for as long as you like. You know National Taiwan University has a really prestigious engineering program too—you've studied there and loved it—"

"No," Jany replied, stopping Lingyi short. "I've had enough of hiding like a fugitive these past few days, and I refuse to run like a criminal." Her dark brown eyes swept over the dingy apartment. "After my MacFold is safely put away in the vault, I'm finishing my studies here and getting my doctorate."

"You know what he's capable of." Lingyi put her glasses back on in time to see Jany jut her jaw out in determination.

"I do." Jany touched her forearm. "My knife wound has barely scabbed over." She winced, whether from pain or from the memory of the attack, Lingyi didn't know. "But promise me something." She paused. "It's an unfair thing to ask."

"Anything," Lingyi said.

"If something were to happen to me, don't let Jin get my invention," Jany whispered in a hoarse voice. "I made this to help others, but also to help my own family. Don't ever let him profit from it."

"You speak like this, and you refuse to go to Taiwan with me?"

Jany gave a resolute shake of her head. "My home is here; my studies and my family."

Lingyi reached across the rough table and squeezed Jany's hand briefly. "Only you and I have access to your MacFold. It's safe."

"Thank you," Jany said. "For everything. I'm so grateful for your help." She stood and began clearing the table. "You go sleep on the bed tonight. You've been working nonstop and look like a ghost risen from the grave." She grinned, flashing her dimple. "Get a good night's rest."

Lingyi didn't have the energy to argue. Instead, she brushed her teeth in the small closet that served as their bathroom. A cloth separated the squat toilet and sink from the main room; there was no tub or shower. The single yellow bulb cast a sick pallor over her face. Lingyi hadn't washed herself for days; she didn't want to think about what she must smell like. She'd take a long bath the minute she returned to Taipei. She crawled into Jany's narrow bed in the windowless bedroom without changing, falling immediately into a deep sleep.

▲▼▲

A loud, crashing thud made Lingyi shoot straight up in bed. She fumbled, instinctively searching for her glasses, then pushed them up her nose. She had been so exhausted she'd forgotten to remove them when she went to sleep. The bedroom door was ajar, and faint light slanted in from the main room. There were footsteps, then—

"No!" Jany screamed. "What do you want?"

Lingyi broke out in a cold sweat from hearing the terror in Jany's shout.

Whoever had barged into the room didn't speak. Instead, there was the sound of furniture scraping against the stone floor, then toppling over. Scuffling noises followed, and Lingyi knew Jany was trying to fight off her attackers. Lingyi sat frozen in place, her body rigid with fear. Her heart beat wildly, and she saw in her mind again Jin Corp's shuddering floors before the building collapsed inside, heard the loud booms from the wall screen as she followed the cam Iris had worn clipped to her shoulder. Lingyi had not been there that night

Jin Corp went down, had not been there when they lost Victor, but she had relived the noise and chaos many times in her mind since.

She fisted her palms, nails digging into her flesh, willing her legs to move. She had to run into the other room and help Jany. Her breath hitched when she heard Jany's muffled scream, then the sound of a body falling to the floor.

"We have it," a gruff male voice said after a short silence. "Search the place. Make sure there aren't witnesses."

The stranger's voice catapulted Lingyi from her paralysis. She slid out of bed, her limbs shaking so hard she was sure the men in the other room could hear her. There was nowhere to hide in the cramped room, except for under the bed. She eased herself beneath the dusty space, trying to control her body's trembling. It was only after she was underneath that she realized her glasses had fallen from her face. Panicked, she swept her arm out, hoping her fingers would find them.

She couldn't see anything except for the blurred smudge of light from the other room. Footsteps stomped over just as her fingertips connected with her glasses, and she grabbed them, tucking them against her chest right when the bedroom light buzzed on.

"Anything?" a man asked from the other room.

Lingyi watched the man walk in, stopping beside the bed. He was so close that if she reached over, she could untie the laces of his thick-soled black boots. "Nothing in here," the man replied. "What a shithole."

"I'm done," his companion said. "Let's clear out."

The man turned on his heel and left the room, not bothering to flick off the light. Lingyi let out a small breath but stayed under the bed for a long time, even when she could no longer hear any noises from outside. Tears streamed down her face, then snot from her nose, but she remained still, noiseless, clutching her glasses to her chest until all her limbs had gone numb.

She stayed hidden for over an hour until past eight a.m., according to her Vox; it felt like an eternity. Finally, Lingyi dragged herself from underneath the bed. Her limbs tingled, and she could barely drag a sleeve across her face before dropping her glasses by accident. They clattered against the dirty stone floor, and she flinched. But there was no noise from the other room. Stooping down, Lingyi picked up her glasses and slipped them back on.

She crept toward the half-open bedroom door, like an elderly woman who needed the aid of a cane. Peering out, she could see nothing but overturned stools. The room appeared empty—but she knew Jany's body was there. Lingyi hesitated at the threshold, too horror-struck to confirm the death of someone else whom she cared for. Finally, she forced herself to enter the main room. The rotten front door had been kicked down, splintered from its weak hinges, and dim morning light filtered in. Faint honking from the street traffic outside drifted to her. With small steps, she walked to the table where she and Jany had shared their last meal. Jany was sprawled on the ground beside it, one arm covering her face as if she were asleep. But it was impossible to miss the large pool of blood beneath her head.

Lingyi fell to her knees, a silent sob shuddering through her body.

Tears blurred her vision. "Jany," she whispered. "No." Lingyi touched her hand, but there was no need to search for a pulse. Jany's other arm was flung out, and there was a gun dropped there, casually, with a piece of paper beside it. A suicide note, Lingyi knew without looking. A lie. The thug had used a silencer. Another murder by Jin covered up so he could take what he wanted. "Oh, Jany." Lingyi's hands fluttered over her friend's body; she didn't know what to do. "I'm so sorry."

She jumped to her feet and searched the apartment, knowing in her heart that it was futile. There weren't many places to look. The dining table had also served as a work space, and that was where Jany's MacFold would be if she had been working. The table was empty except for a can of Coca-Cola that had fallen on its side, spilling dark soda across the top.

The men had gotten what they came for.

Lingyi collapsed to the ground beside her friend again, bringing her knees to her chest. She had to go. Run. It wasn't safe here. Even if Jin's men had what they wanted, there was no telling whether they might return. She should book a flight, fly back to Taipei. Fly back to safety, to Iris. Her love. "I've done everything I could," she said in a soft voice. "I tried, Jany." But she'd failed her—just as she'd failed Victor. She'd let Jany be murdered while she sat immobilized with fear in the other room.

She buried her face in her folded arms and her body shook with sobs, but no more tears came. *Don't ever let him profit from it,* Jany had said to her, just hours before she was murdered and robbed. Lingyi suddenly saw Dr. Nataraj's warm brown eyes. *We have to keep doing right,* she had said. *We have to keep fighting. It's a destructive path our world is currently on.*

Then Victor emerged in the darkness behind her eyelids. *Is this worth dying for?* he had asked before they had embarked on bombing Jin Corp. *You'll get us all killed.*

I miss you, Vic, Lingyi thought. The tilt of his sarcastic grin was the last thing to fade into blackness. *Was* this worth dying for? Worth fighting for? And if she left Shanghai, returned to the comfort of her home, and her bed, could she live with herself? Could she leave Jany's dead body and pretend this had never happened?

She took long, slow breaths, trying to steady her racing heart, ease the tightness in her chest. No; she wouldn't be able to live with herself. Her friend had been cruelly murdered, and Jin was again behind it. He had gotten away with Dr. Nataraj's death—but he wouldn't get away with this one.

She tapped on her Vox's watch face and sent Iris a cryptic message—a coded one that they had agreed upon before she left. Her first message to Iris since Lingyi had landed in Shanghai. It signaled to Iris that she was in trouble, that she needed her help.

Jany's death would be avenged, and Lingyi would get her laptop back.

By the time Lingyi stumbled out of the hovel Jany and she had been hiding in, the morning was in full swing. Taxis and mopeds swept by on the main street, and pedestrians hurried past the narrow opening of the alleyway. She jumped when she saw an older woman standing with her arms crossed outside her dingy doorway. It was the same woman who had been washing vegetables the first day she came looking for Jany. She stared at Lingyi suspiciously. "I don't know what happened in there," the woman said. "But I've called the police. I heard the door crash, then saw those men leave ten minutes later. Are you a witness?" She reached out a gnarled hand, as if to grab Lingyi's wrist. Lingyi dodged her reach. "You need to stay," the woman rasped.

Lingyi had no way of knowing who might show up next: the police or more of Jin's men. And Jin was capable of bribing anyone with his money and power, including the police. It was too dangerous to stay. She shook her head and headed down the alleyway. As she rounded the corner, she nearly collided into someone. A policewoman with a bun pulled low against her neck brushed past her, followed by two colleagues. She appeared to be around thirty, with dark, intense eyes. Lingyi ducked her head, but the woman half turned, giving her a once-over. She wore a silver badge on her black police uniform that bore her name: *Lu Qining*.

Lingyi kept walking and could feel the other woman's eyes on her back. She forced herself to keep a normal pace. Then she heard a man calling from farther down the alleyway. "Detective Lu, here is the woman who placed the call," he shouted, his voice echoing.

Lingyi didn't slow, then turned onto another narrow street. She peered around the corner, but the policewoman was no longer there.

CHAPTER FIVE

ZHOU

Daiyu was a bundle of frenetic energy, and I watched her with an arm half-slung over my eyes, still sprawled in bed as she darted back and forth from my wood-paneled walk-in closet. It was bigger than the dank Taipei studio I had rented for a short time. She had taken over the closet in my apartment in the 101, because, let's be honest, my interest in clothes was basically nil. Daiyu had been living with me almost full-time for three months now, and I couldn't imagine life in this apartment without her.

"But is black too somber?" she asked, draping a long black dress in front of her. "Or should I wear the purple-and-silver qipao?"

"You look great in everything," I replied. "And even better in nothing."

Daiyu threw the black dress on the bed, then picked up the pillow beside me and pushed it onto my face.

"Hey!" I shouted. We struggled, and I could hear her laughing with glee. "You can't smother me for telling you the truth."

She cast the pillow aside and climbed onto the bed, straddling me.

"That's a dangerous game you're playing, Ms. Jin," I said, looking at her through half-lidded eyes. Sunshine from the floor-to-ceiling windows limned her in a hazy morning glow; she grinned down at me. "I thought you said you had a busy day ahead," I said. "I'm going to try and keep you in bed if this continues." I lifted an eyebrow and ran my hand down her thigh. She had put on a black lace bra since getting up. I wished she hadn't.

She laughed again and put both hands on my shoulders, pinning me to the bed. "You are coming tonight, right, Jason?" Her expression suddenly turned serious. I touched the slight furrow between her dark eyebrows. The last thing I wanted to do was spend hours with boring *you*s at a masquerade fund-raiser all night. But Daiyu had organized this gala, to raise awareness and donations for pushing through environmental laws in Taiwan. The *you*s had deep pockets, especially for what they perceived to be a trendy cause. "Of course I'll be there," I replied. "But I thought it was a costume masquerade gala. Where's your costume?"

She slid off me, and I resisted the urge to reach for her wrist. Half the morning was gone because I had lured her back into bed earlier. Daiyu picked up the black dress again, shaking it out. "I need to dress formally as hostess and show my face. The gala tonight will have wide coverage."

In the past six months, Daiyu had become the unofficial spokesperson for pushing for stronger environmental laws through the Legislative Yuan. She had even deferred her acceptance into National Taiwan University for a year to focus on this. Her family's wealth and name made her someone the *you*s could easily trust, and her natural charm and candidness had slowly won over the *mei*s. Unfortunately, her dedicated work had failed to win over my friends. We hadn't really talked much since . . . that night.

"Will you wear a costume?" she asked.

I grinned and rolled out of bed. "I was thinking of going as Aramis from *The Three Musketeers*. He was handsome and charming; all the women loved him."

She let out a low laugh. "Was he as modest as you?" She crossed her arms and slanted her head, her eyes following me across the vast room. "You're right—you're even better in nothing too."

"Ha!" I said, disappearing into the walk-in closet. Rifling through the small section that held my clothes, I finally found the black, satin-lined cape I was looking for. "This would be perfect." I came back out and held up the cape. "Vic—" I paused, clearing the sudden knot of emotion rising in my throat. "Victor was into capes and these billowy shirts for a while." It was still hard to say his name. "So he got me one too. . . ."

Then Daiyu was standing before me, slipping her arms around

60

my waist, her brown eyes bright with sympathy. She knew how much I missed Victor. But what she didn't know was how guilty I felt over his death. It wasn't anything I'd been able to speak aloud.

"You'll look very handsome as a rogue—"

"Musketeer," I said.

"That too," she replied, and tilted her chin up, pressing herself against me. We kissed, slowly at first, languidly, until she ran her palms up my back and I could feel the heat rising from her skin; then she did that thing with her tongue that rendered me helpless. She knew it too.

"Oh," she breathed after a long moment. "We're crushing your cape."

I let it slip to the ground. "Forget the cape," I said. "I thought you had things to do?"

She smiled and took my hand, leading me back to my ridiculously huge bed. "What's another ten minutes?" She lifted her eyebrows.

I laughed.

It was never just ten minutes.

▲▼▲

Daiyu finally swept out the door a little after noon, giving me a quick kiss on the lips. "I'll see you there tonight. Wish me luck!"

"Luck!" I winked. I knew she'd be amazing, both gracious and articulate.

Attending one of Daiyu's official functions on these rare occasions meant hanging in the back and never speaking with her directly. As far as Jin was concerned, I was dead, tied up in Jin Corp's basement before the building exploded. It wouldn't have taken much digging by Jin's thugs to know his daughter was seeing someone, but we'd been left alone for now, since Jin had fled to Beijing and set up base there to avoid prosecution for bribery and coercion. Was this too good to be true? Zhou, high school dropout and orphan of the streets, dating someone who had been the richest heiress in Taiwan? It was ludicrous and implausible—a fever dream.

I was rifling through the hangers in the large closet, trying to find a white shirt that could pass for that of a musketeer, when the Vox on my wrist chimed. Expecting a message from Daiyu, I froze when I saw Iris's face flash across my watch screen. I had heard from Lingyi a few times in these last six months, but never Iris. Iris had barely spoken to me when we were on good terms. I quickly read her terse message: Can you meet me tonight?

Yes, I dictated back without hesitation. I'd have to make time before heading to Daiyu's event, but I knew Iris. She wouldn't reach out directly unless it was important.

▲▼▲

If I were meeting Arun, it would have been at a cybercafe, and if it had been Lingyi, an actual cafe, preferably filled with well-loved manhua. We used to sit for hours in these cafes, me reading on my Palm as Lingyi paged through the thick comics, exclaiming every once in a while, then explaining to me what was happening in the series. And Victor. Well, Vic would have arranged for us to meet at a trendy bar. But Iris asked to meet in a dark alley behind a garbage bin.

Seven p.m. on a Saturday night and the Tonghua night market was just beginning to fill with people—teens like me looking for cheap eats, browsing the latest gadgets and knickknacks, while the adults gathered to drink, eat, and complain about life. I could have made my way to the meeting point through emptier streets, but I reveled in being among the crowds. Leading the life of a *you* in my outrageously expensive 101 apartment was isolating. The rich lived constrained and carefully curated lives. Walking the streets of Taipei was to feel its heartbeat, to take in the city's vibrancy through all the senses.

Music boomed through old speakers, mingled with the sounds of hawkers selling their food or trinkets as mouthwatering scents wafted from all sides: dumplings, buns, stinky tofu, fried chicken, and sausages. The choices were delicious and endless. I think if it were the end of the world, the food vendors would still push their carts out for their customers. And we would be there to buy it all.

Most young people chose to go bare-faced for a fun night out, but the summer air was oppressively hot, humid enough that I could feel the sweat trickle down my spine. Exhaust and smog mingled with the aroma of food and sweat, and with a pang, I missed the comfort my Jin suit had provided. The unbidden thought disgusted me. It was so easy to be rich. Too easy.

I meandered down two dark alleyways before my locator could pinpoint Iris's meeting place.

Fingering the knife tucked against my thigh, I sidestepped slick puddles, their surface barely reflecting the neon signs behind me on the main street. I swallowed and held my breath against the over-whelming stench of piss and vomit. Near the giant garbage bin, a figure emerged from the shadows like a phantom, and my fingertips twitched over my knife handle. But then the person crossed their arms, and I recognized Iris's predatory stance—one that gave no lee-way in her territory.

"Hey," I said in a low voice, my hand relaxing.

"Gods, Zhou," she replied. "What's happened to you?"

I paused, then remembered the costume I was wearing: tight black pants, a white shirt with billowing sleeves, and a black leather vest, with that cape from Vic draped over my shoulders. I had decided to skip the felt hat but wore a black face mask instead—one that cov-ered the top of my face for once, decorated with black feathers. No wonder I was sweating like a rookie about to rob a bank.

"Oh." I awkwardly adjusted my mask. "I have a gala to attend after this."

Iris shook her head. "Somebody will try to mug or kill you. Easy pickings."

I slipped out my knife and spun it in the air, catching it a moment later by its handle. "I'd like to see somebody try."

"You can't even see clearly out of that mask," Iris said.

"True," I conceded. "But did you ask to meet to critique how I'm dressed, or was there something else?" I grinned; it was good to see Iris. I'd missed my friends. Then it hit me like a punch in the gut. "Where's Lingyi?"

Iris and Lingyi were pretty much inseparable. Since I was closer to Lingyi, it was odd that Iris had been the one to reach out, then meet me without her. "What's going on?"

Iris took so long to answer, I thought she was playing with me, but when she finally let out a low breath and spoke, I realized she was trying to rein in her emotions. "I don't know. She disappeared somewhere in Shanghai." Her voice cracked.

"Shanghai?" It was the last thing I had expected. "Why?"

"She wouldn't say," Iris replied. "She left two days ago, but this morning I received a coded message from her. One that we had agreed on if she got in trouble." She tapped on her Palm, and a song lyric played, echoing hollowly in the quiet alleyway.

"Is that . . . is that a Jay Chou ballad?" I asked. "That's your distress code?"

Her Palm disappeared, and she glared at me. "Zhou, I'm worried."

Then I felt crappy for trying to make light of it. This wasn't like Lingyi, to take a secretive jaunt to China and then disappear. "I know. But Lingyi's one of the best hackers out there. If she needs to go dark and be untraceable, no one can do it better than her."

Iris nodded once, but I didn't miss the gleam of fear in her dark eyes. "She's vulnerable," Iris whispered. "Things haven't been the

65

same since—" She broke off abruptly, but I knew what she meant.

"How can I help?" I asked.

"Come with me to Shanghai, Zhou," Iris said. "I need backup, and you're the best I know."

That was a serious compliment coming from Iris. "When?"

"Tomorrow," she said. "I think she's in danger."

I didn't hesitate. "I'm in. You know I'd do anything for you and Lingyi." I might have kept my distance from my friends in these past months, but I never stopped loving them like family. That's how families were, right? Even the happiest ones had disagreements and fought.

Her lips pulled into a grim line. "One more thing." She paused. "Don't tell your girlfriend."

"What?"

"Tell her you're taking a short trip to the south, or Penghu. Whatever," Iris said. "You can't trust her."

"I *do* trust her," I said. "She saved our lives, remember?"

"She's Jin's daughter." Iris's tone was resolute. "You seem to have forgotten that."

"They haven't been in contact since he fled to China," I said.

"She told you that?" Iris asked. "And you believed her? I mean, *look* at you."

I felt the blood rush to my face. "What does that mean?"

She jerked her chin up, and a strand of her platinum hair glinted in the dim light, more silver than blond since I last saw her. "Dressed up like some fancy pirate, enjoying your *you* girlfriend and luxe apartment in the 101." Her features were shadowed, but I didn't need to see Iris's face to hear the disdain in her voice. "Have you forgotten who you are? Where you come from?"

"None of us had any trouble spending the money I took from Jin—"

"Happily," Iris interjected. "I'd steal from that asshole all day long. But I'm not the one shacking up with his daughter."

I shook my head. "She's not like him."

"She's the heir to Jin Corp—"

"No way," I said. "Not anymore."

"Did she tell you that, too?" Iris took a few steps toward me, and I could see her dark brows lift in question.

"Not in so many words." I didn't have to ask. I knew how she felt about her father and his unscrupulous ways—always putting profit above all else. She had never wanted to be the heir to Jin Corp, and she certainly would have refused it now, after everything that's happened. "But—"

Iris snorted. "Don't be a fool, Zhou. You're drunk on love and money."

Infuriated, I turned on my heel and said over my shoulder, "Just message me the flight info." I retreated down the dank alleyway with brisk steps, clenching and unclenching my hands.

This wasn't the way I'd expected to start the evening.

▲▼▲

By the time I arrived at the Shangri-La Hotel, where Daiyu was hosting her gala, I felt more like a half-drowned highwayman than a dashing musketeer. I headed straight to the bathroom lounge, passing many *you*s who were obviously there to attend the fund-raiser. One woman was dressed as a swan princess, her dress strategically layered with white feathers gleaming under the chandelier light, exposing glimpses of supple flesh dusted with glitter. A group of men dressed like wealthy warlords from *Romance of the Three Kingdoms* in brocaded robes with curved sabers strapped at their waists followed close behind. The grand marbled lobby vibrated with a low hum of excitement as the beautiful gala guests glided toward the elevators that would whisk them to the ballroom above.

The men's bathroom lounge was, incredibly, empty. I went to the sink and removed my black mask. It had left faint imprints across my brow and cheekbones, and I placed it carefully on the ivory sink before washing my hands and face, trying to scrub the city's grime and my own sweat off. My mind kept returning to the fear I heard in Iris's voice when she spoke of Lingyi. Lingyi couldn't beat the crap out of you like Iris could, but she certainly could outsmart anyone. Still, something was very off about the whole situation—dangerous—and I felt a foreboding I couldn't shake. I chose not to dwell on everything else she had brought up about not trusting Daiyu or calling out my life as a *you*. Hadn't we done enough by destroying Jin Corp's headquarters? Suffered enough? I'd never fathomed we would lose Victor in the process. It had always been mission first—we agreed. But what would I choose now if I could go back in time?

I stared at my own reflection, my face damp from the water I had splashed on it; my dark eyes appeared haunted.

I blinked.

It should have been me.

Drying off with a plush monogrammed towel folded into a woven basket for guests, I then ran a hand through my hair, cut short except for the front. I had styled it as best I could with product that Vic had recommended, but the hour walk in Taipei's summer heat had proven to be too much, and it flopped into my eyes now. Giving up, I put my mask back on.

Disheveled rogue it is.

A gold "magical" coin given to every attendee granted me access to the private elevator. I rode the high-speed elevator with a couple dressed like a dragon and a phoenix. The man's dragon mask looked heavy, etched with blue and green scales, with deep green jade horns jutting from his brow. The woman was attired in vermilion with a phoenix mask to match her partner's. I politely ignored the way she giggled and swayed, crashing into her date. He wasn't any steadier on his feet. Already drunk or high, they were making the most out of this gala. I was the first to step out of the elevator when it dinged a short time later.

The doors opened into another world. I knew the theme had been fairy wonderland, and Daiyu had discussed her plans with me extensively, asking for suggestions when she needed help or wanted to brainstorm, but it was incredible to see the results of her hard work. Flowers and ivy erupted from the ballroom's ceiling in colorful bursts, and a golden banyan tree dominated its center, growing, it seemed, upside down from above. Vibrantly colored silk butterflies and birds fluttered between the blooms. The floor, in turn, was lit with swirling constellations, so it appeared that the guests danced in the center of the galaxy, among the stars.

I scanned the room for security, always present when rich *yous* were gathered to party, quickly noting the dozen or so people dressed in dark suits. Then I searched for anyone who might be part of Jin's team—they usually looked meaner, more keen on killing than protecting. No one caught my eye, and I edged along the wall, making my way deeper into the magnificent ballroom.

The costumed guests only added to the otherworldly feeling of it all. Silver and golden light accentuated bejeweled throats, glowing horns, and glittering wings. One woman dressed like an ice queen clasped a staff that emitted a bright silver flame at its top. The hotel's servers were all dressed as huli jing—it was easy to spot their pointed fox ears as they circled among the guests bearing trays of bite-size food and flutes filled with sparkling champagne.

I craned my neck, searching for Daiyu in the expansive ballroom. There were probably three hundred people in attendance, and it took me some time to find her. She was standing by the raised dais near the front, speaking with a small circle of men and women, rich donors, no doubt. She looked stunning in the purple qipao embroidered with silver chrysanthemums, her long hair swept up in a loose twist. She had threaded flowers through her hair, her nod to the evening's theme. Daiyu looked like a mortal queen being paid tribute to by a throng of fantastical creatures. The glimpse of her in the crowd still did this *thing* to me—like seeing an unexpected surprise—delight and tension all at once.

I didn't like the idea of lying to her about the Shanghai trip. Our relationship had had its basis in deceit, and I had tried my best to change that, to be forthright and honest with Daiyu now that we were officially together. And I knew she did the same for me. We trusted each other, and what Iris was asking would undermine that trust. Remembering the contempt in Iris's voice made me bristle again. Who was she to judge me?

Although she isn't wrong, Zhou. The thought emerged like the proverbial demon sitting on my shoulder. *What have you been doing with yourself? Other than being complacent and comfortable?*

I would have stabbed that demon with a knife if I could.

Keeping my distance, I lingered at the edge of the ballroom, watching the *yous* from behind my feathered mask. I ate a few appetizers and drank one flute of champagne, the drink fizzing through my nose, but in the end, my favorite foods were still home-style or street food. Not bite-size morsels. About an hour in, a tall women slinked toward me. There was no other way to describe it. She wore a skintight dress with a train that trailed behind her like a long tail.

71

It wasn't until she was closer that I saw the dress was decorated with gold and emerald scales, mimicking a snake. She glided in front of me. Her eyes were emerald too, with dark vertical slits as pupils.

"Hello," she said in a low, husky voice. "What's a handsome young man like you doing lurking in the shadows?"

I raised an eyebrow. "I have a mask on. You can't see my face."

She lifted her glowing champagne glass and took a long sip, before saying, "I can see your mouth and that jawline." Her crimson lips curved into a smile, and the tips of her long fangs flashed briefly. "It is enough."

I laughed. It was short and humorless. "This isn't my scene."

"Let's get out of here." She dragged a sharp nail down my sleeve. "I have the penthouse to myself."

I pushed away from the wall. "I have a room in the hotel tonight too, with my girlfriend."

She threw her head back and laughed. "Your girlfriend? How quaint. Are you playing at monogamy? You must be even younger than I thought."

I didn't respond, and she took another long swallow from her glass before letting out a long sigh. Then she sashayed away without another word, serpentine eyes set on someone else more willing to play her game. There must be something about covered faces that made people lose their inhibitions. But then, *yous* considered anything good sport, including sexual escapades.

Right before eleven p.m., the orchestra stopped playing, and

Daiyu took to the large dais at the front. Her image was projected on four wall screens across the massive ballroom. "I wanted to thank everyone for attending the gala tonight and donating so generously to the fund-raiser," she said. "Your money will help raise awareness of the importance of introducing and pushing through environmental laws in our Legislative Yuan. Our beautiful Taiwan *is* our fairy wonderland—" She paused graciously as the audience burst into loud applause. After a full minute, the guests finally stopped clapping, and Daiyu flashed that killer smile. The one that would stop anyone in their tracks and make them forget everything. "It means the world to me that you're here to support this very important cause to ensure a better future for us and our magical Taiwan." She bowed her head, and the audience erupted into applause again.

It seemed she was finished speaking when an older man dashed up to the dais. He whispered to Daiyu, and with a puzzled expression, she handed her microphone to him. "Hello, everyone. Good evening," he said in a resonant voice. "My name is Mr. Li, and I'm here to present a surprise donation to Ms. Jin this evening."

The audience murmured in anticipation, and I straightened from where I had been leaning against the wall. Mr. Li was grinning from ear to ear, and Daiyu waited with the rest of us, her expression unreadable.

"One million yuan from Mr. Jin himself!" Mr. Li exclaimed. All four screens were replaced with an image of Jin standing with Daiyu by his side, and the guests erupted in surprised gasps. "Your father is so proud of you, Ms. Jin."

A young woman dressed in a black skirt and red tuxedo jacket threaded in gold stepped onto the stage carrying a huge check, smiling widely at the cheering crowd below.

Daiyu's expression hadn't changed, but she appeared paler in the spotlight, and she gave Mr. Li a tight-lipped smile. "Thank you."

I glared at the image of Jin, always glowing with vigor and larger than life. He loved to put on a show and take center stage. This would make him look good, an atonement, given the convictions brought against him in trying to stop the passing of environmental laws. I waited for Daiyu to refuse the check, to politely but firmly reject her father's donation. She'd worked so hard these past months fund-raising and getting huge sponsors to help pay for this gala. She'd even charmed her way into getting the ballroom space for free, compliments of the Shangri-La hotel; they knew it'd garner great publicity and a lot of booked rooms. I'd watched her, been by her side the entire time—she didn't need this from Jin. It was tainted money.

Daiyu seemed to be glancing down at her hands clasped in front of her, then lifted her chin and nodded once at Mr. Li, but remained silent.

A moment later, glittering confetti erupted from overhead, showering down on the guests, as the orchestra began playing again. Everyone laughed, some lifting their hands to the ceiling as the shimmering paper drifted down on them, their mouths open in surprise and delight.

But my own surprise was leaden, heavy in my chest. Why hadn't she refuted her father? To accept his money only implied to the public that Jin was still in control over her life—hell, that he was possibly the one behind all Daiyu's own hard work. It gave him good press when he didn't care anything about the environment at all or about the *meis*.

Disgusted by how Jin had inserted himself into Daiyu's event, I slipped into the elevator and headed for the hotel room Daiyu had booked for us, unable to shake my disappointment that she had accepted his money.

I got a message from Iris with our flight info as I made my way down the wide hotel corridor. The ticket was already booked. Don't tell her, she reminded me. Annoyed, I didn't bother to reply.

CHAPTER SIX

When Daiyu finally came to our hotel room, I had already showered and pulled on a bathrobe, leaving the musketeer outfit in a heap on the floor. It was past one a.m. I had wanted to confront her straightaway but softened when I saw how tired she was. She leaned against the wall, taking off her high heels, then the pins from her hair. She shook the locks out and massaged her scalp. "Thank gods it's over," she said, unclasping her diamond necklace. She casually dropped the jewelry, probably worth more than six figures, onto a side table.

I went to her, and she turned around so I could unzip her dress.

I massaged the back of her neck as she slipped out of her qipao. She pivoted again and wrapped her arms around my waist, resting her head against my shoulder. "You smell nice," she murmured against my chest. "I can't believe my father did that."

I rubbed her back, feeling the tension slowly seep from her body, as she leaned into our embrace. "I can," I said.

Now that she was in my arms, tucked securely against me, I began to feel the leaden weight in my chest lighten, slowly begin to break loose. We'd hardly spent any time apart these last three months, ever since she moved in with me. I was certain there was a misunderstanding, and we could work our way through anything.

"But why did you take the money?" I murmured against her ear.

She stiffened, then pushed away from me. "What did you expect me to do?"

"Say no?" I replied. "Thank you, but no."

"He's my *father*, Jason." Daiyu slipped out of her lace bra with a speed and ease that could have won her a medal. "And you don't know him," she said with exasperation.

"I know that he made himself look good tonight. At your expense."

"I've had to choose my battles with him my entire life—live with his controlling ways," she retorted. "This wasn't worth fighting over. If I had rejected his donation publicly, he'd lose face, and it'd turn all his attention back on me—on *us*. That's the last thing I want. Instead of making a donation, he could actively work against me. You *know* that."

"Has he been in contact with you, then?"

"I don't want to talk about this right now." She stalked away, only pausing to bend over and pull off her underwear. I completely lost my train of thought, and she disappeared into the bathroom. Frustrated—and horny—I almost followed her inside, but stopped myself. Daiyu was right. As much as I hated Jin, I didn't have to deal with him like Daiyu had to. She probably knew him better than anyone.

Instead, I grabbed my Palm and opened up my robot apocalypse game, hoping to find Arun online. But he wasn't, so I had to content myself with shooting robots on my own, trying to forget about our argument—and my hard-on.

I heard the shower turn off. When Daiyu finally emerged, she also had a bathrobe wrapped around herself, and her face had been scrubbed of the makeup she had worn for the gala; her wet hair clung to her like she had just risen from the sea. She climbed into the king-size bed, burrowing beneath the plush duvet. "Come to bed, love."

I hid a smile as I joined her. It was a truce then. She only used that term when she was feeling especially tired or vulnerable. We settled against each other like a matched set, like celadon teacups or ceramic spoons. "I'm sorry I said anything. My reactions are strong when it comes to your father." She didn't respond, but nestled closer to me. I stroked away the wet strands of dark hair that clung to her cheek. "I need to take a short trip tomorrow," I said. Her breathing had already slowed, and I think she had been on the verge of sleep, when her eyes snapped open.

"You do?" she said. "To where?"

"Just a quick trip to Taichung." I hesitated only one second before telling the lie. "Arun asked me to go with him." I regretted it the moment I did it, but I convinced myself that it was a harmless untruth. I almost believed it.

"Arun?" she murmured, and closed her eyes. "I'm glad. You haven't seen him in a long time." She let out a small sigh, draping a hand over my hip.

"No," I said. "I haven't."

"I see him in media news a lot," she said. "He's been busy."

I nodded against her shoulder. Arun had become somewhat of a celebrity after his new antidote helped to curb the deadly avian flu epidemic, and he had become a multimillionaire in his own right. He'd used part of his earnings from the antidote to open a clinic in Taipei—patients paid what they could afford. Often, they couldn't pay anything at all. We had met once after the bombing, but I hadn't made an effort to see him in months.

Daiyu was asleep a minute later, and I watched her, ignoring the demon perched again on my shoulder. I imagined he was dressed in an expensively tailored tuxedo with better styled hair than I could ever manage on my own. He rubbed his hands together, cackling. "One small lie never hurt anyone, Zhou. She'd only worry anyway."

I voice-commanded the dimmed lights to turn off and gazed out the windows at Taipei below. Our room had a clear view of the 101, my home for the past year. The building was lit in violet tonight, a familiar icon in Taipei's shimmering neon skyline. Airlimos circled in the distance. For many *yous*, the night was only beginning. Feeling Daiyu's familiar warmth against me and the soft curves of her body, I closed my eyes and tried to sleep.

Instead I only saw little demonic me cavorting beneath my eyelids. It was a long time before I finally fell asleep.

▲ ▼ ▲

Restless, I woke at dawn the next morning, just as the gray-smudged city beneath began to take on more distinct shapes and colors. Daiyu was curled against me, her head resting in the crook of my arm, still in a deep sleep. We had both shed our bathrobes in the night, too hot beneath the heavy duvet. I stroked her arm, and she murmured dream words as I tried to go back to sleep. Instead, my mind was filled with the impending trip to Shanghai with Iris, and my lie to Daiyu. *What she doesn't know can't hurt her,* I told myself. So why did I feel so crappy about it?

Giving up, I slipped out of bed and pulled on a black tee and some gray sweats, then headed down to the hotel gym. It was empty so early on a Sunday, and I spent the next hour and a half trying to jump rope, lift, and do chin-ups to the point of exhaustion. But when I finally returned to our hotel room, drenched in sweat, one glimpse of Daiyu sitting up in bed, rubbing the sleep from her eyes, confirmed that you can't sweat your guilt away. She stretched her arms overhead like a languid cat, and I stood near the door, basically just staring.

"Jason," she said in a voice still husky with sleep. "For a moment, I was scared you had already left for your trip with Arun."

I pulled off the soaked tee and threw it on my pile of clothes collecting on the floor. "I wouldn't leave without saying goodbye."

"Come here," she demanded. Daiyu was staring at me as unabashedly as I had been at her.

I felt the corners of my mouth tilt up. "I stink. I was going to hop into the shower."

"Mmm," she replied, and waved me over to the bed.

I laughed but obliged, sitting on top of the duvet. "Good morning." I leaned over and kissed her on her bare shoulder. "Really, though, I need a shower."

"After I give you a gift."

"A gift?" I searched my mind, wondering if I'd forgotten some special occasion.

She reached over and picked up a long rectangular box from her nightstand. "It isn't the most romantic gesture." Daiyu appeared almost shy when she passed the box to me. "But it's been on my mind for some time—your safety. And now, especially since you'll be traveling . . ."

It was a black leather case with my name embossed in silver on one end. Curious, I lifted the top, and it creaked open at the hinge.

Two silver throwing daggers rested against a black velvet lining inside. "Daiyu," I said, and lifted one dagger out of the box. The blade was so pristine it reflected my warped image, and a slender calla lily was engraved on its hilt, like the one tattooed above my heart, in memory of my mom. "You're wrong. This is *very* romantic."

She let out a low laugh. "Do you like it? Is it weird?"

I felt the heft of the knife; the hilt fit perfectly in my palm. "I love it. I love weird. Thank you."

"There's one more thing," she said. "There's a button at the top of the knife's hilt. If you press it, it'll release a poison on the blade."

I flipped the knife over to look at the top of the hilt. It was so well made, it was impossible to tell you could depress a hidden button there. "Really?"

She nodded, her expression serious. "The poison incapacitates almost instantaneously and kills within a few minutes after contact."

I gave a low whistle. "But why do you think I need this? My aim is usually true."

She reached for my hand. "I know, Jason. It'd just give me peace of mind. You're a target now that we're together. My father has left us alone so far, but I feel his attention could turn to me at any time—especially after what happened last night. And once he focuses on you, he's relentless until he gets the results he wants."

I shut the box, and it closed with a sharp snap. "And the best result when it comes to me is if I were dead."

She didn't respond, but her gaze said enough.

I kissed her softly on the mouth. "Thank you. Don't worry about me. You know I can take care of myself."

Daiyu smiled, but it didn't touch her eyes. "This makes me feel better."

"I'll always carry them on me."

"When do you see Arun?"

And for a moment, I had no idea what she was talking about. That was the danger of lies. "I'm heading out around noon. I need to get a few things from our apartment first." Sometime in these past months, I had begun to think of my apartment as ours. I averted my face and ran my hand over the smooth box, before slipping it into my open backpack. I hated lying to her.

She nodded. "You go shower then, and I'll order room service."

I went into the bathroom, then ducked my head out, wanting to say something more.

Thanks again.

I love you.

Daiyu had already settled back into bed, voice-commanding through the hotel's extensive menu on our wall screen.

Instead, I turned on the shower without saying anything more.

▲▼▲

I left the hotel a few hours later, giving Daiyu a quick kiss, not wanting to linger.

83

"I'll see you in a few days?" she asked.

"Sure," I said.

"Message me when you get there?"

I nodded. "I'll have your knives on me."

She smiled. "I always carry my taser."

I opted to walk back to the 101 from the Shangri-La Hotel. At noon, the streets were filled with families and pedestrians enjoying the day off, almost everyone wearing a mask to cover their faces. But not many meandered on the streets, because the heat and humidity were too much this time in August. Everyone headed for air-conditioned spaces: food courts, restaurants, department stores. The 7-Elevens were filled with customers getting iced drinks and parents buying their children ice pops and ice creams. The automatic doors kept sliding open, emitting a sudden whoosh of cool air as I walked past, before closing again.

The sun hung overhead—a dirty orange—and the skyline was blanketed in a thick brown smog. I stopped to buy some candied yams, which the vendor scooped into a clear plastic bag, pushing a toothpick in one for me to use. I pulled down my face mask and enjoyed the warm treat even as I felt the sweat slide down my neck. The doorman, Xiao Huang, greeted me when I entered the building.

My apartment felt empty without Daiyu there, and I packed without much thought, throwing some black T-shirts and jeans into a leather bag. Vic had protested when I said I didn't need any luggage cases, so instead, he got me two beautifully made brown leather duffel bags for my travels. I smiled, remembering our argument. "You can't claim to be a *you* boy and be half-assed about it, carrying your clothes in a plastic bag like you're homeless," he had huffed, more angry over a topic I hadn't given a second of thought to in my entire life. The next week, he presented me with the hand-sewn leather bags.

I carefully slipped my new knives into the duffel. As much as I liked to have a knife on me at all times, security would only hassle me at the airport. Checking through my pockets, I came across something in my jeans. Curious, I pulled it out. A note, folded into a triangle. I opened it and recognized Daiyu's writing; her written characters were elegant, even when she was just using a pen.

I will miss you.

She had written only those four words, then doodled a few hearts and blossoms around them. I grinned, feeling a surge of emotion that I didn't want to dwell on, and tucked the note back into my pocket. Glancing at the time, I requested that Xiao Huang hail a taxi for me downstairs for the airport, before grabbing my bag and heading out.

It was a fast drive without much traffic to the Taoyuan airport. I gave the taxi driver a generous tip on my cashcard and spotted Iris's silver hair near one of the entrances right away. I raised my chin in greeting, and she nodded once as I navigated my way between cars and travelers toward her.

"I wasn't sure if you'd show," she said when I was within hearing range.

"Don't you know me well enough to know that I always keep my promises?" I asked.

"I *thought* I knew you—"

I brushed past her. "I'm the same, Iris. I haven't changed. Now let's go find Lingyi."

I checked my duffel, as I had all my knives carefully packed in it. Iris also checked her small luggage, and I didn't bother to ask what she had in it that she couldn't walk through security with—you never knew with Iris. She had booked us first-class tickets; I suspected for the convenience and lessened scrutiny from officials and security alike as opposed to the luxuries it offered.

We waited to board in Empress Air's "Elite Lounge." I wasn't sure if its classist branding was a case of lost in translation or totally deliberate, but it lived up to its name. There were private luxury pods for sleeping, as well as showers and even one oversize whirlpool tub claiming the best and newest in water-jet technology. An extravagant buffet featuring light appetizers to full-course meals was laid out for guests, with two bars on either end of the opulent lounge. Empress Air waitstaff dressed in silver jackets were ready to assist at the wave of a hand.

Iris and I retreated into the farthest corner of the lounge, to hide on a high-backed sofa that faced the wall-to-ceiling windows, away from everyone else. A woman delivered the two shots of espresso I had ordered soon after we settled onto the velvet cushions. I downed one shot at that critical moment when it had cooled enough not to scald, but was still hot enough so that its rich, earthy aroma was at its finest. That was one thing I'd gotten used to living the life of a *you*: enjoying as many expensive espresso drinks as I wanted.

"You didn't tell her," Iris stated without preamble.

I swirled the second shot of espresso, watching the steam rise. "I didn't. But you had no right to ask me to lie to her."

"Even after what happened last night?"

I met her sharp gaze, trying to pinpoint what she was referring to.

"The donation from Jin himself at your girlfriend's fund-raising gala? It was blasted through all-media news."

"Oh, that," I said. "Daiyu didn't even know her dad was going to make a donation. It's what Jin does—he can't pass up an opportunity to make himself look good. They haven't been in contact since he fled to China."

"They *have* been in contact, Zhou. Since day one." Iris gave a shake of her head.

I felt the blood drain from my face. "What? How do you know?"

"Lingyi hacked into Daiyu's Palm—"

I placed the remaining espresso shot onto the table in front of us, but it clattered against the glass, because my hand was shaking from anger. "You had no right—"

"You wanted us to trust her, Zhou. But your safety—our safety—came first. It was the only way we could know for sure if she could be trusted. . . ."

I wanted to slam my fist down on the tabletop, but instead crossed my arms, gripping them with tight fingers. "What did you find?"

"They've been messaging each other about once a week."

"And Daiyu has been conspiring with him? On whatever he's trying to start in China?" I swallowed hard; the taste of espresso was too bitter in my mouth now, revolting.

"Nothing incriminating, exactly," Iris said. "But we were only looking through her messages. Who knows what sort of communication they might have had through face chat?"

"Let me see," I said. Iris passed her Palm, and I scrolled through boring and innocuous exchanges between Daiyu and Jin, whom she had labeled "the Father" on her end. "If it's nothing incriminating—"

"She lied to you, Zhou," Iris cut me off. "About keeping in contact with Jin. Can you fully trust her not to lie to you about anything else?"

I clasped my head between my hands. "I can." My words were directed to the floor. "After all that we've been through, I trust Daiyu with my life." But my stomach still felt sick. Iris was right—why had Daiyu lied to me?

"Well, I don't trust her with ours," Iris replied.

Before I knew how to respond, her Vox chimed. She glanced down immediately.

"It's Arun," Iris said. "He said he tried to contact you, but you didn't respond."

I had turned off my devices as soon as I left Daiyu, not wanting her to be able to track my movements. But how long could I avoid her without explaining myself?

"Daiyu tried to get ahold of you, but when she couldn't reach you, she messaged Arun, since you were supposedly meeting today for a trip." Iris showed me her Vox.

What the hell is going on? Arun had messaged in orange text.

"Zhou and I are headed to Shanghai," Iris dictated into her Vox. "Don't tell Daiyu. Cover for us."

He responded with giant red exclamation points. !!! Why?

"To find Lingyi," Iris replied. "We're staying at Les Suites on the Bund if you need to reach us. We might be offline."

Her Vox chimed then to take an incoming call from Arun. Iris dismissed it.

"That's cold," I said.

She shrugged. "The less he knows, the better. And he's your cover."

I shook my head, feeling the effects of the espresso course through my bloodstream. A pleasant female voice announced the boarding for our flight, and Iris and I rose at the same time.

Somehow, it didn't seem like a fortuitous start to the trip.

CHAPTER SEVEN

I had never been on a plane before, and although the flight was short, I still hated it. I hated feeling trapped in a machine in the sky with a bunch of strangers. I hated that we had basically handed our lives over to a faceless pilot droning on about the weather and time and the landmarks below us if we looked to our left. I hated the surge and plummet of my heart and stomach with the plane—an entirely different feeling from flying an airped, because I had no control over anything that was happening. When our plane finally jounced onto the runway, then parked at our gate, I was the first to deplane, grateful to step on solid ground again.

Iris and I followed the crowd of people who seemed to have done this a million times before toward the immigration area. Some spoke in Chinese dialects I couldn't understand, and others spoke Mandarin tinged with an accent I wasn't used to hearing. Luckily, we made it through immigration without incident. We grabbed our bags, and Iris hailed an airlimo for us. "It's faster," she said. I never knew Iris to be loose with her spending, even with her cut from the ransom money. I had a feeling she was eager to reach our hotel, so we could set out and find Lingyi as soon as possible. My last airlimo ride had been to Jin Corp with Daiyu months ago, and I tried not to think about it. I kept my devices turned off, knowing there would be messages from her waiting for me. I didn't know how to deal with the information Iris had shared.

Lost in thought, I hadn't even been looking out the window until Iris said under her breath, "There it is—the Bund." Our airlimo swept past in an arc, giving us an expansive view of Shanghai's famous skyline, recognizable on both sides of the Huangpu River. The stately and ornate buildings lining the Bund were almost all historical landmarks that had previously served as banks and trading houses from all over the world. They said that someone familiar with the Bund from centuries ago would be able to recognize it today. I believed it; because looking at these architectural landmarks felt like a glimpse into a time warp, the low buildings dwarfed by the modern steel-and-glass giants across the river.

It was late afternoon, and the sun's hazy light gleamed off the glass windows on the tall buildings. Throngs of people were walking on the Bund along the river; boats and barges of all sizes drifted slowly on the water.

"And there's Jin Tower," Iris said, pointing at the tallest building, a curving silver shard piercing the polluted skies.

I studied the structure. It was beautiful if not grandiose—exactly what Jin loved. "Of course it's the tallest building in the world now."

"He's got to make money somehow, since the suits are not back on the market yet." Iris smirked.

We had done exactly what we had set out to do in bombing Jin Corp, but we'd paid a high price for it. Was Victor's life worth what we'd accomplished? Sure, there was a moratorium on Jin suits production, but then they'd be back on the market, newer and better than ever. In the meantime, Jin continued to use his wealth, network, and power to expand his reach in China. Had we done anything to deter him in a significant way? Or was it like ants fighting gods? Had we lost Vic for nothing?

The airlimo glided into the garage of one of the buildings near the end of the Bund, and we took the elevator down into our hotel lobby. Iris had booked us into Les Suites, a small and modern boutique hotel. We checked into a large two-bedroom suite overlooking the river. She made a clean sweep of our accommodations, noiseless as a panther stalking prey, searching for hidden bugs and cameras. Vic had left us with one of the best detectors on the market—at least half a year ago. I felt his presence again, stronger than ever, now that I was reunited with Iris. And damn, I missed him.

Iris nodded at me once when she was done. "We're good," she said. "Lingyi knows we're staying here."

"So she's coming to us, instead of us having to find her?"

Iris nodded. "Ideally. That's the hope." She walked to the windows and glanced out toward the city near dusk, a truly magnificent view, even if swathed in smog. The Pearl Tower's neon lights had already turned on, and a commercial played across the entire length of Jin Tower, before firework images erupted, and then an announcement of the opening ceremony for Jin Tower appeared in gold characters. "That must mean he'll be in the city, if he isn't already," Iris said.

"Jin's in town, all right," a familiar, quiet voice replied from behind us.

And our suite door, which neither of us had heard open, snicked shut.

In spite of the familiarity, I had already pulled one of Daiyu's knives out, palming it for a throw. But Iris ran toward the door, flinging her arms around Lingyi. Lingyi drew a shuddering breath that sounded like a sob. "My heart." The two girls hugged, and I felt a knot of emotion rise in my own throat. Over these past months, Lingyi had tried reaching out to me, messaging to check in, gently suggesting we might meet to talk. I had agreed once, but then bailed at the last minute. I wasn't ready to face her—to apologize for leading Victor to his death.

It should have been me.

Lingyi and Iris clung to each other for a long time; Iris's tall, lean frame seemed perfectly matched to Lingyi's more petite one. Their embrace made me think of Daiyu. I didn't want to think about her, either, and shoved the thought from my mind. Finally, Lingyi lifted her eyes and looked at me, standing like an interloper by the windows. "Zhou," she said with a timid smile. "You're here."

"I'm here," I said, and slipped my knife into its hidden sheath.

Lingyi stepped away from Iris, but not before kissing her on the cheek. She came to me, and I remained where I stood, motionless.

"I'm sorry, Zhou," she said, opening her arms to me. "I'm so sorry."

I shook my head in confusion. What was Lingyi apologizing for? Then she wrapped her arms around me, and I felt the grief swell in my chest, my eyes stinging with tears. I hugged her back and tried to speak, but nothing came out. "Shh," she whispered. "It's all right." Her voice cracked.

But nothing was all right.

"I've missed you," she whispered.

"Me too," I managed to reply.

"Are you willing to help me make things right?"

I grinned even as I wiped the wetness from my eyes. "Always." I paused. "How did you get in?"

Lingyi grinned back and lifted a shoulder. "I made my own key. These hotel rooms are ridiculously easy to hack. I stayed in a posh hotel room along the Bund, much to the confusion of the house-keeping staff after I left, I'm sure."

Iris joined us, shaking her head. "You *are* damned messy, love."

"Am not," Lingyi retorted with indignity, but not much conviction.

"They probably wonder what typhoon swept through," Iris replied.

I smiled.

"Are we safe here?" Iris asked.

Lingyi's expression turned serious. "For now. But time isn't on our side. Jin's hunting for me."

Iris gripped Lingyi's hand. "What?"

I felt the heat rise to my face. "Tell us everything," I said.

▲▼▲

We sat huddled together on the plush sofa of our hotel suite, together again. Connected. Lingyi told her story in small bursts, having to pause often to gather herself. Her hands visibly shook when she recounted Jany's murder and seeing the body. She recounted the scene with halting words, and the rage I felt toward Jin filled me with hate. It wasn't enough that he murdered *mei*s without a second thought, but he never had to deal firsthand with its devastating effects. We were soldier pieces in a chess game existing only to serve his own agenda, completely dispensable.

By the time Lingyi was finished, we were sitting in the dark; the only light was the golden glow of the buildings on the Bund and the flickering neon from the skyscrapers across the river. We were starving but reluctant to order room service and give a stranger access to our suite. "There's an executive lounge by the reception area, Zhou," Lingyi said. "I scoped out the hotel before you arrived. There's food there—only light snacks and desserts, but free for the taking."

"I'll be quick," I said, leaving the girls. When I glanced back, Lingyi had laid her head on Iris's shoulder, and Iris was stroking Lingyi's purple hair, whispering softly to her. My heart swelled with love for them, for the feeling of being with family again. Quietly, I shut the door behind me.

The executive lounge was empty on an early Sunday evening. I imagined all the tourists staying in the hotel were out on the streets of Shanghai, enjoying the sights and food from its varied restaurants, from street food to five-star establishments. I walked along the tables laid out with finger foods and desserts, piling two large plates with everything: sandwiches, custard and red bean buns, small platters of cold cuts with seaweed, marinated tofu steak, and stewed eggs. I was filling another plate with small strawberry sponge cake, biscuits, and mango pudding cups, wondering if I could manage to carry everything back to the suite, when a family came into the lounge. The mom passed me, giving me a once-over. I was dressed in a faded gray T-shirt (actually designer: Vic told me we paid for the "expert" fading) and black jeans, but with my hair falling into my eyes, I knew I looked like someone who had just walked off the streets.

"Mommy," a girl with two pigtails exclaimed. "Is he gonna eat *all* that?" She pointed directly at me, mouth agape. Her mother tugged her hand, shushing her, and went to a table in the farthest corner of the room.

I tried not to laugh.

"Yeah, bro," a familiar voice said behind me. "*Are* you gonna eat all that?"

"Arun," I said, setting the plates down.

We hugged, and he clapped me on the back. His spiked hair was still orange at the tips, but more red at the roots. "It's good to see you," I exclaimed.

"Really?" He grinned. "I wouldn't have guessed it with the way you and Iris left me behind in Taipei like you were criminals about to rob the imperial palace."

I laughed. "Really, though"—Arun and I bumped fists—"it's been too long."

"That's the truth," he replied. "Can I help you with that?"

We loaded up a fourth plate with as much food as we could carry, much to the consternation of the mom as she whispered to her husband about us. I flashed her a smile and winked as we left the lounge. Her eyes rounded at that, and I heard her daughter saying, "Did you see the greedy man smile at us, Mommy? He's friendly!"

"Man, Zhou," Arun said. "You're shameless."

I laughed again. "I had to steal food for so long to survive. . . ." I paused, remembering those endless years of gnawing hunger, of fighting to live. "I guess it's second nature still."

Arun snorted. "Please. Enough of the sob story. I know those leather boots you're wearing cost at least a few thousand yuan."

I glanced down at my shoes. "Vic got them for me."

"That Victor," Arun said. "He always did have great taste." But the humor had died from his voice.

Arun's surprise appearance elicited happy exclamations from Lingyi and Iris when we entered the suite. We caught Arun up on what was happening as we made a meal of our makeshift feast. We were enjoying our espresso drinks, and tea in Lingyi's case, when Arun finally said what was on all our minds. "So what do we do now?"

"We have to get Jany's MacFold back," Lingyi said in a quiet voice edged with a fierceness I recognized. She wouldn't back down until she accomplished what she aimed for.

"But how?" I asked. "Are we able to track her device?"

Lingyi shook her head. "That was the reason Jany asked for help. I encrypted her computer and secured it—its location is untraceable."

"Then it's impossible," Arun said.

"There is one way," Lingyi replied, staring into her tea mug. "I left a signature on the device—a personal stamp that I'm the architect behind the encryption."

"Why would you do that?" I asked.

"For emergency purposes," Lingyi replied. "I can only be found if I want to be found. I've been dark so far."

"But why would Jin look for you? He can hire whoever he wants to break the encryption," Arun said.

"It would take months, and there's no guarantee," Lingyi said. "Jin doesn't have months. I'm his best, possibly only bet to get his hands on the data."

"Are you suggesting that you want to get kidnapped by Jin to get to Jany's device—" I asked, but was cut short by Iris.

"No," Iris said. "No fucking way."

Lingyi rested a hand on Iris's arm. "Darling . . . ," she said in English.

"Don't try and sweet-talk me, Lingyi!" Iris looked furious, but I knew she was bordering on panic. "What do you think Jin will do when you unlock the machine for him? You'll just be another person he kills to get what he wants."

"I can bide my time . . . ," Lingyi said. "Until you come to get me."

"How?" Iris demanded. "The first thing they'll do is get rid of all the devices on you. We won't have a way to track you!"

"We could implant a tracker in me," Lingyi said.

"What?" Iris and I exclaimed at the same time.

Arun nodded. "It's true. They are barely the size of a grain of rice."

Iris rounded on Arun. "Are you actually agreeing to this scheme?"

"I'm only listening"—Arun lifted his hands—"and offering my expertise. This falls in the realm of biotech."

"It's not the same without Vic," Lingyi said in a soft voice.

"No, it's not," Arun agreed. "He'd be up on the latest and how to get it. But I think with some research, I'd be able to get my hands on this fast."

I rubbed my temples, suddenly overcome with exhaustion. "So we let Jin find Lingyi and take her; the tracker will lead us to her and to Jany's device."

Iris shook her head. "You have no idea where Jin might take her—it could be another country. It could be to some maximum-security fort we could never break into." She grabbed Lingyi's hand. "I can't let you do this. Not after Vic; we can't lose you, too." She kissed Lingyi's fingers. "*I* can't lose you. Please."

"It'll work out, my heart." Lingyi touched Iris's cheek. "Trust me."

Iris leaped off the sofa and stalked away, looking like she was ready to punch a fist through the wall. She knew Lingyi as well as I did—better. There was no changing Lingyi's mind.

"Iris is right," Arun said. "There's a high chance that we might not get to you in time. Then Jin has the tech, and he'll have you, too."

"I know." Lingyi met my and Arun's gaze with clear eyes. "But do any of you have a better idea? I'm open." Then she looked toward Iris's tense back, and her brow knitted together. "I made a promise. I couldn't save Jany's life, but I can do this."

"Well," I said. "You know I'm here to back you."

"You too, Zhou?" Iris asked. "You support this? When we're all still grieving for Victor? Lingyi, you just witnessed another murder. You're in shock. You aren't thinking straight."

I stood, palming my knife, filled with too much nervous energy not to do something with my hands. "I'd take her place if I could, Iris. She's made up her mind. All we can do is make sure we get her back as fast as we can from Jin. Safe."

"It doesn't have to be for nothing, even if my life is at risk," Lingyi said in a soft voice. "I can send the data to you and destroy the device if I have to." She nodded once at Arun. "Jin might have me, but he won't ever have Jany's design. Not if I can help it."

Arun's mouth was drawn in a taut line. "The man murdered my mom. I'm willing to do whatever I can to stop him from profiting further from innocent people's deaths."

Iris had looked furious, as if she could argue for days, but then she closed her eyes at the mention of Dr. Nataraj. We had all loved her, looked up to her as someone actively fighting for a better world. And she had died senselessly for it. Her death, like Jany's, was on Jin.

"I'll look into getting the tracker I can inject under your skin. It shouldn't take too long on the Shanghai undernet."

"Thank you, Arun," Lingyi said.

I spun my butterfly knife, and none of us said anything else, but the air felt heavy with words unspoken.

▲▼▲

We all slept in the next morning, exhausted, as if in an attempt to delay the inevitable. Arun had arranged to buy the tracker from a seller at midnight near Yuyuan. He met the seller alone, but I tailed him, not far behind the entire way in case he ran into trouble. But the exchange went without a hitch.

"My sources say this guy's reputable," Arun said as we walked back to the hotel. "As reputable as one can be for selling stolen or banned goods on the black market."

I rolled out of bed at noon and took a quick shower before heading out in search of food. I roamed through the backstreets, behind the Bund. Pedestrians were grabbing lunches from roadside carts frying omelets or selling stacks of fried chicken and sausages. I pushed my way past a small crowd of older men, all smoking cigarettes between hacking coughs, their face masks hanging loosely around their necks. I peered over one man's shoulder and saw that there was a small table set up. Two men with close-cropped hair were playing an animated game of chess, ignoring the suggestions that were shouted at them by others who looked on.

Not far from the chess game, I smelled the delicious aroma of fresh cakes. Within half a block, I came upon a corner store bakery, an open stand really. Suddenly starving, I was tempted by everything I saw. I waited behind three other customers before buying sponge cakes, sesame rolls, and red bean rice cakes for everyone.

When I returned, my friends were all up, converged in the main sitting area once again. Arun lifted his chin at me in greeting, before accepting a large sponge cake. "I've injected the tracker under Lingyi's skin. We've already tested it, and I was able to track her, no problem."

Iris crossed her arms and didn't say anything, obviously still upset over our plan.

I made espresso drinks for us with the machine in our room and brewed a large mug of green tea for Lingyi as everyone shuffled through the bags of fresh-baked goods I had brought back. But no one said anything. The tension was thick in the room. If anything happened to Lingyi, Iris would never forgive us. Hell, I would never forgive myself.

A part of me thought that no matter how hard we fought or tried, we could never best Jin in the end. But a larger part didn't want the bastard to get away with anything else. I trusted that Lingyi could handle herself, but I knew that, once again, the odds were stacked against us.

I carried the hot drinks over to the group, allowing myself to enjoy the rich aroma of the espresso, before sitting down beside Lingyi on the sofa. Her face was pale, and there were dark circles under her eyes. "I can tail Lingyi too." I downed my shot of espresso before going on. "This way, we have both me and the tracker on her. Unless you want to follow her, Iris?" Iris was faster than I was and more agile.

"No," Lingyi said. "I don't want it to be Iris." She looked toward Iris, who was hunched against the wall away from the group. "It'd be too personal for her."

Iris turned her face away and gazed out at our expansive views of the river.

"It's a good idea," Arun said. "If Zhou can follow Lingyi discreetly from the start, we can be there as backup soon after, using the tracker."

"I'm stocked up on my throwing knives," I replied.

Iris nodded. Her weapon of choice was the sleep spell injection that knocked anyone out within seconds and wiped their memories.

Arun handed Iris and me cheap imitation Palms. "We can use these to message, call, and track each other. I've programmed all our temporary numbers into them. Stay offline with your own devices."

I pocketed the dummy Palm.

"Iris, could I speak with you alone?" Lingyi asked. She had barely made a dent in the giant sponge cake on the plate in front of her. But her tea mug was almost empty.

At first, it was as if Iris didn't hear her. Then, with long strides, she walked into their bedroom, and Lingyi rose to follow.

Arun and I sat in silence for a long time. Finally he spoke. "Everything will be okay."

But it sounded more like a question than a statement.

CHAPTER EIGHT

Lingyi and I set out in the afternoon. She left first, disappearing into the throng of pedestrians and tourists on the sidewalks. I followed half a block behind, glimpsing a flash of her bright purple hair every so often. The side streets were filled with taxis and cars, but as we passed the main boulevards, men and women had enough space to ride past on bicycles, some precariously stacked with boxes and goods in the back, tied down with cords. They teetered on the edge of the wider streets, as cars and trucks honked at one another, trying to inch their way forward in the congested traffic.

The simplified writing on store signs and trucks was disconcerting; some characters were close enough that I knew the word, and others were so changed it was unrecognizable—a strange dissonance. Lingyi had her Palm and would have turned it on by now, letting Jin's men know her exact location if they were looking for her. I thought of Daiyu with a pang. She would be really worried by now because I'd completely dropped off the grid. Yet why should I be the one feeling guilty, when she had lied to me for so long about being in contact with her father?

I pushed past the pedestrians, focusing on Lingyi. They threw dirty looks but gave way. Lingyi took her time, pausing outside a bakery window, then lingered in front of a woman selling embroidered slippers set out on a woven blanket. She examined the shoes, never glancing up to look over her shoulder or toward the cars on the narrow street. I was more nervous for her than she appeared.

She moved on to the next block, and I followed, the pedestrians stepping aside for me, probably because I looked like I was ready to knife someone.

Lingyi paused again, peering into a shop window while checking the messages on her Palm. She looked so vulnerable, exposed, as others tramped past her, all noise and bustle. In contrast, she was a study in stillness, her shoulders tense, her eyes focused on her device.

She'd been online for almost thirty minutes. I wondered how long we'd have to wait—or if Jin wouldn't come for her at all. The thought had barely emerged in my mind when a black sedan pulled up right next to the shop Lingyi had stopped at. My heart lurched. Lingyi was still turned toward the shop window, oblivious, when a tall man jumped out of the car.

I was already on the move, pulling myself up onto the bamboo scaffolding that lined the buildings along the sidewalk. All of Shanghai seemed under construction. It gave me a perfect view as the stranger threw an arm around Lingyi, knocking her Palm from her hand, before forcing her into the sedan. She struggled, but the brute was big, and it was like watching him drag a rag doll into the car.

Even though I had been expecting this, my adrenaline spiked, and I had to force myself to stop from running forward and punching the thug.

Some pedestrians glanced at them but did nothing to intervene. Her Palm got kicked by a few people, before a kid who looked about twelve picked it up and slipped it into his pocket. The sedan jerked back into the street, but lucky for me, the traffic was terrible, and it crawled forward slowly. I ran along the scaffolding, hidden above them by the shadows of the tall buildings, easily following the car. I dictated a quick message to Iris and Arun, never letting my eyes off the black sedan.

We were nearing the end of the first long block, and I was just considering my next move as the scaffolding was ending, when the car hummed. I knew that sound. It was an aircar and about to fly. There was no way I could follow it then. Just as I was trying to suppress my panic, some rich *you* kid glided past me on his airped. He looked about my age, with his indigo hair cut short and spiked. He sported some designer sunglasses and was grinning widely, enjoying the ride.

"Hey!" I shouted. We were almost level, and he looked at me in confusion. It was long enough a pause that I lunged at him and tugged him off the airped, thumping him onto the scaffolding. He bounced off the bamboo, howling with surprise and pain.

"Help! Thief!!"

But I had already leaped onto his airped, feeling the strong hum of the propulsion system as I surged higher into the air, away from the *you* boy screaming at my back. The sedan Lingyi was in had already flown a short distance off, but my airped was fast, and I followed at a reasonable distance, flying higher than the aircar. There was enough traffic in the skies that I didn't appear conspicuous, but I had no idea where our final destination might be, and as I followed farther from the city center, there were fewer and fewer air vehicles around us.

I feared I would become too noticeable soon.

As I decided what to do, the aircar glided back onto the street below. We hadn't gone far, maybe ten miles or so, and were on the outskirts of Shanghai proper. Throngs of people pushed along on the streets below, and I saw canals, their waters a muddied brown. The sedan was caught in light traffic, but moving toward one of these canals. I followed above as it turned and drove along the water, past a few streets overrun with shoppers and tourists. A number of stone bridges arched over the dirty waters, and there were many sightseers on them, taking photos and videos.

But the car kept moving, past the busy city center. Ramshackle houses emerged. I continued to tail the car at a safe distance, until I saw them pull into a narrow alleyway beside a run-down house farther along the canal, far from the shopping and crowds. Electrical lines crisscrossed above the low, dirty buildings, their facades thick with grime. I glided onto the flat concrete rooftop of one of the buildings nearby, which offered a bird's-eye view. Soon enough, the sedan car doors opened. A driver wearing dark sunglasses stepped out; then Lingyi was pushed out of the car, followed by the thug who had kidnapped her. She was awake, and walked on her own, sandwiched between the two men. Jin probably didn't want to risk knocking Lingyi out, wanting her to be able to work on Jany's MacFold and give him access to the tech as soon as possible.

They disappeared into the squat, two-story, dilapidated home—the last place I thought they would take her. But then, it made sense that Jin wanted this all done far from Jin Corp in Beijing, with no ties back to him if anything went wrong. As far as he knew, Lingyi was alone and vulnerable. My guess was there were a couple of more thugs in the house at most. Jin would think four or five goons were enough to keep Lingyi in line.

I let Arun and Iris know where Lingyi and I were.

"We're almost there," Arun replied. "Hang on, Zhou."

I waited another five minutes, watching for any movement that might suggest Lingyi and the men would be on the move again. But no one entered or exited from the old wooden door. A blanket was hung on the inside of the single window next to it, but the few windows on the second floor were uncovered.

I steered the airped onto a side street a little ways behind the house and slinked my way toward it. There was a narrow back door hidden in darkness that faced an alleyway. I used the exposed pipe running along the corner of the house and climbed up, stepping onto the ledge of the second floor, which made it easy for me to navigate. An old air-conditioning unit hung out from one of the windows in the front of the house, appearing as if it would topple any moment. I peered inside. An empty room except for a dirty mattress on the floor and a side table.

I quickly scanned the main street and my surroundings. There was no one in view, but I felt better when I turned the far corner into another alley so I was not exposed on the main street any longer. There was a window on this side of the house too, and I glanced inside, but quickly leaned back again. A man was standing right next to it, his back turned to me. The same man who had dragged Lingyi off the street, if his thick shoulders were an indication. Lingyi sat at a table in the center of the room, typing away on a MacFold.

She didn't look frightened—more so determined—her eyes narrowed in concentration. But her face was pale under the single lightbulb hanging overhead, casting a harsh light in the cramped room.

Seeing her like this, trapped, elicited a visceral reaction, and I forced myself away from the window, pressing my back against the rough wall. I slipped down the pipe easily and went back to where the airped was parked, reporting to my friends what I had seen.

"What are our odds?" Iris asked.

"Better than good," I replied. "Probably four at most securing the property. You could take them out yourself."

Iris gave one short laugh, but it was humorless.

"I'll stay outside as lookout and backup," Arun replied. "Stay put. We're headed to you, Zhou."

Not five minutes later, I saw Iris's familiar lope farther down the alleyway, followed by Arun's bright orange hair behind her. Iris and I nodded at each other, and Arun bumped fists with me. We quietly discussed our plans in the shadowed alleyway; then Iris and I set out together. I watched her climb onto the second floor of the house as easily as if she were walking up stairs. I navigated it almost as swiftly, since this was my second time. We had agreed that we'd enter from the second floor so we could reach Lingyi immediately, but that would also give us the element of surprise.

When we returned to the narrow window looking into where Lingyi was, nothing had changed. The thug still stood near it with his back to us, and Lingyi was working on the laptop. Iris and I situated ourselves on either side of the window. Our eyes met, and Iris nodded once.

I rapped on the glass pane hard and heard the deep voice of the guard cursing. We had both sidled back from his view, so the guy, just as we had guessed, lifted the window open and stuck his head out. He saw me first, and I grinned. "What the—" But Iris jabbed a sleep spell injection into his thick neck before he could finish his curse. He roared but went limp immediately after, half slumped over the windowsill. I didn't have enough leverage to haul him out or push him back into the room, but then Lingyi was there, dragging the man back in by his legs.

"You're here already," she said, and sounded out of breath.

The thug had barely bounced onto the floor before Iris had climbed into the room, giving Lingyi a quick hug. "We're here," she said. "Now let's disappear."

Lingyi ran toward the table to get Jany's MacFold.

But heavy steps were already thumping up the wooden stairs. "What was that noise? Shortie, what's going on?"

Without a word, Iris was across the room, pressing herself against the wall behind the narrow door. I palmed a knife, loving the perfect balance of it in my hand, when the door burst open. A man stood in the doorway, stared at Shortie knocked out on the floor, then lunged straight for Lingyi. There was nowhere for her to run in the small room. He put her in a choke hold and was so much taller than her, Lingyi's feet lifted off the ground. She grabbed at his thick arms, her face reddening as he squeezed. "Drop your weapon," he growled.

I kept eye contact with the thug, trying to assess how much of him was exposed that I might be able to get a good stab in.

"Who else is with you?"

"No one," I lied. Iris was still hidden behind the door. I slowly circled around the small table toward the open window, to draw his attention away from her.

But whether it was from instinct or luck, the thug twisted halfway so he could keep me in his view and spotted Iris pressed against the wall behind the door, which stood ajar. She had a sleep injection ready in one hand—but it was tucked behind her palm, not visible to Jin's henchman. I'd seen her use this grip a hundred times.

"Stop," he said. "Or your friend dies." He tightened his squeeze around Lingyi's neck and lifted her entirely off the floor. She struggled, kicking her legs, and it took all my willpower not to rush him. But I wasn't fast enough. He could snap her neck before I could stop him.

Fuck.

"I'm sure you've been instructed not to hurt her," I spoke loudly to distract him.

"You know nothing." He sneered, showing stained teeth. And as if to prove his point, he squeezed his arms harder around Lingyi's throat. I watched in horror as her eyes rolled back, and then her head lolled against the man. I didn't think she was dead, but if he kept that clamp on her neck, she soon would be.

Enraged, I charged, a primal shout erupting at the same time. He held Lingyi like a rag doll and protected himself with her body. It gave me limited choices as to where I could strike. Desperate, I depressed the button on the bottom of the knife hilt. A dead man wouldn't be able to keep a choke hold.

The thug was twisting this way and that, trying to keep an eye on both me and Iris; Lingyi's legs swung loosely in the air, and the sight of it was horrifying. I charged again, and he jerked my way. It gave Iris enough time to leap on the man, stabbing him in the side of his neck with her sleep injection. She then wrapped her own arms around the brute's neck, forcing his head back. He swayed, and his grip loosened around Lingyi. She slipped to the wood floor, thunking against it like a corpse.

I rushed to her side, my heart in my throat. The thug dropped to the floor then, and Iris shoved his body aside, running to crouch on Lingyi's other side. "Shit, shit, shit," Iris kept saying without even realizing. Her hands hovered over Lingyi, too afraid to touch anything. I pressed my hand against Lingyi's wrist. Her pulse was weak, but there. And her face was slowly returning to a normal hue.

"She's alive," I said. "She'll be all right."

"How do you know?" Iris turned her wrath on me. "She almost died. He could have"—she seemed to struggle for words—"broken her neck. Her face was *purple*."

I was sick to my stomach but had to pretend to be calm, for our survival's sake. I spoke into my dummy Palm. "Arun, are you there?"

"Yep," Arun replied immediately. "One of the goons tried to run. He was about to report to Jin on his Palm, but I knocked him out and dragged him back into the house. All clear down here. Let's head out."

I tried my best not to sound panicked. "The thug got ahold of Lingyi. She's out."

"Coming up," he said. Within moments, we heard stomping on the stairs. Both Iris and I tensed, but Arun appeared in the doorway.

He immediately went to Lingyi, checked on her pulse, then peeled her eyelids back. She groaned when he did that. "What happened?" he asked. Iris told him, describing the scenario with her eyebrows drawn in anger. But I knew it was fear and panic that fueled her rage—those were easier feelings to deal with.

"Lingyi?" Arun said softly, cupping her face. "Are you awake?"

She opened her eyes and winced, as if the room was too bright. "What happened?" she asked, echoing Arun.

"You lost consciousness for a bit," Arun replied. "You'll have some bruising on your throat and feel sore, but it'll be okay." He glanced toward Iris. "Could you get some water for her?"

Iris ran down the stairs and returned in a few minutes carrying a small pot. "There weren't any glasses."

Arun gently helped ease Lingyi into a sitting position, and Iris tenderly lifted the pot to her mouth. Lingyi drank, but we could all see how much it hurt for her to swallow. "Are we in the clear?" she managed to ask after several slow, painful sips. "For now," I said. "Do you think you can stand on your own and walk?"

Iris helped Lingyi to her feet. She swayed a little, but then gripped Iris's arm and nodded. "I can manage."

Arun grabbed Jany's MacFold off the table and slipped it into his backpack.

"We better clear out," I said.

Lingyi stepped over the brute who had choked her and Iris followed, a hand clutching Lingyi at her elbow. I patted the men down, finding a Palm in the pocket of the goon who had kidnapped Lingyi. There was a message on there from someone simply dubbed "Boss": Is everything on track?

It had been sent recently, right before the fool stuck his head out a window. I considered the message, then scrolled through previous exchanges. Nothing incriminating, but I got the language that was used by both men. Yeah, boss, I dictated. The girl's working hard.

Good, came Jin's immediate reply. I'll stop in tonight.

I left the thug's Palm on the ground beside him. They'd be knocked out still when Jin showed up, but the exchange had bought us some time.

I rose and swept my eyes across the barren room, before following my friends down the cramped stairway.

▲▼▲

I abandoned the airped I had stolen. There were no taxis near the crush of old houses where Lingyi had been taken, so we made our way toward the city center. I learned we were in Qibao, an ancient water town on the outskirts of Shanghai proper. It was late afternoon, and sweltering, so hot that I could smell the stench of the water rising from the canal we walked along.

Arun was leading the way, followed by Lingyi and Iris. I brought up the rear, my hand resting against one of the knives Daiyu had given me just a few days ago. It felt like my entire world had changed since our last morning together. Although I knew Jin didn't realize yet that his target had escaped along with the design he so desperately wanted to get his hands on, I still scanned our surroundings, leery. From my experience with Jin, I knew you couldn't underestimate him, and when he struck back, he did so without a second thought or mercy.

Instead of taking the smaller side streets, Arun led us straight into the heart of the shopping area of Qibao. Mobs of people moved like cattle along the narrow streets, between stores offering everything from steamed buns shaped like panda and pig faces, to dried goods ranging from fruits to meat, and cheap trinkets and souvenirs. The storefronts were made to look like architecture from past dynasties, with curved tiled eaves overhanging the two-story buildings, and redwood panel windows thrown open in the oppressive August heat. I bumped into people as they meandered through the crowded street and stopped frequently to buy food or inspect wares. Vendors enticed potential customers with samples and shouted about the unique deliciousness of their noodles or braised tofu. I kept my eyes on my friends, easier to do with their bright hair colors. It seemed like an older crowd enjoying the tourist town today, wearing large sun hats and caps, their faces covered by masks.

Arun dropped back when Iris stopped to buy an iced tea for

Lingyi. "I thought it'd be safer to go through the crowds."

I watched as Iris bought a bag of small fried buns, probably also for Lingyi. "I think we have a few hours before Jin finds out. I'm glad Lingyi seems all right now, but she could have died."

"I know." Arun's tone was as morose as I felt.

Lingyi turned right then and glanced back at us. Her face was pallid in the glaring daylight. We began walking again, side by side, as Iris and Lingyi had moved on to another storefront. "We got damned lucky," Arun said.

We could have easily lost her—anything could have gone wrong in the heat of the moment. We had succeeded in our task, but it wasn't a triumph. It didn't feel like a time for celebration or relief. Lingyi's life was still in danger—all of our lives were—as long as we had what Jin wanted. We were walking targets in a different country without any resources. And even though we spoke the language, we still stuck out like foreigners. We did not fit in; not in our manner-isms, nor the way we talked or dressed.

I was damp with sweat by the time we had pushed through the crowds to finally emerge onto a main boulevard where we hailed a taxi. Brown haze hung over the skyline and the air reeked of exhaust, even through my face mask. Aircars were few this far from Shanghai proper, so we sat in the congested traffic instead, mostly in silence, unable to discuss anything until we had privacy. Arun was in the back with the girls, and I sat on the passenger side up front. The driver's seat was blocked off from me and the back with thick, clear plastic, something I had never seen before. When I asked about it, the driver joked that the screen made it harder for anyone to mug him.

When we finally arrived back at our hotel, I was antsy, eager to discuss what we needed to do next before we flew back to Taipei. Eager to put plans into action and move. The suite was as we had left it, and after Iris and I swept through and made sure it was safe, it still didn't feel safe.

"How soon can we book flights back to Taipei?" I asked when everyone regrouped in the sitting area.

"Jin's flagged me to prevent me from leaving China. I can change my identity as much as I'd like, but he took my retina scan. His thug told me I couldn't leave the country unless Jin allows it." Lingyi sank back into the sofa, and Iris wrapped an arm around her. Lingyi looked exhausted, worn. Dark bruises stood out on her pale throat. "To bypass that would take more work than I have time for right now. Our priority is to keep Jany's design safe." She coughed, her voice rasping. "I'll work on securely transferring her data, then wipe this device. It'll take at least a day."

I cursed under my breath. That was too much time; Jin could easily track us down. "Is it safe to stay here?"

Lingyi sighed, then stood and stretched. Her skirt was wrinkled, and another purple bruise was blooming on her arm where the damned brute had grabbed her. I went and got an iced tea from the hotel fridge. She took it gratefully, taking a long sip before continuing. "It's as good as anywhere for now. I'd rather stay put and get this done as fast as possible. I'll work on manipulating my passport info after, so I can leave the country without being flagged."

Arun nodded, and I resigned myself to being holed up here and waiting, until Lingyi was finished.

"In the meantime," Arun said, "I'd suggest we all stay offline. I don't know if Jin is tracking any of us, but he knows I'm the person who made the antidote that curbed his flu epidemic. I'm definitely on his radar. And Zhou—"

I flipped my butterfly knife and stopped him from going on. "I know. I'm with his daughter." *Or was, anyway.* It hurt me to think how panicked she probably was by now, since I'd been out of touch. But I wasn't ready to speak with her, confront her, deal with what might be the remnants of our relationship. I was grateful for Arun giving me a good reason to stay dark.

"Actually, I was going to say you were the one who kidnapped his daughter and held her for a large ransom," Arun said.

"Oh," I replied. "That too."

Iris leaned back against the sofa, her arm still wrapped around Lingyi's shoulder. "Is no one going to say it?" she asked in a tone so fierce I nearly took a step backward. "You almost died today." Iris slipped her arm off Lingyi and pressed her face into her palms, then doubled over as if in pain. Or in an attempt to protect herself. She made no noise; her shoulders didn't heave. Instead, she sat hunched over and dead still.

The thick silence that fell across the room felt worse than any sound Iris might have made. I rubbed my temple, slipping my butterfly knife back into a pocket.

Arun and I avoided eye contact. Lingyi leaned forward and put a gentle hand on Iris's shoulder. "But I didn't die," she whispered. "I'm here. I'm all right."

"From luck," Iris said in a muffled voice. "From sheer foolish luck."

"No," Lingyi said. "Because you were there like we had planned. Because Zhou and Arun were there. We worked together and we took back what Jin had stolen."

"But what if I had failed?" Iris finally lifted her face and stared at Lingyi with red-rimmed eyes. "And I lost you."

Lingyi grabbed for Iris's hand, holding it against her own chest, but couldn't seem to meet Iris's imploring gaze. "I'm sorry, love."

Iris stood. "I'll take first shift tonight," she said in a rough voice.

We had all known what the risks were, and it had very nearly become reality again today. But if Iris had hoped Lingyi almost dying might have changed her determination to avenge Jany's death—it obviously hadn't. Lingyi was not going to run home; she would see this thing through.

"Let me come with you," Lingyi said. She still clasped Iris's hand.

Iris shook her head. "I do surveillance better alone. And you need to work on transferring Jany's data. The sooner that's done, the sooner we can leave here"—she swallowed—"and you'll be safe."

Lingyi did meet Iris's eyes then, and nodded once.

Iris leaned over and kissed Lingyi on the lips before heading out the door. Arun pulled Jany's laptop from his backpack, and Lingyi took it to the desk in the corner of the room. The determined look I had seen when she was trapped with Jin's men had returned, and she went straight to work.

Arun left soon after to gather plates of appetizers and desserts for us from the executive lounge. I cobbled together a meal of finger sandwiches and Thai chicken satay skewers. The hours dragged on, the passing of time marked by the fading daylight as the neon lights brightened on the skyscrapers across the river. Iris checked in on the hour with no news. Jin Tower was almost directly across from our hotel, and I watched the commercials and images play across its glass panels. It seemed there was no escaping the man—he was omnipresent like some amoral god in a Greek tragedy.

Suddenly, Jin himself was projected on the tower, dressed in an expensive suit, literally bigger than life. He was speaking, but without sound, and subtitles scrolled vertically beside his image. *I would like to welcome everyone to an opening ceremony like Shanghai has never seen.* He lifted his arms. *Jin Tower is the first self-contained vertical city, and all retail and residential spaces are almost sold out. Contact Jin Corp if you'd like to be a part of history.*

I was pressed against the window, glaring at the broadcast. Arun came and stood by my side. "The man never quits, does he?" he murmured.

Then Daiyu was plastered onto Jin Tower's glass surface, and I stumbled back from the window. It was an image of her dressed in her purple qipao, accepting the one-million-yuan donation check from Jin Corp at her fund-raising gala.

"Shit," Arun said.

My daughter, the heir of Jin Corp, will be by my side for Jin Tower's grand opening ceremony. The words scrolled down the building in simplified Chinese, and each character felt like a punch in the gut.

Arun clasped my shoulder. "Zhou."

I stared blindly at Arun, then looked back at the building in time to see an image of Daiyu standing regally beside her father in a red sheath dress, before the image scattered into a million bright pixels, and a commercial for Jin Tower took its place.

"Zhou," Arun repeated.

"How could I have been so foolish?" I asked.

Arun shook his head. "You don't know what the circumstances are. Maybe Jin is coercing her. Jin's all about saving face and showing a united front. It's no surprise he wants to bring Daiyu back into the fold. She *is* his daughter."

Of course.

I wanted to pound my fists against the glass but clenched them at my sides instead, unable to put my jumbled thoughts and emotions into coherent words. She had been visiting her father's mansion once or twice a week still, but none of Jin's staff asked about her comings and goings. And I knew Jin had stopped supporting her financially since he'd fled to China, closing accounts and shifting his assets abroad. "I don't think on purpose," Daiyu had said to me. "But I'm just an afterthought."

Until Jin needed to use her again.

"Even if her father is forcing her to do this, she's still the *heir* of Jin Corp," I finally managed. "I had assumed when she cut off ties with him . . ."

But she had never cut off those ties.

"I'm sorry, man," Arun said after a long silence. "I know you like her."

The hotel room's phone rang in that moment, and I turned from the window, glad for the distraction. It was ten p.m., and Iris was reporting that things were all clear. "Come back," I said. "I'll head up to the roof."

"I'll give you five minutes," Iris replied, and disconnected our call, even more sparse with words than I was.

"Jin will know Lingyi has escaped by now," I said to Arun. "He'll regroup. The longer we remain in Shanghai, the more dangerous it'll be."

Arun glanced toward Lingyi, who had been hunched over the laptop this entire time, rising only to use the bathroom. I had been keeping her mug full of hot tea the whole evening. "You call on the hour too, Zhou," he said.

I nodded, patting my clothing, checking on where all my hidden knives were tucked.

"Will you be okay out there?" Arun sounded concerned.

"I'm good," I said. I didn't look back when I shut the heavy suite door behind me.

CHAPTER NINE

The summer heat lingered in the air, like cloying perfume that wouldn't dissipate. I took the elevator to the roof first, needing to be away from people, needing time to think, and breathe. Unmasked, I took long breaths of the humid air, the pollution feeling worse than inhaling secondhand smoke blown directly at me. Still, I left my face bare, an anomaly now in Taipei, and also in Shanghai. It seemed humankind wouldn't be satisfied until our entire world was smothered in smog.

I walked along the edge of our hotel building, peering over the shoulder-height concrete wall. The crowds had thinned this late in the night, but the Bund was by no means empty. Shanghai was a city that never slept. The historic buildings on the Bund were lit in golden light, juxtaposed against the flashing neon and advertisements on the modern skyscrapers across the river. I paced along the wall until I was above the main entrance of Les Suites. I could see two doormen standing outside as cars and taxis swept past. Aircars and limos hovered in the distance, headed to the exclusive restaurants and clubs that dotted the Bund.

The night was still, with little breeze. Ignoring the warning signs plastered on the walls, I pulled myself easily up, sitting down and taking in Shanghai's breathtaking skyline. Jin Tower continued to project its advertisements, and I wrenched my gaze away, the hurt and confusion taking hold again, clamping down like a vise on my breath. *A fool indeed.* I had thought dating Jin's daughter—someone completely out of my league anyway—was an impossible dream. Well, I was right.

Has he been in contact with you? I had asked Daiyu the last night we spent together in the Shangri-La Hotel after her gala. She had been annoyed, dismissive. *I don't want to talk about this right now.* Now I knew why—they'd been in contact all these months, and Daiyu had chosen to lie to me about it.

But part of me still couldn't believe that Daiyu had lied to me maliciously, that her feelings for me hadn't been true. Or maybe she'd finally realized that I would never be good enough—a street urchin, pretending to be someone I wasn't. An outsider. Maybe she knew all along that our relationship would only be temporary. I pounded my fists into the concrete wall again and again, letting the pain bolt up my arms.

Pathetic, Zhou.

I surveyed the street below, taking in the pedestrians on the sidewalks and the cars coming and going. A silver BMW pulled up to the hotel entrance, and a black man in a tuxedo stepped out before reaching over to lend a hand to his partner; a beautiful black woman wearing a slinky red dress emerged from the car. Nothing suspicious. Maybe we'd get lucky tonight and it'd pass without incident. I jumped off the wall. When the lights along the Bund and across the river dimmed to darkness at eleven p.m., I took the elevator down to the sleek hotel lobby and rang up our suite to check in.

"Iris is sleeping," Arun said. "She'll relieve you at four."

I agreed. "How's Lingyi doing?"

"Still working," he replied. "I tried to get her to rest, but she refused."

"Iris was right to be terrified," I said in a quiet voice. "It all happened so fast—she was choking to death."

Arun didn't respond right away, and the silence was heavy. "I know. She's all right now, thankfully."

From sheer foolish luck.

I hung up and took a quick sweep of the lobby, empty this late at night except for the attendant behind the counter, before grabbing an apple and a cookie from the executive lounge and heading back up to the roof. It offered the best view of who went in and out of our hotel, but also, I'd know if Jin's men decided to access it from the rooftop. The cars and pedestrians dwindled the later it got; the hours passed without incident. Iris met me on the roof.

"Are you okay?" I asked.

She nodded, her eyes hooded. "But I barely slept."

If it had been any of my other friends, I would have given them a hug, but Iris wasn't a hugger. Instead I said, "That's rough." We talked a little bit about what I had observed in these last hours canvassing, but not about anything that was really on our minds. She gave me a fist bump before I headed back to our suite.

Our once immaculate sitting area was in disarray, with mugs and plates strewn all over the coffee tables and large glass tabletop. We'd opted out of housekeeping during our stay here. Lingyi was curled up on the sofa, and Arun sat across from her with his chin resting against his chest, dozing. His spiked orange hair had lost some of its stiffness from the long day, and he reminded me of a bedraggled rooster. Again, despite the maelstrom we were facing, with the odds piled against us, it felt good to be with my friends. I began gathering the dirty dishes and mugs as quietly as I could, setting them on a credenza where our espresso machine was. Arun jerked awake on my last trip, his hand tightening on the taser resting next to his thigh.

"Zhou," he said. "You're back. Get some rest."

"I didn't mean to wake you," I said in a low voice, watching

Lingyi clutch a quilt to her chin, obviously in a deep sleep.

"I've slept." Arun rose, stretching. "Go."

I didn't argue with him and retreated to the other bedroom in the suite, climbing onto the plush bed and falling asleep instantly.

▲▼▲

I woke to a string of loud curses from Arun in the main room. I glanced at my Vox; it was after eight a.m. I rolled out of bed and ran a hand through my hair. A boat's horn sounded loudly on the river; I squinted against the hazy light that filled the main sitting area of our suite. Everyone, including Iris, was sitting on the sofas.

"What's wrong?" I asked, glancing around, making sure nothing looked out of place.

"I discovered in Jany's notes just an hour ago that she had made a fully functioning prototype," Lingyi said, sounding exhausted. "Arun and I were discussing what to do about it."

For a moment, I didn't follow, and then understanding dawned. "Where is it?"

Arun nodded at the wall screen. "Looks like we might be too late."

The screen was muted with subtitles, but I voice-commanded the volume up.

A news reporter stood in front of a single-story building. Its walls had once been white but were a dingy gray now, and much of the paint had flaked off years ago. Double glass doors with faint blue trim were flung open, with paramedics streaming in and out. Above the doors was a faded wooden sign with the characters QIBAO BLESSED MERCY CHILDREN'S CLINIC, originally etched in black, but long since worn away.

"This is an image of the robbers responsible for stealing the air filter from the clinic two nights ago," the reporter, a woman dressed in a sleeveless silk shirt and tan skirt, said to the cambot. A grainy image of three men in dark suits flashed across our screen. I immediately recognized them as Jin's thugs—the ones who had kidnapped Lingyi. "This single image was provided by the director of the clinic, Ms. Wang, as the facility is not equipped with a security system or cameras."

"No wonder they took Lingyi there," I said. "Jin's men were already in Qibao."

"It's no coincidence," Lingyi agreed. "Jany's notes indicated that she donated the prototype to a clinic on the outskirts of Shanghai. She included an image, and it's an exact match."

The program cut to another woman, older, with her hair cut short. She had been crying. "These are poor children from the city and countryside, abandoned or given to us by heartsick parents who didn't have the money to take care of them. These men robbed us. I knew these kids' lives were at risk if the filter was taken." The woman's hand shook as she swiped at her eyes. "I begged. I offered my life savings." She took a quivering breath that turned into a sob. "We didn't have the equipment to help these kids when the air quality worsened." Ms. Wang bowed her head, unable to look directly into the cambot.

"Shit," I said.

The news program cut back to the reporter. "To make matters worse, much of Qibao is suffering from a brownout since yesterday, and electricity has been off for large sections of the Minghang District—where Qibao is located—including the clinic. Due to lack of funds, the clinic has only one old generator that is not functioning." The reporter shook her head. "Three infants and two children have already died. The situation is dire."

The director grabbed the mic from the reporter. "We're in desperate need of a new generator, incubators, ventilators, and hospital-grade air filters. Please help!"

I muted the program. "What can we do?"

"I have to go on-site," Arun said. "Iris can stay here with Lingyi. Come with me, Zhou."

"It's too risky," Iris replied.

"I can't *not* help," Arun retorted. "Kids are dying. *Babies.*"

Lingyi stood and wrapped her arms around Arun. She looked worn out, but Arun appeared somewhere between enraged and panicked. "Go with Zhou. Iris has her temporary device. We'll be in contact. I should be done by the end of the day."

"You're not safe, Lingyi, even if Jin has the prototype now," I said. "His men got their hands on it *before* they took the time to kidnap you the next day." I took my butterfly knife out and spun it, too restless not to have something in my hand. "Jin doesn't like loose ends. You're a loose end."

"You're right," Arun said. "And the reverse engineering on the catalyst could take at least a month, if not longer. Jin has no patience for that."

"Don't worry about me," Lingyi said. "Go. Keep your hair unspiked and covered, Arun," Lingyi said. "You're too recognizable now. Keep your faces hidden."

We nodded in agreement. Arun and I took fifteen minutes to get ready and were out the door before nine a.m., headed back to Qibao.

▲▼▲

We hailed an aircar along the Bund. The day was already hot, and the Bund was crowded with pedestrians, including two large tourist groups. Their guides held colored flags, and the tourists all wore color-coordinated caps. A long barge drifted down the river, hauling what appeared to be heaping piles of dirt. Smaller tourist boats navigated past it, with people pressed against the railings on the deck, taking photos and videos and admiring the views. I was relieved to settle into the cool aircar as it soared into the sky, away from the masses. I stared at Jin Tower as we arced past, last night's revelation about Daiyu hitting me again like a bad hangover. I concentrated on the city views from above, trying to distract myself.

The aircar glided gently to a stop across from the Blessed Mercy

Children's Clinic's front entrance. The low building was farther away from the canals and the popular shopping areas, surrounded by a six-foot-tall stone wall. It was tucked at the end of a residential street filled with older traditional houses with slanting tiled roofs. Although it was less crowded than when we had seen the news broadcast, a few reporters still lingered on the perimeters.

The area wasn't policed, and Arun and I stepped easily over the yellow-and-black caution tape that had been haphazardly pulled across the main entrance leading into the clinic's courtyard. We both wore dark caps pulled low on our heads and large face masks that obscured everything but our eyes. No one gave us a second glance. We waited at the front entrance as two paramedics carried a tiny covered body out on a stretcher. Its entire length was smaller than a hand towel. Arun made a strange choking noise beside me, and I averted my eyes.

"We have to find the director," Arun said brusquely, pushing his way in after the stretcher had moved into the courtyard toward the main gate.

I followed him and almost reared back at the wall of humid heat in the dim clinic. Emergency lighting flickered overhead, not providing enough light in the long, narrow hallways. The clinic was eerily quiet, except for the occasional shrieking cry of a child. The silence was also punctuated by thick, ragged coughs that reminded me of my mom on her deathbed.

Arun cursed loudly; his voice sounded too loud and out of place in these somber surroundings. "If they don't die from the bad air quality, they'll all die from heatstroke." We passed a reception area with one lone woman sitting at a desk, frantically dictating into her Palm. Her words slowed when she saw us, and she put her Palm onto the table. "We're in crisis here," she said. "What do you want?"

"We're here to help," Arun replied, going up to the faded blue counter. "Can I speak with your director?"

The woman gave Arun a doubtful look but appeared too exhausted and stricken to argue. "I'll page Ms. Wang," she said. She picked up her Palm again and dictated a short message into it.

Five minutes later, I recognized the woman with the short hair from the news broadcast. She was wearing dark blue hospital scrubs, but her pink face mask hung around her neck. "Yunli said you're here to help," Ms. Wang said without so much as an introduction. "Unless you have a stable of doctors or top-notch hospital equipment to give or a working generator on hand, you won't be of any use to me."

Arun pulled off his face mask, and Ms. Wang's dark eyes widened with recognition. He was well known in the field for manufacturing the antidote that had saved Taiwan from suffering Jin's avian flu epidemic. "My name is Arun Nataraj, and this is my friend Zhou. I'm not a doctor, but I help run a clinic in Taipei, and I want to donate equipment. We can start with a working generator. This kind of heat will only raise the death toll."

Ms. Wang grabbed for Arun's hand and clasped it for a moment. "We don't have time."

"Do you have leads, anywhere we can get equipment fast?" Arun asked. "Money is no object."

She nodded emphatically. "I know someone who can sell us a good generator and deliver it right away. I just didn't have the money the seller was asking." She looked Arun in the eyes. "The one we have, I was forced to buy on the black market for cheap. It failed us."

"Buy everything you need," Arun said. "My one request is that I remain anonymous. No one can know I'm here."

Tears had sprung into Ms. Wang's eyes. "We won't say a thing." She turned to the younger woman, who was standing behind the counter now, gawking at Arun. "You heard him, Yunli. Make the necessary calls for us."

Arun leaned over the counter. "I've a cashcard account that'll cover everything. I already let my assistant know to expect and approve forthcoming equipment purchases."

Yunli nodded and bowed when she proffered her Palm. Arun added the info she'd need, and the woman returned to the desk, her mouth thinning in determination as she got to work.

"Can you show us around, Ms. Wang?" Arun asked. "I'd like to see the kids and assess how best we can help."

The older woman let out a loud sigh, and I could feel the weight of the world on her shoulders in that one breath. "They're all in danger, Mr. Nataraj. Only some are closer to death's door than others." She swept an arm out down the dim corridor. "Please follow me."

I hesitated and walked behind the director and Arun, not certain I was ready to face this.

"The children came to us with compromised health already, many with pulmonary issues caused by diseases like cystic fibrosis, chronic asthma, and bronchitis," Ms. Wang said.

Arun shook his head. "They don't have a chance under these conditions."

"The government never responded to our pleas," Ms. Wang said. "We've been running on donations for years. It's why that air filter was such a gift." She wiped a hand over her eyes. "It was able to purify the air of an entire wing of our clinic. It truly was a miracle machine. Then those men came." Her voice cracked and she stopped herself.

"Who gave you the air filter, Ms. Wang?" I asked.

Her gaze slid to my face, scrutinizing. I hadn't removed my mask, and I could tell she tolerated my presence only because of Arun. I didn't inspire trust at a glance.

"Why are you asking?" She didn't bother to hide her suspicion.

I had to tread carefully, and treading carefully was not my strength. Arun gave me a sidelong glance in warning.

"Because," I said, "this air filter seems one of a kind. Powerful and unique. We know someone, a friend, who has invented something like this. I think we might know the same person. . . ."

Ms. Wang stopped mid-stride and turned to face me. "The person who donated this filter to us made me swear I'd never mention it." She flushed. "I tried contacting them after the theft but have not been able to speak with them. I had to report the theft to the police; I was desperate. But the police have been of no help either."

I nodded. "We're here to help Ms. Tsai—"

"You know her too!" Ms. Wang looked relieved. "I feel awful that she donated this so generously, and it was taken right in front of me."

"It's not your fault," Arun said. "We're dealing with brutes."

"Arun's right. You did everything you could." I paused. "Are you friends with Ms. Tsai?" She didn't need to know that Jany had been murdered by Jin.

Ms. Wang gestured, indicating we should move on, and we continued down the hallway as she talked. "We're only acquaintances, but I admire her so much. We are indebted to her."

The emergency lights flickered and buzzed overhead. I pulled my mask off, unable to breathe in the humid and still air within the clinic.

"She just appeared at the clinic one day carrying a box," Ms. Wang went on. "When she showed us what that compact filter could do! Well, I thought the heavens had sent her to us." She cleared her throat, and I felt her studying me again. "Jany said that no one knew about this filter except me."

I heard the suspicion creeping back into her voice. "It was true. But she came to us for aid—"

"Is she all right?" Ms. Wang interjected.

Arun said, "We're doing our best to help her."

It wasn't a lie.

Ms. Wang glanced at Arun, and something in his expression stopped her from pressing further. "I'm glad, because I didn't like the looks of those men. They were dangerous," she said instead, then opened a door to our left.

Arun paused at the threshold, and his dark complexion paled. He entered the room, and I stopped short just behind him.

"We've lost three infants already." Her gaze flew to an empty incubator. The white blanket and sheets dotted with elephants and giraffes were marred with specks of bright red blood. "These incubators are very old and barely functioned, but we had to make do." Ms. Wang's voice broke. "When the power went out, we scrambled, but we couldn't save them."

Two more incubators were in the small room, both draped with white sheets. The sight evoked an ominous dread in me, and my skin prickled despite the heat.

"Their health was always in delicate balance," Ms. Wang said.

Arun scrubbed his face with his hands, his shoulders drawn so taut I was worried for him. "Are we too late?" he finally asked in a hoarse voice.

The older woman patted Arun's shoulder, sensing the same distress I did. "I think there is hope for some of the older children with less severe illnesses. Come."

Arun followed, and I trailed behind, closing the door on the room that had been decorated with cute animal wallpaper in pastel colors. My chest constricted suddenly, and I remembered holding my mother's hands in those last days. Her skin was so frail—paper thin—so the veins stood out on the back of her hands. She, too, had coughed up blood in the end. Grief rose, unexpected and staggering, and I leaned on the closed door as Arun and Ms. Wang walked farther away from me, speaking in low voices.

I had to get out of there. It didn't feel like I could take a full breath in the oppressive heat of the building. I stumbled back the way I'd come, passing Yunli, who was speaking rapidly into her Palm, and tripped on my way out the glass doors. The daylight was blinding for a moment, and I covered my eyes, taking a long breath. It was hot out here, too, but a faint breeze stirred, giving some respite. I pressed my hand against the wood frame of the door and took a second to steady myself, when I felt a presence in the quiet courtyard.

I spun around, my eyes sweeping across the few trees and stone benches, when I glimpsed a figure half-hidden behind a large ginkgo tree. They wore a jacket despite the heat, their features shadowed by a hood and face mask. But the familiarity of the figure, in the curve of her neck and her wide stance, as if claiming the space, made her instantly recognizable to me.

Daiyu.

I almost turned around to disappear into the dark clinic again. But I knew she had seen me before I had spotted her, our awareness of each other like passing through a magnetic field. She stepped out from behind the tree.

There was no running away.

"What are you doing here?" I asked.

She shook her head but didn't lower her hood. "What are *you* doing here? I've been trying to reach you for days."

I might have felt guilty before, but not now. Not after everything my friends and I had gone through. Not after knowing how she'd deliberately lied to me for months. Not after seeing more blood-stained sheets.

"Arun and I are here to help," I said. "I might have lied to you about where I was going, but you lied to me, too."

She tensed.

"It's been all over the news, Daiyu," I continued. "Hell, I even saw you broadcasted across Jin Tower—the heir of Jin Corp come to Shanghai to celebrate your next moneymaking venture."

"Jason," she said in a voice so low it barely carried to me.

"Tell me I'm wrong." I couldn't keep the pain or anger from my voice. "Tell me it's not how it seems."

"It's not," she said.

"Are you still the heir of Jin Corp?"

She didn't reply for a long time. Then finally, "Yes, but—"

I laughed; it sounded cold and cruel. "I guess in the end, you really are your father's daughter."

She flinched.

"How did you find me?" I asked.

"I didn't know you were here." Her fists were clenched in front of her, pale against her dark jacket. "I came to help too."

"Help? Did you know about this beforehand, Daiyu?" I gripped the splintered doorframe. "Your *father* did this. The blood is on his hands."

"Jason," she said again.

I could barely keep from shouting. The rage I felt was all-consuming; my vision went dark for a moment. "Do you know how many deaths—" I saw my mother in my mind, Dr. Nataraj sprawled on her office floor, the man who'd caught Jin's avian flu and collapsed in the square beside me, Victor grinning, saying something sarcastic but taking the sting away with his wicked humor, the tiny body carried away beneath a thin sheet, specks of blood—bright red blood everywhere. A relentless montage that grabbed me and wouldn't let go. "Could you have stopped this?" I managed to choke out.

Daiyu stepped forward and lowered her hood. I knew her features, every line of her body, better than I knew myself. She looked tired, and her eyes were bright with tears. I glanced away, unable to hold her gaze. "I didn't know. I saw it on the news." Her voice wavered. "If I could have stopped him, I would. No one knows I'm here."

"Why not?" I asked.

"Because I didn't want the publicity," she replied. "It'd just be an all-media news circus."

"Or did you not want your father to know you were helping?" I asked. "Because you know deep down that what you're doing—

spending *his* money to help those in need—is everything he would be against?"

"Why are you judging me for using my trust fund for good, if I can?"

I lowered my head and drew a slow breath to try and calm myself, to quiet the rage inside of me. Finally, I looked Daiyu square in the eyes. "I know you want to do good." I had no doubt about that. She had showed me she cared, wanted to change the world, in everything she did. "But I don't know if things can work"—I struggled to keep my voice even—"between us like this. Lying to each other. Always hiding from your father. How can I ever fit into your life?"

She took a stumbling step backward, as if I'd hit her.

Shouting from outside the clinic walls startled us both, and Daiyu slid behind the gingko tree again, hiding from two beefy men who maneuvered a huge generator resting on a large four-wheeled dolly through the main entrance. "Where should we leave this?" one of the guys yelled at me.

"Zhou!" Arun emerged at the door. "Come help."

Ms. Wang followed behind, and her face lit up at the sight of the generator. "This way, men."

I followed them and glanced back once, but could no longer see Daiyu.

CHAPTER TEN

Arun worked with Ms. Wang, determined and relentless in his focus on saving the children. The generator got the air-conditioning working again in the clinic, and the temperature dropped so the kids were no longer living in an oven. It couldn't have come at a better time, as the day only got hotter by the afternoon. A handful of volunteer doctors and nurses showed up, and around three p.m., six new state-of-the-art incubators arrived along with ten new ventilators and two hospital-grade filters. Ms. Wang accepted the delivery with cries of joy, but when we were wheeling the equipment past Yunli with the help of the volunteers, she said in surprise, "I guess they could deliver the ventilators today after all."

"What do you mean?" I asked.

"I ordered a dozen new ventilators for the kids, but no one could deliver them today," Yunli replied. "The company who could have them here the soonest promised me tomorrow morning."

"Only eight ventilators were delivered today," Arun said.

"And six of the newest incubators," Ms. Wang added.

Yunli's forehead creased. "I didn't order any incubators. You hadn't asked specifically, Ms. Wang, so—"

"I think I know what happened," I said in a low voice. Arun glanced at me and I nodded at him. Daiyu's purchases had arrived first. "You can expect more ventilators arriving tomorrow morning."

Ms. Wang, eager to get the equipment in place, had barely been listening. "You've been far too generous, Mr. Nataraj," she said. "We are forever indebted to you."

Arun shook his head. "If you need anything else, buy it. These kids now actually have a chance."

I came to help too, Daiyu had said to me. And I never doubted it. But how tied she was to her father, how beholden she was to him, I didn't know. It was more than I could contemplate at the moment, because there were lives to be saved.

▲▼▲

Everyone worked tirelessly past midnight. Almost all the children's conditions were stabilized, and for the few who needed better support and care, the volunteer doctors were able to find places for them in the bigger hospitals where they worked. I mostly helped move equipment, did grunt work, and stayed out of people's way.

We were kept so busy that I was able to check in with Iris only once. She said in her succinct way that Lingyi was still working on establishing a secure VPN to transfer Jany's data, but we'd regroup and discuss the situation when we returned to Les Suites. I didn't even think of Daiyu again until Arun and I finally left the clinic, and I walked past the giant gingko tree she had hidden behind. The hairs on the back of my neck stood on end, and I almost expected her to appear again, so she could explain herself. So I could explain myself, too. But knowing Jin, he was probably keeping tabs on her, and she couldn't stray far or for long while in Shanghai. Not when she was the star of his opening ceremony at Jin Tower.

Exhausted and emotionally worn, I found it impossible to think straight. I almost brought up seeing Daiyu to Arun, but then decided not to say anything to him or my friends. What was the point? My heart wanted to trust Daiyu, but I knew my friends didn't. And for good reason. We staggered down the empty, dark street toward a main boulevard, hoping to find a taxi so far out from Shanghai's city center. If anyone decided to attack or mug us, we would have been easier prey, but despite looming shadows and the occasional strange night noises, we managed to find an old taxi reeking of stale cigarette smoke willing to take us back to the Bund.

It was past two a.m., and most of the streets were empty of pedestrians and traffic. But when we saw a still-lit corner shack near Yuyuan with tables and a few customers sitting outside, eating large bowls of noodles, Arun asked the driver to stop. He ran out and disappeared into the tiny shop, emerging again some time later holding a cardboard box filled with round containers. He thanked the taxi driver when he climbed back in. "I don't know about you, but I'm starving," Arun said.

I hadn't thought about it, but my stomach grumbled loudly at the smell of beef broth and scallions. "Me too," I said, suddenly ravenous.

We arrived back at the hotel soon after, and Arun and I stumbled out of the taxi, but I carried our box of noodles like precious cargo. Iris met us at the elevators. "You're back," she said.

"With food," I replied. "How's it been here?"

We entered the elevator and headed up to our suite. "I've been alternating between staying in the suite and canvassing the hotel," Iris said. "Lingyi fell asleep while working."

We found her sprawled over the desk. Iris must have pushed Jany's MacFold out of the way. But Lingyi's brow was creased, as if she were worrying over a puzzle even in her sleep.

We quietly settled in the sitting area and ate our beef noodles, and it was the best thing I'd ever tasted. Arun had gotten hand-cut noodles with vegetables and tofu for himself. But toward the end of our meal, a shriek rang through the room. I palmed a knife before seeing that Lingyi had sat bolt upright in the chair at the desk. She was hyperventilating, tears streaming down her face. Shocked, I froze, not knowing what to do.

Iris was beside her in an instant, wrapping her arms around her. "Hey," she murmured. "We're all here. We're safe. You fell asleep."

Lingyi nodded, trying to slow her breathing. She drew long, shaking breaths.

I looked toward Arun, whose dark brows were furrowed in concern. We must have mirrored each other in our expressions.

"She's not had a good night's sleep in months," Iris said to us. "A doctor prescribed sedatives, but she doesn't like to take them." Lingyi had pressed her face into Iris's shoulder, and it was jarring to see her like this. She'd always been our leader and guided us with quiet assuredness. Lingyi had always taken care of *us*. Iris's eyes were dark and wide as she stroked Lingyi's hair. It was obvious she'd done this many times before, and how worried she was for Lingyi.

"Go to bed," I said to Iris. "You both need some proper rest."

"Zhou and I will take turns keeping a lookout," Arun said.

The girls headed to their bedroom, and the door clicked firmly shut behind them.

"Will she be okay?" I asked Arun in a low voice.

"She's traumatized." Arun stared down at his hands. "You know, she witnessed Victor's death on cam."

I rubbed my eyes with the heels of my hands. It had never even occurred to me. I had never bothered to ask. Instead, I'd distanced myself from my friends so I wouldn't have to see them and remember who was missing from our group, miss Victor's teasing and banter, the familiar sight of him sprawled in an armchair, long legs crossed in front of him. I had withdrawn from them in an attempt to deal with my grief and guilt, not wondering once how they might be suffering.

"Then all this happened with Jany," Arun said. "Knowing Lingyi, she'll pull through. But we need to be there for her."

I nodded. I didn't know how much Lingyi had been hurting. But why would she have told me? I had rebuffed her every time she tried to reach out. "Fuck," I whispered. "I've been such a little shit."

That made Arun crack a smile. "Yes, you have. But that's nothing new."

I punched him in the arm, but then his expression turned serious. "We've all been grieving in our own ways. But if getting into another dangerous venture has shown me anything, it's that our strength is in each other. Especially if we want to bring Jin down." He paused. "And I *really* want to take him down."

Arun was a scientist, observant and analytical; he was a literal genius. I stared at him and was suddenly overcome with emotion. He was right. We were putting our lives at risk again fighting someone who seemed incapable of losing. But I knew we could do this together. "That's eloquent and deep for so late in the evening."

Arun snorted, thinking I was teasing, but I reached out a fist and hit the top of his fist, and he reciprocated. Rising from the sofa, I said, "I'll take the first shift. Get some sleep."

"You don't have to ask me twice." Arun stood too, and stretched, then disappeared into the other bedroom.

I woke him three hours later and fell asleep on the sofa. Next thing I knew, Lingyi was gently shaking my shoulder. "Wake up, Zhou. We need to have a group meeting." Her eyes were a little swollen, but the quiet determination was back in her voice.

I shot up, my hand going to where a knife was tucked out of habit. "What time is it?"

"Just after seven," she replied. "I told Iris to stay for this too."

It must be important, if she'd taken Iris off surveillance.

"Let me just shower real fast," I said.

Lingyi gave me a playful shove, wrinkling her nose. "I agree. Arun's already showered."

Arun was sitting in a velvet armchair, scrolling through his Palm. He lifted his head and tilted his chin in greeting. "Yeah. I feel almost human again," he said.

After I showered and changed, I rejoined my friends in the sitting area. Iris was pacing around the room, restless. Lingyi was still a target, and there wasn't much we could do about it. If anyone could protect Lingyi, it'd be Iris. But we both knew it'd be an ugly fight when Jin turned his full attention back to us again, assuming his focus had ever strayed. I wouldn't have bet on it.

Arun made tea and brewed espresso drinks, and I gratefully picked up my mug, letting the strong, earthy scent wash over me before I took my first sip.

"I'll be done transferring Jany's data today," Lingyi said after everyone had time to drink their beverage. Her no-nonsense approach was back, and she gave no indication of what had happened last night. She raised a hand when she saw our excited expressions. "I still need to manipulate my passport info to safely leave China . . . but our work here isn't done."

"The prototype," Arun said.

Lingyi let out a small breath as she stared into her teacup. "Yes. We have to get it back."

"What?" I said. "Jin *stole* it. The invention is willed to Jany's family. We just need to push the patent through for them."

"It doesn't matter if Jin stole it," Lingyi said. "Once he figures out how to replicate the catalyst, he'll manufacture it. He's got enough money to bury Jany's family in court. Big corporations do it all the time."

Arun set his empty espresso cup on the table. "Lingyi's right. Nothing will stop Jin once he has his hands on the design. Like I said, the reverse engineering might take some time, but when he's got it figured out, he'll produce the catalyst and do whatever he likes with it."

"Why didn't Jany tell you about the prototype?" I asked.

"She might have forgotten, given the danger she was in," Lingyi said. "But I think more likely she chose not to tell me. Her notes indicated that the prototype was working better than she had hoped and was crucial to the health and survival of the children at the clinic—which was true. We all saw what happened when Jin stole it. She wouldn't have removed it even if I asked her to."

"Shit," I said under my breath. "How can we get it back?"

"The prototype is traceable," Lingyi said. "Jany made certain of that. I know exactly where it is. It's at the Peninsula Hotel, right here on the Bund, where Jin is staying."

We sat in silence for some time, letting the new info sink in. "I don't like it," Iris finally said. "You don't *owe* this woman anything. You can't risk your life again—"

"It won't come to that," Lingyi said.

Iris stopped and slammed a fist on the glass table. Everything clattered on its surface, and we all jumped. "Things go *wrong*." Her throat worked, and her eyes gleamed with unshed tears. "Things *went* wrong! Victor is gone. There's no rewind button, Lingyi, no take-backs. And in the end, Jin will always win."

"We can't think like that," Lingyi said vehemently. "We can't just give in—"

"We blew up Jin Corp!" Iris retorted. "How much do you think we hurt Jin? He's on to his next venture! We can't touch him." She glared at each of us, furious. "It's how the system is set up. I survived on the streets by myself my whole life, and that's how our world works. Jin will be rewarded over and over again no matter what he does—who he steals from, who he kills."

Lingyi dropped her face into both hands, and her shoulders heaved. I thought she was crying, but when she spoke, there was a hard edge in her voice. "Jin takes everything because he can." Lingyi lifted her face; it was flushed with determination. "Well, he can't have this. Please, my heart . . ."

Iris's expression gave nothing away, as if carved from stone, but her dark gaze was sharp as ever. I agreed with her. To stick our necks out again to get the prototype back was risky and dangerous. If Jin caught us, he'd kill us on sight. But I never had a problem following my friends to the cliff's edge—or leaping off, for that matter. My life was my own to risk. But each of them had the right to choose too.

"I get what you're saying, Iris. I'd lived on the streets for five years, and it was enough for me to give up on humankind at times. Or just give up." Iris crossed her arms, listening. "I witnessed viciousness and cruelty—endured both. Our world is not an easy world to live in right now," I said, trying to process all my thoughts and feelings. I wanted Iris to know I understood, knew exactly where she was coming from. The hard line of her mouth softened a little. "But I found kindness, too . . . and friends." I looked around the room at each of them. "I found family."

Arun nodded.

"This might feel personal"—my knee jittered, and I stared at my hands—"hell, maybe it is personal." I had probably lost Daiyu because of this path I had set upon with my friends. The thought felt like a knife twisting into my heart. I swallowed hard. "But when it comes to Jin, there are bigger things at play. We have the choice to fight or give up. Your friends"—I glanced at Lingyi—"your love. We want to keep fighting."

"I'm in until the end of days," Arun agreed. "Smite the fucker."

Lingyi extended a hand toward Iris. "I know you're afraid for me, love. You don't want to see me in danger. I didn't choose this lightly, but I *have* chosen."

Iris stared at Lingyi's hand, and for a second, I was uncertain if she'd take it. But then she entwined her fingers with Lingyi's, leaned close, and whispered in her ear, soft and low. But I still caught the shape of the words: *You're my everything.*

Lingyi cupped Iris's cheek and kissed her. Arun and I actively looked anywhere but at the girls as they shared this tender moment.

After they drew apart, I cleared my throat and said to Lingyi, "We'll work on getting the prototype back. You can do your magic and guide us through it—off-site." And safe from Jin's thugs.

Lingyi nodded, then smiled. "I've already hacked into the Peninsula's system," she said. "The hospitality industry is ridiculously easy to infiltrate."

"You mean as opposed to the retail industry?" Arun asked. "Or gaming?"

Lingyi grinned wider. "True. Jin's in the presidential Peninsula suite. He's throwing a big gala at the hotel tonight—this is our best opportunity to get into his suite and steal the prototype back," she said. "Zhou and Iris can go up. Arun, I need you there as backup in case anything unexpected happens."

Unexpected, like if Jin's thugs kill us and dump our bodies into the Huangpu River.

"I know you can give us access to his suite easily enough," I said. "But where's the prototype? I assume it's not just sitting on a desk for us to take."

Lingyi gave a frustrated shake of her head. "I can see the comings and goings outside in the hallway, but for privacy reasons, there are no cameras within any of the rooms. I only know from the filter's tracker that Jany had built within the machine that it's there. I can pinpoint the location, but don't have a visual."

"What time is the gala tonight?" I asked.

"It begins at eight and runs until midnight," Lingyi said. "All the richest, most influential people of Shanghai have been invited— everyone with deep pockets—and the highest government officials. He'll be occupied schmoozing the entire time."

"I'm game," I said. "Iris is my best partner in crime." I flashed her a grin, and she arched one eyebrow. "What's the plan?"

"I think the best way is if you and Iris dressed like the hotel staff," Lingyi replied, and showed us images of a man and woman. The man was dressed in black trousers and vest with a matching brocaded jacket. The woman was wearing a deep blue qipao with silver embroidering. "You'll be less likely to be questioned that way." She looked toward Arun. "Could you get two sets of the trousers, vests, and jackets for them? White shirts. You know their sizes?"

"I'll take their measurements on my Palm," Arun said. "No problem. I'll be able to get something within a couple of hours."

"We'll all be connected on our earpieces Iris brought so we can communicate with each other. If the prototype is in the hotel safe, I'll have a decoder for you. The hotel safes tend to be easy to crack," Lingyi said. "But it's impossible for us to know how it's stored until you get into his suite."

A low boat horn sounded outside on the river. The hazy skies were slowly brightening, and at eight a.m., Jin Tower flickered to life with advertisements. All the other buildings across the Bund didn't turn on until dusk, but who was Jin to follow along like the rest? The Jin Tower celebration announcements began broadcasting across its glass panes, reminding all of Shanghai to come out and participate.

"Sounds good," I said.

"Let me show you my camera access views within the hotel," Lingyi said. "And its layout so you can familiarize yourself. I'll manipulate the cameras so security won't see you on Jin's floor or have any recording of it." She brought out her own MacFold and connected to the hotel's camera, and the Peninsula's grand lobby appeared. She showed us an image of the prototype from Jany's laptop. "We'll steal this back so fast, Jin's head will spin," Lingyi murmured.

I hoped she was right.

CHAPTER ELEVEN

Iris and I entered the lobby of the Peninsula at eight thirty p.m. It was a vast space with dark marble floors and marbled reception desks with gold accents. A massive chandelier hung over the lobby, and a luxury boutique was still open for business on our left. Three automatons in the window going through a set of seamless motions showcased designer dresses. They looked like real-life Chinese women except for the vacant brightness in their eyes and the unnatural way they were programmed to blink every so often. The high-end stores had begun using these lifelike models, but they creeped me out.

We might have appeared out of place, hotel staff entering through the main entrance, only the lobby was so filled with elegantly dressed people headed to Jin's gala that no one noticed us. The women wore diamonds, rubies, and sapphires on their throats and at their wrists, the precious stones catching the low ambient light in the lobby. Sparkling jewels swayed from their earlobes as they made their way to the elevators. A low hum of excitement filled the air as the guests spoke to one another, wondering what they could expect from Jin, who was famous for his grandiose parties.

Iris and I stayed near the wall, our dark clothing providing cover juxtaposed to their bright silks and brocades. No one gave us a second glance—we weren't worth another look. The women rustled by, patting their hair, and adjusting their heavy jewelry. We waited for the crowd to ebb before going to an elevator and using the card Lingyi had given us to access Jin's presidential suite. While we were ascending, Lingyi spoke into our earpieces. "I didn't want to say anything before, but Daiyu is in Jin's suite."

"What?" I asked, feeling my pulse quicken at the mention of her name.

"Unfortunately," Lingyi said. "She went back to the suite twenty minutes ago and has been there since."

"She must be sharing a suite with Jin," Iris said.

"Just our luck," I murmured, remembering Daiyu's wounded expression before our conversation was interrupted the previous day. It twisted me up inside.

"You two can wait out of sight, and I'll let you know when I see her come out again on the hotel hallway cam," Lingyi said. "I expect she's the hostess for Jin's gala—she can't be gone for that long."

The elevator doors opened noiselessly, and Iris and I made our way around a corner, out of sight of the presidential suite's door. I hadn't been nervous before, but knowing that Daiyu was within shouting distance changed everything. Feeling antsy, I slipped my butterfly knife out and began flipping it, the motions so familiar, I didn't even think about what I was doing.

"Put that thing away," Iris whispered to me. "Stay focused."

Sheepish, I tucked the knife back into a pocket, running my hands across the hidden places where I had my other knives. We waited mostly in silence, with an occasional update from Arun, who entered the lobby soon after we did. But he was dressed in a tuxedo. "There're a few stragglers," Arun said. "But the gala must be in full swing in the ballroom upstairs."

By 9:40 p.m., Daiyu was still sequestered in the suite.

"It's getting too late," Iris said. "We have to get her out somehow."

"I agree," Lingyi replied. "Zhou, go in."

"What?" I asked.

"Knock on the door and say you want to speak with her," Lingyi said. "Get her to leave somehow."

I felt a cold sweat gathering at the back of my neck. "Are you serious, boss?"

"It's the easiest way," Lingyi said into our earpieces.

I held back on my expletives. The last thing I wanted to do was speak with Daiyu in Jin's suite. And showing up like that at her door was just strange and creepy, especially after how I had ended things last time. What if she actually wanted to *talk*? I was only there to distract her so we could steal from her father.

I pushed away from the wall, and Iris grabbed my jacket cuff. She pointed at her ear. I removed my earpiece and tossed it to her before turning the corner and ringing the doorbell at the grand wooden door. If I hesitated, I might have lost my nerve. There was no movement or noise from the other side for some time. Maybe she had fallen asleep? Relieved, I was about to turn on my heel when the door cracked open, and I could see Daiyu peering out.

"Jason?" she said. "What are you doing here?"

Fuck.

"I . . . I wanted to see you," I muttered. "I was hoping we could talk. I heard about your father's gala tonight and guessed you'd be staying in the hotel too."

"How'd you get access to this floor?" she asked.

I shrugged uncomfortably and stuck my hands into my pockets. "Do you want to go somewhere?"

She pulled the door open wider, so I saw all of her. She was dressed in a soft gold qipao embroidered with butterflies, and her hair was swept up, revealing the elegant column of her neck. I dropped my eyes, embarrassed that I had been staring. Daiyu twisted the single jade bracelet on her wrist—a nervous gesture. Part of me wished she'd shut the door in my face, but that wouldn't help us gain access to the suite.

I had used her from the start, and here I was doing it again. If we were working toward the same ends, why did I have to keep deceiving her? Why did we have to keep lying to each other?

"Is there a bar or restaurant in the hotel?" I trailed off, expecting her to politely decline.

"I can't," she said in a soft voice. "I begged off from the gala and told my father I had a terrible migraine. If one of his guys spotted me out talking with you instead . . ."

"I see." I half turned, eager to disappear.

She reached out a hand. "Wait. We could talk inside?" Daiyu opened the door all the way.

My heart lurched. Daiyu looked stunning and so vulnerable. She was choosing to trust me. It made me feel like crap. "I"—I cleared my throat—"I wouldn't want to get you in trouble."

She shook her head. "It's all right. My father and I are sharing this suite, but he'll be gone till well past midnight. There are too many important people at the gala for him to woo."

Daiyu stepped back, as if giving me berth to enter, and the floral perfume with a tinge of citrus she wore on special occasions drifted to me. Without saying a word, I went inside, and she shut the door behind us. I could imagine Lingyi watching the entire exchange on camera, relaying to Iris and Arun what was going on. I felt like a hero confronted with an unexpected roadblock who needed to be cunning and debonair to carry the scene, only I was clueless and bumbling instead.

Now what?

Iris could access the suite with the card key Lingyi had given us, and she had her motion detector to know if the room was clear. The presidential suite had two bedrooms, and I needed to get Daiyu into her room to give Iris an opportunity to sneak in. I took in the vaulted ceilings and the gold drapes, which were pulled open, giving a wide view of the river and the buildings lit in flashing lights across from the Bund. A giant crystal chandelier hung over the sitting room, casting a soft glow. A grand piano was set in the corner, and it opened into a more intimate study. This presidential suite was bigger than most houses.

Daiyu swept a hand toward one of the deep velvet chairs, indicating we could sit, and I shook my head. "Could we go to your bedroom instead?" I winced inwardly.

Smooth, Zhou.

I saw the color instantly rise to her cheeks.

"I don't mean—I meant"—I took a deep breath—"I don't feel comfortable in the sitting room. I know you said your father's occupied at the gala, but what if he needed something and walked in on us?"

"I didn't assume . . . ," she said. "It's just—" Daiyu pressed her lips together, looking as uncomfortable as I felt. "My bedroom is this way."

I nodded. My hands were still stuffed into my trouser pockets, bunched into fists. It was painful to feel so awkward with her—like strangers—after months of being so in sync.

Daiyu led the way, and it was impossible for me not to admire how her hips moved under the silk sheath of the qipao.

Get a grip.

I followed her down a hallway with thick carpeting, and she stopped at one of the wide doors and opened it. "You're right," she said, and waved to indicate that I should enter first. "There's no telling with my father. We have never shared a suite before, but he insisted this time. Good bonding time." The sarcastic note in her voice didn't escape me.

I entered the luxurious bedroom, decorated in ivory and beige. The king-size bed was meticulously made, with gold and silver cushions stacked against the large plush pillows. The housekeeping staff had left a single red rose and a small plate of chocolates on a tray on the bed after the turndown service. I knew they must have come through in the evening, because Daiyu tended to be messy, even more so than me sometimes. This intimate insight, rising unbidden, felt intrusive and out of place.

Suddenly, I wished I was anywhere but here, with the girl who I loved but had probably lost, both of us weighted beneath too many lies.

She sat on the edge of her bed. I saw a pair of high heels flung on the ground to the side. Daiyu hated high heels, complaining how much they pinched her toes and made her feel like she was waddling. "So . . ." She smoothed the duvet with her palm. "What did you want to talk about?"

I stared at the thick carpet, trying to find the right words. "I wanted to thank you," I finally said after a long pause. "For donating the new equipment to the clinic."

"Did it help?"

I nodded. "We weren't able to order ventilators to be delivered same day. And yours prevented more serious illness and possible deaths."

Her eyes brightened. "I'm so glad. I had to do something."

She tried to capture my gaze, but I couldn't look at her. There was so much more I wanted to say, but the words felt jammed, stuck in my chest and caught in my throat.

I'm sorry I lied.

I want to trust you.

"Will you tell me what you're doing in Shanghai, then?" she finally asked after an uncomfortable silence.

"I came for a friend"—I cleared my throat—"a friend who was in trouble."

"I didn't know I'd be coming to Shanghai until my father gave me an ultimatum—support him publicly or he'd actively work to take away my sponsors and donors."

I stared at her. After all that Jin had done, I didn't believe I could still be surprised by his ruthless tactics. But I was.

"In the end, I had no choice," she said. "I'm not sure I would have known how to tell you either."

"Yet you're still the heir to Jin Corp."

She had been focused on her jade bracelet, turning it on her wrist, but she lifted her head. "I am—"

"Why?" I cut her off. "Why, Daiyu? I thought what your father does, what Jin Corp represents, is everything you're against. He *threatened* you to get what he wanted—and he's done so much worse."

I thought we were on the same team.

"I know," she replied. "But what better way to change everything? From *within*. My father has built an empire with power, money, and reach. I could fight him from the inside, or from the outside as a disgraced and disinherited daughter." She rose and came to stand in front of me, close enough that I wanted to reach out to her from instinct. From habit. "Which hand would you play?"

She touched my shoulder—the lightest touch. I fought the urge to lean in, drawn to her despite my uncertainty, despite all the questions running through my mind. I took a step back, and she dropped her hand. "I've thought more about what we said to each other outside the clinic—" I said.

"So have I," Daiyu interjected. "And it's not fair. It's not fair for you to punish me for the wealth I was born into. I know you despise *you*s, yet you know yourself that major changes require funding. I'm in the perfect position to use my father's name and money to my advantage, use them to undermine him."

I shoved my hands deeper into my pockets and stared at my feet. "I don't hate *you*s, Daiyu. I hate the deliberate turning of the eye from those in need, the idea that a life is only as valuable as someone's net worth."

"I'm not like that, Jason."

"I know you're not. But your father has stolen and murdered in the name of profit and personal gain. What does it mean that you remain silent and stand by him?" I shook my head and finally lifted my gaze to meet her eyes. "It *sends* a message. It taints everything you're trying to do."

Her face paled, despite the heavier makeup she had put on for the gala tonight. "But in the end, he's still my *father*, Jason."

I thought about my own father, whom I'd lost when I was five. My memories of him were amorphous: a deep voice, his rumbling words a soothing backdrop when I played with my blocks on the living room floor, and his large, calloused hands that would envelop my own. I didn't remember much, but I remembered my love for him, and how much he loved me back. This was something Daiyu had never had and would never have with her father.

"I know, and he'll always be someone I'm fighting against," I said. "If you had to stand against him, could you?"

She drew a step closer, almost in challenge, and raised her chin. "Yes," she finally replied after a long pause of consideration. I knew it wasn't in fear, or to cover a lie. She wanted to give me the honest truth.

"Even if you could lose everything?"

Daiyu gave a humorless laugh. "I will never be poor, Jason. I have a trust fund set up that even my father can't touch. And my mother is a successful designer in Hong Kong in her own right. I'll always be a *you*."

"You know what I mean," I replied. "Because you *do* have a choice when it comes to your father."

A buzzer rang and we jumped apart from each other. I was suddenly aware of my heart thumping hard against my chest.

"It's Da Ge," Daiyu said, glancing at the monitor set by her bedroom door. It showed an image of Jin's right-hand man, who did all his dirty work, standing outside the suite.

Shit.

"My dad must have sent him to check in on me." Daiyu was already ushering me out of the room. "You have to hide. Go into my father's bedroom. He won't go in there. Everyone knows it's off-limits." We rushed through the main sitting room and down another hallway. She opened an ornate door at the end and pushed me inside. "Wait here."

I almost laughed at how ludicrous the situation was. This wasn't the first time I'd had to hide from Da Ge. But the last time, I thought with a pang, it was Vic who had hidden me at the Rockaroke. Daiyu had left the door ajar, and I pressed my ear against the small crack. I could hear her speaking to Da Ge, saying she was feeling better after resting. She'd grab her shoes and return to the gala. I strained my hearing, praying the thug didn't find an excuse to wander down this hallway. Instead, a while later, I heard Daiyu murmuring something and the heavy front door closing shut. Then silence. The bedroom was dark, and I searched for an old-fashioned light switch, not wanting to use voice command. As I fumbled around, someone whispered from the cavernous room, "Zhou."

I leaped out of my own skin, suppressing a shout of surprise.

A Palm screen flickered on, and I saw Iris's features barely illuminated.

"You're in," I said, feeling relieved. "Have you found the prototype?"

She nodded and stood from where she had been crouching behind the huge bed, and disappeared down a hallway. I followed, and the lights turned on from Iris's motion, showing an expansive walk-in closet large enough to have a seating area. Shirts, jackets, and trousers hung from hangers in a neat row. At least a dozen pairs of leather shoes were lined up perfectly on a shelf. Iris handed me my earpiece, and I tucked it back in.

"Boss," I said.

"You're back," Lingyi replied. "Great work, Zhou."

I felt my cheeks burn. I wouldn't have called it that.

"Lingyi was able to help me pinpoint where the prototype is being kept." Iris pointed at a large black safe tucked inside a built-in cabinet. It took up the entire space, measuring probably three feet across and six feet high.

"It's Jin's personal safe. It's top-of-the-line and basically bomb-proof," Iris said. "Unfortunately, it utilizes voice recognition for the twelve-digit security code."

"So even if we were able to crack the code, we'd have to speak the numbers in Jin's voice to open the safe," Lingyi said. She sounded subdued. "It's basically impossible."

I cussed under my breath.

"You should all clear out while you can," Lingyi said. "We tried, but I don't want to risk you getting caught by Jin."

And getting killed.

She didn't need to say it. But it felt like giving up.

Iris and I took the side streets behind the Bund and headed back to our hotel on the opposite end of the Peninsula. We passed dark storefronts and the occasional hole-in-the-wall eatery that was still open, but didn't speak one word to each other. I knew Iris had thought this venture was foolish and dangerous, but once invested, she hated to lose.

It was past eleven p.m. by the time we made it back to Les Suites. I grabbed some fruit and cookies before following Iris up. Arun was sprawled in the armchair, his tuxedo jacket draped over its back behind him. Lingyi sat on the sofa with her feet tucked underneath a bright yellow skirt. They looked as defeated as we felt.

"Hey," Arun said.

Iris went to sit down beside Lingyi, and Lingyi caressed her cheek, giving Iris a light kiss. "It's a small setback," Lingyi murmured.

Iris's mouth tilted up at the corner, despite her dark mood. "You never give up, do you?" She gave Lingyi a tender look. "I love you for it. But even you can't work miracles."

Lingyi's gaze flicked toward me. I was still standing, too weary to decide if I wanted to join my friends or just crash and let sleep claim me so I didn't have to think. "Can I speak with you, Zhou?"

Surprised, I nodded. "Nothing happened between me and Daiyu, if that's what you're wondering."

Iris rolled her eyes.

"I'm headed for bed," Arun said. Which meant I'd get the sofa.

"I'll take the first shift," said Iris.

Lingyi squeezed Iris's fingers, then got off the sofa and went to the bedroom she and Iris had claimed for themselves.

"I'll come and relieve you in a few hours," Arun spoke over his shoulder.

Lingyi waited for me to enter the bedroom, then closed the door behind us. She sat down on the large, rumpled bed and pulled her knees up to her chin. I fell into the green armchair near the bed. The room looked lived in, but not messy. I saw a book on the bedside table: *Notes of a Crocodile*.

"Qiu Miaojin?" I asked.

"I'm enjoying it," Lingyi replied. "Have you read it?"

I picked up the book. "I have. I liked it. But it wasn't always lighthearted reading."

"No." Lingyi fell silent for a moment, then said, "I can't imagine feeling shame for loving Iris. Or self-loathing. Qiu's storytelling hits me here." She jabbed three fingers against her chest. "It twists me up inside. Iris and I are so lucky to live in a time like now."

I smiled, even though I was so tired, my cheeks ached. "Honestly, I can't imagine you with anyone else—"

"Really?" she interjected. "What about Victor?"

I clamped my mouth shut. Lingyi and Vic had dated for several months, and as much as he tried to hide it, I knew he had fallen hard for her. "Lingyi . . ." I smoothed my hand over the paperback cover of the book. "What do you want me to say?"

She shook her head. "Nothing. There's nothing you can say."

"Victor had feelings for you," I replied in a low voice. "But he also wanted you to be happy. Anyone who knows you and Iris can tell how happy you are together. It's so obvious."

Lingyi nodded and rocked on her heels, gazing out the bedroom window. The lights had long gone dark outside along the Bund. "I only wish I had worked up the nerve to tell him how much he meant to me. If not as a boyfriend, then as a friend." Her arms tightened around her knees, as if this could bring some comfort.

"He knew, Lingyi."

"Did he?" she asked.

"He did." I sensed the sadness enveloping her, like a living thing. "I'm sorry," I managed to say, feeling as if my throat was snapping shut. "It was my fault. . . ."

It should have been me.

"What?"

"Vic had said from the start how dangerous our mission was, but I kept pushing for it." My heart hurt to speak these thoughts aloud, but if I were to admit my guilt to anyone, it'd be to Lingyi. "I insisted we try, and when I was kidnapped"—I looked away, because I could no longer hold my friend's gaze—"Victor died because of me."

"Oh, Zhou." Her face had flushed with emotion. "I blame myself."

"No." I was stunned, not knowing what else to say. "How?"

"I'm the *boss*, Zhou," she replied. "I've been the leader of the group from the start. I knew that targeting Jin Corp was a risk, but I never imagined"—she faltered—"if I had known Vic would die . . ."

I rose and went to her, sitting on the bed, and she leaned against me.

Lingyi was silent for a long time. I stared at her hands, clasped in her lap. A tear fell into her palm, and only then did I realize her face was wet from crying. "Lingyi."

Her throat worked, and I could see she was trying to gather herself so she could speak. "He came to me, Zhou," she finally said. "After you and Iris had broken in and gotten access to Jin Corp's backup system. He came. To talk." The words came in spurts. I reached for a tissue from the box on the bedside table and she took it gratefully, wiping her face and blowing her nose. "It was getting real. We were getting close." Her breath hitched. "Vic wanted to warn me again what a bad idea it was. Someone could die, he kept saying. Do you understand?"

I hugged Lingyi closer, but it felt as if the breath had been knocked from me.

"I knew the risks, I told him. We all did," she went on. "It was so easy to *say*, but . . ."

It was something entirely different when you had to pay the price for taking that risk. It was something entirely different when your friend died. "I'm sorry," I said. "I'm sorry. But it's not your fault—"

"You're the boss, Vic said to me. Followed by that grin." Lingyi swiped at her eyes furiously. "I knew how he felt about me, and I didn't take the chance to tell him how much he meant to me. It seemed so awkward. A chore." She lifted her gaze. "I was a coward."

I shook my head. "No," I replied. "You were only being human."

Lingyi stopped mid-sniffle and gave a hiccuped laugh. "That's such a Zhou response. Do you have a book example to share?"

"Probably on any other night." I gave her a lopsided smile, then squeezed her hand, the one not clutching a damp tissue. "It's not your fault," I repeated in a hoarse voice.

"Well, it isn't yours, either," Lingyi said back.

We sat like that for some time, in silence, taking comfort in grieving together. Finally, she gave me a sad smile and kissed me on the cheek, just as a big sister would her little brother to try and make him feel better. I noticed the dark shadows beneath her eyes. "What about you and Daiyu?" Lingyi's eyes were red-rimmed, but her gaze sharpened when she posed the question.

I placed the book back on the bedside table. "Gods. Do we need to talk about this now?"

The corner of her mouth curled up. "I think we do."

"The boss is back," I replied, only half-jokingly.

"What happened in the hotel room?" she asked.

"Nothing." I stared up at the ceiling. "It was awkward. . . ."

Lingyi nodded, easing back so she could see my face, pulling her sweater sleeves over her hands. I decided to come clean; now I definitely felt as if I were being interrogated by a big sister.

"Especially after what happened at the clinic yesterday," I went on. "Daiyu was there."

"What?"

"She had equipment delivered to help—it arrived sooner than what we were able to order."

"Why wasn't this all over the news?"

I shook my head. "She donated anonymously. She wanted to be certain the equipment got delivered, but she was hiding from the reporters. Daiyu said she didn't want it to be all-media news."

"Or maybe she was keeping it from Jin?" Lingyi arched an eyebrow.

"That, too. She's still the heir to Jin Corp."

"You talked about this?" Her eyes brightened. "Tell me everything."

I didn't want to talk about it. I didn't want to think about Daiyu. But I told Lingyi what had happened tonight in Daiyu's hotel room.

Lingyi leaned forward while I spoke, seeming to hang on every word, as if I were recounting the plot from one of her manhua.

"And do you believe her? What she said about changing things from within?"

I closed my eyes and pictured Daiyu in my mind; the way she always claimed her space with assurance and that stubborn tilt of her chin when she was ready to tackle a challenge. I thought about how she had lied to me and kept in touch with Jin all this time, and her possible reasoning behind the deception. "I do," I finally replied. "I believe her."

"But do you trust her?" she asked, barely above a whisper.

My head snapped up, and our eyes met. "I instinctively trusted her before I had any reason to, and I've never stopped."

"Because she is in the perfect position to steal the prototype back," Lingyi said. "Can we trust her to help us take Jin down?"

CHAPTER TWELVE

DAIYU

Daiyu forced herself to stay at her father's gala until midnight, when it officially ended. She managed to make polite talk with possible buyers and investors for Jin Corp's future "vertical cities" but wouldn't have been able to say who she spoke to or what the conversation was about. She couldn't stop thinking about her encounter with Jason earlier—how her heart had lifted when she saw him unexpectedly at the suite door, and how painful it was to stand so near to each other, but feel worlds apart.

The crowd had thinned only slightly. Even though the gala was supposed to end at midnight, many of the guests would stay as long as there was food, drink, and entertainment. Her father's parties usually lasted well into the night. Daiyu wove her way through the crowd, hoping no one would stop her to chat. She found her father engaged in an intense discussion with a woman wearing a jade-green jacket and black trousers. Daiyu recognized the woman as a high government official her father had been wooing and giving large bribes to in order to acquire all the permits needed to build Jin Tower. Not wanting to interrupt, Daiyu managed to catch her father's eye. He gave a slight nod of his head when she lifted a hand, indicating she was leaving. It meant she was free to go.

Although her father had been an absent parent for most of her life, Daiyu had learned to follow his rules or suffer the consequences. After her parents divorced, her contact with her mother had been limited, because her father hadn't allowed it. Daiyu had grown up knowing that although her father usually paid no attention to her, one misstep when his eyes *were* on her meant she'd pay the price: the birthday card and gift from her mom she had eagerly been waiting for thrown in the trash bin in front of her or a childhood pet gone with no explanation. Like she had told Jason, Daiyu had learned early when to pick her battles. And even when she had chosen to go up against her father, she had always done so subversively—never challenging him openly.

Daiyu couldn't leave the ballroom quickly enough. Thousands of Swarovski crystals threaded through silver wire hung from the ballroom ceiling, dangling at various lengths over the guests. They threw sparkling light across the space, shimmering the room with magic. Larger-than-life emerald and ruby dragons with glowing scales decorated one ballroom wall, matched by sapphire and gold phoenixes opposite. The servers wore bejeweled and feathered masks covering their eyes and brows, adding to the feeling of enchantment. She hurried past a large holographic projection of Jin Tower, which was lit in a floor-to-ceiling silver column in the middle of the room, rotating slowly so the attendees could admire the building from all angles. Whatever she might think of her father, Daiyu had to admit that he knew how to throw a party.

After taking the special elevator up to the presidential suite floor, Daiyu stripped off her high heels the moment the heavy door swung shut behind her. She left them in the entryway beneath an inlaid table adorned with orchids in ceramic pots.

And despite knowing it made no sense, she went down the long hallway leading to her father's master suite. The door was closed firmly, and she turned the handle, part of her expecting Jason to still be there, hidden somewhere in the darkness. She voice-commanded the lights on, and they showed her father's immaculate room—it looked unlived in. He had a fixation on being orderly and keeping everything in its place. As a child, any toy, barrette, jewelry, or item of clothing that was left on a table or chair in their huge mansion was promptly thrown away by the housekeeper, as instructed by her father.

The room smelled faintly of her father's cologne, the only indication he occupied it. She glanced at her Palm for the time, then headed into the master closet. Detecting her motion, the lights slowly turned on to a warm glow when she entered. Jason had said that her father was the cause behind the tragedy at the Qibao clinic, and he was right. She had seen the air filter herself the following morning and hid behind a corner to listen in. . . .

Dr. Shen, Jin Corp's lead engineer from Taipei, crouched in front of the device, which was set on a low glass table. The filter was dark gray and about the size of a small antique printer—rectangular and clunky.

"This is no ordinary filter, Mr. Jin." Dr. Shen had removed the outer shell and was scrutinizing its inner workings. "It uses a chemical catalyst that converts pollutants. The reverse engineering would take time, and there's no guarantee the prototype won't be destroyed in the process." He stood; Daiyu didn't miss that the engineer took a step away from her father, trying to distance himself. "I'm afraid it's beyond my own scope of knowledge," he said, and bowed his head in apology. "You would need to find a highly skilled chemical engineer."

Although her father's expression betrayed nothing, he drew taller, and the air seemed to thicken with tension. He wasn't happy. She slipped back into her room to change, then reemerged, moving quietly down the hallway, just in time to see her father carrying the filter back toward his suite. The machine was cumbersome, and obviously heavy, but not so much that he couldn't manage it himself.

Dr. Shen was nowhere in sight.

Now Daiyu easily located her father's large safe tucked in the spacious master closet. She was familiar with his safes. Her father had had many of them throughout the years, always upgraded to the highest tech and security. She ran her hand across the cold metal door. There was no keypad, no lock, no indication of how the safe was opened. The only thing that stood out was a glowing red light set at eye level, no larger than a laser point. A voice-commanded safe, then, her father's new favorite.

A wave of nausea hit her. Those deaths, the infants and toddlers who had suffered at the Qibao clinic . . . *Your father did this. The blood is on his hands,* Jason had shouted at her, his eyes appearing wild, the rage and pain clearly written on his face. In that moment, he had looked like a stranger. But he had every right to feel enraged. Daiyu knew how painful his mother's death had been for Jason, leaving him alone in this world. How helpless he had felt that he couldn't save her.

And her father had shown again how little he cared about the lives of others, as long as he could get what he wanted, no matter what the cost.

She remembered the argument they'd had earlier that night and felt again, deep in her chest, his hurt and disappointment in her for remaining the heir to Jin Corp: *It sends a message.* She had no idea he'd feel so strongly about it, but maybe she was lying to herself. Because why else had she never mentioned it in their last, blissful six months together?

Pinpricks suddenly crawled across her scalp, and she left her father's suite, voice-commanding the room dark. Knowing him, he'd be at the party for some time, but he would be suspicious if he found her in his suite. Daiyu retreated to her own bedroom, picking up her high heels along the way. When she finally climbed into bed, her body was exhausted, but her mind kept going, relentlessly playing her exchange with Jason over and over.

If you had to stand against him, could you?

She shoved off the thick duvet and voice-commanded the sounds of a soothing tropical rain to play, yet she still couldn't sleep.

A little after one a.m., she received a message from an unknown number: are you able to meet somewhere? j

Her pulse began to race. It was the last thing she had expected from Jason. She lay on her side, waiting for her heartbeat to slow, before dictating: Tianzifang today at noon. Stall 129.

you can come alone? he replied.

Yes.

see you then.

Daiyu stared at the messages exchanged for some time, until she heard the suite door shut and her father's footsteps echo across the marble floor. Her father never checked in on her, had never even been to this side of the suite as far as she knew. Still, she shoved her Palm beneath her pillow and squeezed her eyes shut.

The few times she had traveled with her father, she always had her own more modest suite. But this time, he had made her stay in the presidential suite with him, sending the unspoken message that her movements would be watched—so she'd better behave.

Instead of drifting to sleep, Daiyu mulled over the different ways she could leave the hotel tomorrow without her father's hired security following.

▲▼▲

Daiyu rarely ate breakfast with her father and only upon his request. They were far from close. If anyone asked, she'd describe their relationship as businesslike. Her father viewed her as another asset—an investment in Jin Corp's future—and she'd always played along. And when her father had requested her presence in Shanghai, she had initially balked, but Daiyu had to consider, as she always did, if this was a fight worth having with him. It didn't seem to be: show up, smile stiffly, and pose for photos.

"Your environmental efforts in Taiwan have been charming," her father had said over their call, offering a close-mouthed smile. "I've allowed you to carry on because it helped Jin Corp's image." He blinked twice, slowly, and she clamped down on the urge to shudder. "But it's time to show everyone where your true alliance lies, Daughter."

The morning after the gala, Daiyu dressed in a silk floral shirt paired with a beige skirt—understated and expensive was what her father liked—and greeted him at the large dining table at eight a.m. He had been reading the news on his Palm and set the device down. "Daughter," he said. "What a pleasant surprise." He indicated the seat to his left. Her father was sitting at the head of the ten-person table.

"Good morning, Father." She slipped into the chair and the suite's butler, a tall man named Mr. Han, entered and poured coffee for her. Daiyu took a small sip; it was hot but not enough to burn, and she gratefully drank until half the cup was gone. She then helped herself to yogurt and fresh blueberries.

"What are your plans for the day?" her father asked, taking a slice of wheat toast from the toast rack, then buttering it with precise motions. He had always preferred a Western-style breakfast, despite all the delicious Taiwanese morning choices.

"I'd like to go shopping for a dress for Jin Tower's opening ceremony," she replied. "A special dress for the occasion."

He nodded in approval. "It's too late to have a couture dress made. But go pick something out—I trust your taste. Put it on my account."

"Thank you, Father." She touched the jade pendant that hung from her neck, a rare gift from him when she had turned sixteen. He saw the pendant and his lips curved ever so slightly. "But I'd like to go alone."

Her father raised an eyebrow.

"Please," she said. "There's nothing worse than shopping for hours for a dress when security is trailing you at every step. It makes all the salespeople nervous too. I'll take Xiao Wu with me. I promise I'll be careful."

Xiao Wu was her chauffeur in Shanghai. Her father thought he had hired him, but it was Daiyu who had sent the man to interview for the job. And Xiao Wu was getting paid double: once from Jin, but with an even higher salary from Daiyu to be discreet and keep his mouth shut. The man was shrewd and took the deal. The advantage to rarely going against her father's wishes was that when she wanted a favor, they always seemed innocent and easy enough to grant as a reward for her obeying.

Her father considered her with those intense eyes that weighed every choice as to how it benefited *him*, then finally nodded. "It'll be a nice day. Enjoy your shopping trip."

Daiyu flashed a demure smile, then felt a sharp pang of hurt, not because it was necessary to lie to her father, but because any other daughter probably would have thrown her arms around her dad in gratitude. Perhaps even given him a kiss on the cheek. Or—and Daiyu couldn't fathom this for herself—maybe the dad would actually kiss his daughter on the cheek, mussing her hair with affection.

All these things she'd never known and would never know.

But her father had seen agreeing to this request as something that cost him nothing and would garner more positive feelings and loyalty from her. Daiyu had counted on this.

He picked up his Palm again and said, "I'll be taking an important call soon and have a busy day ahead."

And with that, she was dismissed. Daiyu grabbed a slice of toast and carried her refilled coffee cup with her back into her suite. She downed the rest of her coffee before messaging Xiao Wu: You're tak-ing me shopping today, but I won't be with you. If my father messages, I'm in the dressing room.

Xiao Wu replied immediately: Yes, Ms. Jin.

Her father was right: It was a nice day. By the time she left, her father had already gone, after speaking with another man for a long time on his Palm. She climbed into her white airlimo from the Peninsula's enclosed rooftop garage and instructed Xiao Wu to take her to Plaza 66 on Nanjing Road, known for its designer flagship stores. "I'll meet you back here in a few hours," Daiyu said when they got there.

Xiao Wu gave her a thumbs-up. "Yes, Ms. Jin."

She tossed her Palm onto the backseat of the car. She wasn't cer-tain if her father tracked her on the device; he had never asked to connect with her. But that didn't mean anything.

Daiyu quickly disappeared down the crowded street of shoppers, most wearing face masks. But the *you*s did not, as the necessity to cover one's face was an affliction for the poor *mei*s. The rich had the privilege of being shuttled by airlimo from destination to destination to regulated spaces. Their time spent outdoors with exposed faces was rare, and usually short, but the way the women scurried in their designer dresses and heels into the huge shopping center with hand-kerchiefs pressed to their noses showed Daiyu they didn't like this ridiculous. Still, she no longer knew where they stood. Their relationship felt like it had gone askew—precarious and on unsteady ground ever since they had uncovered each other's lies. Jason probably felt he had good reason for hiding his trip to Shanghai from her, while Daiyu had never felt she needed to bring up being the heir to Jin Corp again. She'd had no idea Jason had assumed it was something she had rejected outright after the bombing.

She stood at the edge of the doorway, leaning out just enough so she could catch sight of the people moving through the narrow alleyway that led to Aining's shop. The crowd seemed a mix of teens, college-aged kids, and older tourists, the younger set's bright-colored hair standing out. But like Daiyu, Jason didn't bother to dye his hair. Almost everyone wore masks covering their faces, and Daiyu scrutinized the crowd as best as she could.

Then she spotted him, dressed in a black tee, and immediately felt her fingertips tingle from the surge of adrenaline. It wasn't his face that had caught her attention. He wore a mask, and his head was lowered, as if he were studying the pavement. It was the set of his shoulders and his gait that had sent a shock of familiarity through her. Jason walked in a manner that forced people to scatter out of his way. She watched the strange phenomenon unfold in front of her now: two beefy European guys hauled a bunch of shopping bags between them, chatting amiably, but sidestepped and twisted their bodies as Jason approached, then walked past them. Another tall Chinese woman wearing large gold sunglasses visibly leaned away

inconvenience one bit. The *yous*' lives had certainly been affected after losing the use of her father's suits.

She knew that her father would begin production of his suits again in a year's time or so in Beijing. Daiyu was working against the clock in pushing environmental legislation through in Taiwan. She hailed another airlimo easily and asked to be taken to Tianzifang. Even her short time outdoors had brought a sheen of sweat across her forehead, and she coughed, watching the airlimo lift to give an expansive view of the thick brown smog that hung over Shanghai. They drifted above the crowded shopping district on Nanjing Road—all glittering glass and opulence.

Surging into the polluted sky, Daiyu glimpsed the iconic Jing'an temple from above, composed of several large buildings, their roofs tiled in gold, which opened into a large courtyard. The temple appeared ornate yet serene, isolated from the steel skyscrapers that towered around it. The juxtaposition was striking. Shanghai was an ever-evolving city, always building higher, utilizing better and faster tech, and yet its history asserted itself with this temple, with the centuries-old buildings along the Bund. She wanted to visit the temple—it filled her with peace just gazing upon it. Then the airlimo veered toward Tianzifang in the French Concession, and although Daiyu craned her neck, she lost sight of the landmark.

She looked for signs of being followed. Daiyu was fairly certain her father was too preoccupied to send someone to spy on her supposed shopping trip, but it never hurt to be cautious. Thankfully, no flying vehicles tailed them.

The airlimo glided to a stop by one of the passageways leading into Tianzifang, and Daiyu paid the driver in cash before stepping out into the humid day. At almost noon, Tianzifang was crowded with shoppers and tourists. Daiyu had visited only once before but had fallen in love with its charm; the warren of endless boutiques and tucked-away corners felt secretive, an exploration as much as shopping. If Plaza 66 oozed wealth, Tianzifang gave the vibe of creative energy and artistic ingenuity. Many of the boutiques were trendy and catered to tourists, but there were some designers and artists creating beautiful work with a fresh perspective Daiyu truly appreciated. It was how she had met Li Aining, a ceramics artist who owned a small, narrow shop at stall 129.

Aining's dragon teapot had an opalescent glazing Daiyu had never seen before, catching blue and green hues when she held it up to the light. She had carved delicate flowers on the fierce dragon head, its mouth open in a wide grimace to allow the tea to be poured. These blossoms she glazed in gold, so they stood out against the dragon's blue-green scales, appearing almost three-dimensional. Daiyu had purchased the teapot along with the four matching teacups and had bought a few other pieces as souvenirs. Since that first meeting, Aining had been Daiyu's go-to when she wanted to buy a special gift for a friend. In fact, she had been thinking of commissioning a piece for Jason's birthday next May. Daiyu

had been excited by that prospect, but now the idea only filled her with uncertainty.

Who knew where she and Jason would be more than half a year from now?

Aining greeted her with a warm hug; her smile lit up her round face. She wore a loose black blouse with a silver feather print and billowy turquoise trousers. "It's been too long," her friend exclaimed.

"Yes, it has!"

Aining gestured to the curtain behind them that partitioned the small store from her private storage area. "I've cleared out some space for you and your friend for"—she leaned in and dropped her voice, whispering dramatically—"your rendezvous."

Daiyu grinned, despite her nervousness at meeting Jason like this. Aining always had a dramatic flair, and it came across in her craft as well. "It's nothing like that—"

"I thought this was to see your secret boyfriend!" Aining exclaimed, her voice no longer pitched low.

Daiyu winced, and Aining's dark eyes widened. "I see. Young men can be such trouble. I'll say no more." Daiyu squeezed her friend's fingers, before glancing at the ceramic clock against the wall shaped like a giant green tortoise with silver rosebuds on its shell. Almost noon.

She had tried not to think too much about why Jason wanted to meet. He knew that her father was keeping tabs on Daiyu, and to ask her to risk getting caught to discuss their love problems seemed inconvenience one bit. The *yous'* lives had certainly been affected after losing the use of her father's suits.

She knew that her father would begin production of his suits again in a year's time or so in Beijing. Daiyu was working against the clock in pushing environmental legislation through in Taiwan. She hailed another airlimo easily and asked to be taken to Tianzifang. Even her short time outdoors had brought a sheen of sweat across her forehead, and she coughed, watching the airlimo lift to give an expansive view of the thick brown smog that hung over Shanghai. They drifted above the crowded shopping district on Nanjing Road—all glittering glass and opulence.

Surging into the polluted sky, Daiyu glimpsed the iconic Jing'an temple from above, composed of several large buildings, their roofs tiled in gold, which opened into a large courtyard. The temple appeared ornate yet serene, isolated from the steel sky-scrapers that towered around it. The juxtaposition was striking. Shanghai was an ever-evolving city, always building higher, utiliz-ing better and faster tech, and yet its history asserted itself with this temple, with the centuries-old buildings along the Bund. She wanted to visit the temple—it filled her with peace just gazing upon it. Then the airlimo veered toward Tianzifang in the French Concession, and although Daiyu craned her neck, she lost sight of the landmark.

She looked for signs of being followed. Daiyu was fairly cer-tain her father was too preoccupied to send someone to spy on her supposed shopping trip, but it never hurt to be cautious. Thankfully, no flying vehicles tailed them.

The airlimo glided to a stop by one of the passageways leading into Tianzifang, and Daiyu paid the driver in cash before stepping out into the humid day. At almost noon, Tianzifang was crowded with shoppers and tourists. Daiyu had visited only once before but had fallen in love with its charm; the warren of endless boutiques and tucked-away corners felt secretive, an exploration as much as shopping. If Plaza 66 oozed wealth, Tianzifang gave the vibe of creative energy and artistic ingenuity. Many of the boutiques were trendy and catered to tourists, but there were some designers and artists creating beautiful work with a fresh perspective Daiyu truly appreciated. It was how she had met Li Aining, a ceramics artist who owned a small, narrow shop at stall 129.

Aining's dragon teapot had an opalescent glazing Daiyu had never seen before, catching blue and green hues when she held it up to the light. She had carved delicate flowers on the fierce dragon head, its mouth open in a wide grimace to allow the tea to be poured. These blossoms she glazed in gold, so they stood out against the dragon's blue-green scales, appearing almost three-dimensional. Daiyu had purchased the teapot along with the four matching teacups and had bought a few other pieces as souvenirs. Since that first meeting, Aining had been Daiyu's go-to when she wanted to buy a special gift for a friend. In fact, she had been thinking of commissioning a piece for Jason's birthday next May. Daiyu had been excited by that prospect, but now the idea only filled her with uncertainty.

Who knew where she and Jason would be more than half a year from now?

Aining greeted her with a warm hug; her smile lit up her round face. She wore a loose black blouse with a silver feather print and billowy turquoise trousers. "It's been too long," her friend exclaimed.

"Yes, it has!"

Aining gestured to the curtain behind them that partitioned the small store from her private storage area. "I've cleared out some space for you and your friend for"—she leaned in and dropped her voice, whispering dramatically—"your rendezvous."

Daiyu grinned, despite her nervousness at meeting Jason like this. Aining always had a dramatic flair, and it came across in her craft as well. "It's nothing like that—"

"I thought this was to see your secret boyfriend!" Aining exclaimed, her voice no longer pitched low.

Daiyu winced, and Aining's dark eyes widened. "I see. Young men can be such trouble. I'll say no more." Daiyu squeezed her friend's fingers, before glancing at the ceramic clock against the wall shaped like a giant green tortoise with silver rosebuds on its shell. Almost noon.

She had tried not to think too much about why Jason wanted to meet. He knew that her father was keeping tabs on Daiyu, and to ask her to risk getting caught to discuss their love problems seemed ridiculous. Still, she no longer knew where they stood. Their relationship felt like it had gone askew—precarious and on unsteady ground ever since they had uncovered each other's lies. Jason probably felt he had good reason for hiding his trip to Shanghai from her, while Daiyu had never felt she needed to bring up being the heir to Jin Corp again. She'd had no idea Jason had assumed it was something she had rejected outright after the bombing.

She stood at the edge of the doorway, leaning out just enough so she could catch sight of the people moving through the narrow alleyway that led to Aining's shop. The crowd seemed a mix of teens, college-aged kids, and older tourists, the younger set's bright-colored hair standing out. But like Daiyu, Jason didn't bother to dye his hair. Almost everyone wore masks covering their faces, and Daiyu scrutinized the crowd as best as she could.

Then she spotted him, dressed in a black tee, and immediately felt her fingertips tingle from the surge of adrenaline. It wasn't his face that had caught her attention. He wore a mask, and his head was lowered, as if he were studying the pavement. It was the set of his shoulders and his gait that had sent a shock of familiarity through her. Jason walked in a manner that forced people to scatter out of his way. She watched the strange phenomenon unfold in front of her now: two beefy European guys hauled a bunch of shopping bags between them, chatting amiably, but sidestepped and twisted their bodies as Jason approached, then walked past them. Another tall Chinese woman wearing large gold sunglasses visibly leaned away when Jason passed, but leaned forward again, tilting her chin to admire his backside as he strode away.

Daiyu couldn't blame her. She'd done the same countless times before.

He had one hand stuffed into his jeans pocket, probably gripping his butterfly knife. Then he lifted his face, searching for the number at a shop just a few stalls away, and she shifted out of view before heading toward the back.

Aining sat behind her small counter and was hand-painting something with a thin brush, but raised her head when Daiyu rushed past to hide behind the partition. Her friend's face positively glowed with curiosity.

Not a minute later, it seemed, Jason entered the store.

"Hey," he said in a brusque voice.

There was a pause, and the moment seemed laden with uncertainty. Daiyu could sense the caution emanating from Jason, only a few feet away. She couldn't bring herself to peek past the thick curtain.

"In there," Aining said, whispering. She must have pointed, or jerked her chin in Daiyu's direction.

The curtain slid aside and Jason was in the storage area with her. They stood toe to toe, because she didn't think to move to make space. Daiyu could smell the soap he had used—something unfamiliar. Flustered, she took a big step back and stumbled over a box. Jason caught her arm, steadying her; then she pulled away at the same time he let go.

"I'm all right," she said.

He tugged down his face mask and swept a lock of hair out of his eyes. "Thanks for meeting me."

Jason took in the space with one sweeping glance.

Daiyu hadn't looked around before. They were surrounded by packing boxes and shelves filled with Aining's art pieces. The cramped closet was lit by a large ceramic firefly with a yellow bulb at the end of its body dangling overhead. A small door she'd have to duck through if she were to use it was set in the back wall. The air was stuffy and hot.

"Yes," she said, losing her train of thought. "Of course."

"We're safe here?" he murmured. "She's a friend?" He slanted his heard toward the front of the store.

"We can trust her."

"Daiyu . . ." He trailed off.

She had the distinct feeling that if she interrupted, he'd find it that much harder to say what he needed to say. His nervousness fueled her own anxiety.

"I need your help," Jason finally said after a long pause. "It's not fair for me to ask, but you're the only one who can do this."

Daiyu stared at him, stunned. "This is about that air filter my father took—"

"You've seen it?"

"Once," she replied. "He keeps it in a safe in his suite." And this confirmed what she had suspected since Jason showed up at their door the previous night. "You came over to try and steal the filter back—it's why you were dressed like the hotel staff."

His eyebrows rose and he finally met her eyes. "Yes."

"I was in the way," she continued. "You didn't really come to talk." She tried to hide her disappointment, but there was no ignoring the way her entire chest seemed to seize, then twist.

He neither confirmed nor denied what she said. "We need your help to take it back."

"Why?" she asked. "Why's it so important? The clinic is safe now with the new equipment. . . ."

"He stole it from someone," Jason said in a quiet voice. "Your father murdered her for it. He'll claim it as his own and sell it for millions. But it doesn't belong to him."

Daiyu was suddenly dizzy. The heat felt oppressive, but she hadn't expected Jason to tell her about another one of her father's murders. Someone Jason knew? No wonder he hated her father so much. He caught her hand, and she stared down at their entwined fingers.

"I'm sorry to be so blunt," he said. "Are you sure you're all right?"

He hadn't grabbed her hand as he had always done before—because he liked to touch her as much as she did him—but because she had swayed on her feet. Jason looked down at her, concerned.

She shook her head. "It's not your fault." Her throat had gone dry. "Please go on."

He let go of her hand.

The curtain behind them stirred, and they both froze. A female voice asked a question in the outer room, and Aining responded. The stool Aining was sitting on scraped against the stone floor, as if her friend had risen from it, and an animated conversation began between Aining and the customer over one of her pieces.

They spoke for some time, probably five minutes, but it felt like an eternity. It seemed she and Jason barely breathed. She became hyperaware of how close they stood to each other, and she wanted more than anything to reach out, to show that she still cared for him. But it felt foolish and out of place. Instead, she watched Jason's jaw tighten with tension. His eyes were downcast.

Finally, things quieted on the other side. The customer had left.

Jason drew a slow breath and reached into his pocket, pulling out a slender device. "It's a voice-activated recorder."

"For my father's safe."

He nodded. "Once you capture the recording of your father speaking the combination, we can open the safe."

She took it from him, and their fingers brushed. He clenched his hand into a fist after she took the device.

"Will you do this?" he asked.

"Your friends . . . they trust me?"

"I trust you," he said. "I vouched for you."

"How do I know you're not just using me?"

This brought a flush of color to his face. He stared down at his hands, flexing his fingers. She knew he wished he were flipping one of his knives instead. "I want to believe"—he swallowed, the words seeming to catch—"I want to believe that we're on the same side. And that we can depend on each other?" One corner of his mouth slanted upward.

That ghost of a smile made her miss him more than she thought was possible. They stood a hand's width apart, but it felt like a huge chasm. Yet he trusted her, was risking his friendships over it. This gave her hope.

She tucked the small device into her wallet. "I'll help."

"Daiyu," he said, "if your father catches you, he'll never forgive you. You risk losing everything."

She closed her eyes and drew a slow breath, then opened them again to find Jason studying her, unable to disguise his hope. It crushed her, that this wasn't a given, that her willingness to help him was no guarantee. "You asked if I could stand against my father, that I had the ability to choose." Daiyu lifted her chin. "I'm choosing now."

Jason grinned, his features relaxing from relief, and took a step forward. He raised a hand, as if to caress her hair or her cheek—the way he used to. Her heart lurched; for a second, she thought he was going to kiss her. Instead he stopped short, then pulled out a tattered notebook—something nobody she knew even used anymore—and said, "Let's go over the plan, then."

CHAPTER THIRTEEN

ZHOU

"It can't be you who takes the prototype," Lingyi whispered heatedly. "Jin knows what you look like—he knows you're the punk who stole that huge ransom from him."

I flipped the butterfly knife in my hand. "That's good, though. Jin probably thought I died in the explosion. He'll hate that I somehow survived and have stolen something from him again." I had returned to the Les Suites from my meeting with Daiyu and was relieved to find Lingyi alone so we could talk. We were huddled again in her hotel bedroom. Iris was currently canvassing the hotel grounds for us, and Arun had left in the morning to visit the clinic again.

"It's too risky," Lingyi said. "He'll kill you on sight if you get caught."

"I won't get caught." I grinned. "Besides, who else can do it? Iris?"

Lingyi shook her head. "Iris would never agree to working with Daiyu."

"I vouched for Daiyu, and I'll take the risk." I couldn't really blame Iris for not trusting Jin's daughter and the proclaimed heir to Jin Corp. If I didn't know Daiyu so well, I wouldn't trust her either.

She's played you before, Zhou, that small demon me whispered, cavorting on my shoulder. *Are you certain she's not playing you again?*

I ignored him.

"For all you know, Jin already knows you're alive and that you've been dating his daughter."

I shrugged and tossed my knife into the air before catching it and spinning it in my hand. "If he does, he'd think I was doing it in direct retaliation against him. He doesn't know that Daiyu saved me the night of the explosion. Jin always brings the narrative back to himself. It'd only help us—"

"Help us how?" she interjected.

"To incense him. He'll do anything to gain control again, to save face." I tucked my knife back into my pocket. "It means he'll readily agree to my terms to meet at Jin Tower. He'll think he has the upper hand—his security, his grounds. But he'll be wrong." I winked at her.

Lingyi sighed. "I don't like it."

"I know it's dangerous." I felt my pulse quicken in anticipation. I loved a good cat-and-mouse game. And there was nothing I enjoyed more than pissing Jin off. Before, it had always felt I had nothing to lose, but this time . . . this time there was Daiyu. In a low voice, I replied, "I'm more worried about Daiyu. She has nowhere to run right now if things go wrong."

"But you trust her," Lingyi said. "And she'd never have agreed if she couldn't handle this, if she felt she couldn't somehow fool her father."

I thought about how she had played me for so long, with deftness and ease. If anyone could pull this off, it would be Daiyu. Still, if someone was going to take the fall in the end, I always wanted it to be me. "You do your job, and I'll do mine."

Lingyi scrutinized me, before tucking a strand of purple hair behind her ear. She leaned forward and we bumped fists. "Deal."

We had been so engrossed in our discussion, neither of us heard anyone come in until the heavy door slammed shut. I jumped to my feet, Daiyu's knife already palmed into my right hand, when I saw Arun's face on the monitor.

"Where is everyone?" he asked from the outer room.

Lingyi and I exchanged a glance. If we didn't tell Iris, Arun couldn't know either. I tucked the knife back and exited the bedroom, running my hands through my hair lazily as I yawned. "Hey, man. How was it at the clinic?"

Arun cocked his chin at me in greeting. "Things are good. Everything's stable and there've been no more deaths." He lifted his hands, which were clutching a large box. "And I stopped at that noodle shop again on the way back."

I grinned. "You're my favorite."

Arun laughed and set the box on the table.

"I'll go relieve Iris," I said over my shoulder. "She can eat first."

I was hungry, but Iris had already been on shift for almost three hours. And I also needed time to think. Alone.

▲▼▲

A message appeared from Daiyu that night on my temporary device: I have it. I've tested it. It works.

Daiyu had told me that Jin was actively searching for someone who could work on reverse engineering the prototype; he was keeping the job secret and separate from Jin Corp. For now. Our time was running out. Still, I hadn't expected her to get the voice recording the same day.

"I'm headed out," I told my friends.

"Where to?" Iris asked, a note of suspicion in her voice.

Arun was covering for her in surveillance.

"Zhou's working on getting the prototype back," Lingyi said.

"How?" Iris asked. "It's impossible."

"He's looking into it," Lingyi replied.

"I can help."

Lingyi shook her head. "Zhou's got this for now."

Iris opened her mouth to argue, then clamped it shut. They'd been together for almost two years now, but before Lingyi was Iris's girlfriend, she was the boss. Lingyi had always been the boss. And what she said went.

"I'm always here for backup," Iris said after a pause.

I nodded at her. "The best backup." I ran my hands over the places where I kept my knives, trusting that Daiyu had left the recording device at the front desk as we'd agreed, and headed out onto the Bund.

It was after nine p.m., and the temperature had dropped, but there was still a balminess in the air. The thick throngs of pedestrians and tourists had lessened, but many people still walked along the pavement in front of the historical landmarks and beautiful hotels. Even more people strolled along the promenade across the street, admiring the Bund's buildings lit in golden light, contrasted with the sleek structures across the river, flickering in bright blues, pinks, oranges, and greens. They painted a colorful reflection in the waters as late-night boats cruised along it.

It was a beautiful night, and I wished I could enjoy it. Instead, my mind kept returning to my meeting with Daiyu earlier today.

How do I know you're not just using me? she had asked.

Aren't you just using her, though, Zhou? my mini-demon rasped.

"I love her," I said into the night. "We love each other."

Are you so certain of that? The demon chortled, adjusted his perfect bow tie, and flicked imaginary dust from his tuxedo sleeve. *Can a girl like her truly love a boy like you? You're overreaching.*

I clenched my teeth and shoved my hands deep into my pockets. My fingers felt something, and I pulled it out. A small note folded into a triangle. Daiyu's quick note to me before I'd left for Shanghai. Before either of us knew we'd both end up in the same city, working together to steal something back from her father. The demon on my shoulder was right: I didn't know how things would go between us. But I knew for certain what I wanted; I wanted her. I wanted us to stay together. Maybe she was my weakness, and when it came to Daiyu, as Iris implied, I was too easily fooled. But no matter what was thrown at me, or came between us, I never stopped loving Daiyu—or trusting her.

I could only hope that after all that had happened, she felt the same way.

A woman with a yellow head scarf wrapped around her hair meandered through the pedestrians, selling fresh flowers. She held small bouquets and individual flowers in her arms, calling out to the people still wandering the streets, many of them couples. A young Chinese man with indigo hair stopped to select a few long-stemmed roses for his boyfriend. The recipient, a Filipino man, beamed in delight. Their animated conversation carried to me even as they walked away, hand in hand.

One of the sprigs in her bunch caught my eye: a long stem of pale green orchid blooms, the color of crisp jade. It stood out among the red and pink roses, and the large white lilies. Jade was part of Daiyu's name, and on a whim, I approached the woman. "How much for the orchids?" I asked.

"For a handsome young man like you"—she grinned, showing a few missing teeth—"only thirty yuan."

I had a feeling she was overcharging me, but I wasn't bothered and fished out two twenty-yuan notes from my wallet. "Keep the change."

Her ingratiating grin turned into a true smile. "Sir. Thank you, sir! Perhaps you'd like a red rose, too?"

I shook my head. "Just the orchids, please."

"Yes, of course." Tucking her bouquets into a wicker basket at her feet, she then carefully wrapped my delicate sprig of orchids in cellophane, adding some greenery, before tying it with a purple ribbon. She handed the flowers to me and said, "May things go as you wish this evening."

I nodded, forgetting to thank her as I headed to the Peninsula Hotel. It seemed an odd thing for her to say, or was I feeling paranoid? And how would I even get the flowers to Daiyu? I couldn't walk up to her suite—and what, pass the bouquet on to Jin to give to his daughter? Feeling foolish, I strode into the Peninsula's foyer. It was surprisingly busy for this time of the evening, but maybe the *you*s always had something to do, somewhere to go. They bustled in their designer clothes, jewels sparkling on their fingers, earlobes, and wrists.

The automatons still stood in the boutique window, and to my horror, they were moving in unison. The store display had been transformed into a sandy beach, and the automatons wore bathing suits and bikinis with silk wraps, their feet marking grooves into the shallow sand. Their mouths pursed in pretend conversation, and I walked quickly past them to the reception desk.

"How can I help you?" a woman with her black hair pulled into a bun asked from behind the marble counter.

She arched an eyebrow as I approached. Although the air was regulated in the expensive hotel, I hadn't bothered to pull down my face mask. Dressed in black jeans and a faded leather jacket, I definitely did not look like the average customer staying there. "Ms. Jin left a small package for me here," I said.

Her eyes widened in surprise. "I see," she replied. "Under what name, may I ask?"

"Zhou," I said. "Jason Zhou."

"Of course, Mr. Zhou." She turned from me, and I could smell the faint scent of her floral perfume. "I'll have a look."

A man at the counter continued to help people as she went to the back to search for my package. I was more nervous than I thought I'd be. What if the recording device had been intercepted by Jin? It was our last and only chance to take the prototype back.

She returned after a while with a small envelope in her hand. "Here you go, Mr. Zhou."

I couldn't wait. I opened the envelope right there at the counter. Inside was the slim recording device I had given Daiyu and a note. I pulled it out, and seeing her beautiful handwriting brought a visceral reaction, especially remembering the last very personal note she had given me, still tucked in my pocket.

We'll be out for an investors' banquet tomorrow, which starts at 11:30 a.m. It will last at least two hours.

Then the last line, in a messier scrawl, as if written in a hurry.

I trust you, too.

The last sentence brought a flood of warmth to my face, and only then did I feel the other woman's gaze on me. There were no customers waiting, and she had been studying me with interest. I was sure Daiyu had never left a note to give to a strange boy at the front desk before.

"Is there anything else I could help you with, Mr. Zhou?" she asked in a warm voice. Her curiosity was obvious.

"Yes," I replied. My friends always said I often acted rashly. They were right. "Could you get these flowers directly to Ms. Jin?" I set the bouquet down on the marble counter. "Only to Ms. Jin."

"Of course," she said, understanding me. "Would you like to include a note to pass on?"

"No, no note."

"I'll handle this personally," she assured me, smiling graciously, taking the bouquet and setting it under the counter.

"Thank you," I said.

"Ms. Chen." Someone had stepped up beside me without being called, and the familiar baritone in his voice made my scalp crawl. *Jin.* I turned my head from him slowly, fighting the urge to run—it'd only draw his attention.

Shit.

I felt Jin give me a once-over and was grateful for the mask that still covered half my face. Blood thundered in my ears. I didn't belong in this rich hotel, and Jin had sharp eyes. His gaze was heavy against my back as I strolled from the counter, forcing my fingers to relax, my shoulders to sway naturally. The weighted moment passed, and I heard Jin say to Ms. Chen, "I need a favor. . . ."

"Of course, Mr. Jin. You could have called down, or relayed your request to Mr. Han—"

"I could have, but I wanted to instruct you in person." I could hear the warm smile in his words. Jin was charming as hell when he wanted to be. "I know I can trust you to manage things exactly as I like."

I walked away and glanced back. Ms. Chen had her attention turned to Jin, her hands clasped on the counter in front of her. I left through the front doors, the humid air and pollution hitting me like a wall the moment I stepped outside.

I could only hope that Jin hadn't paid attention to the flowers I had set on the counter, or notice when they were delivered to the suite to Daiyu. Or what if Ms. Chen gave the flowers to Jin now, to pass on to his daughter? The thought brought a cold sweat to my forehead and the back of my neck.

This one impulsive gesture might ruin everything.

▲▼▲

I couldn't sleep that night, waiting for a message from Daiyu that we'd been discovered, that Jin was onto us. But no message ever came. The next day Lingyi and I were at the Bank of China on the Bund when they opened at nine a.m. to set up a safe-deposit box together. When we returned, Lingyi spent the rest of the morning placating Iris, reassuring her she was working on altering her passport info so we could travel back to Taiwan soon. Which was true.

I knew Iris was growing impatient and feeling trapped. She also worried Jin would target Lingyi again. I didn't blame her.

Arun left once more to visit the clinic. He wanted to assess the facility and see what other equipment and needs he might be able to provide before we returned to Taipei. I went out just after eleven a.m. with a large duffel bag tucked into a leather briefcase. Lingyi knew the specific dimensions of Jany's filter, but Daiyu had already assured me it was something I could carry in the duffel.

Arun had had a suit made for me when he had ordered the hotel staff clothing, and I appreciated his foresight. "You never know when you might need a smart suit, man," Arun said.

"You sound like Victor," I replied.

"Victor was right."

We smiled at each other but didn't say more. We both missed him.

It might not have been designer or as stylish, but the gray suit was tailored perfectly. I wore a white shirt with a silver-blue tie and managed to get the flop of hair out of my eyes with some styling product. Slipping on a pair of leather shoes, I looked the part with the briefcase.

The heat was unrelenting when I stepped outside Les Suites. And though the sunlight was hazy, it beat down upon us. I took the backstreets this time, avoiding the large crowds along the Bund. Still, there were people everywhere, and despite my mask, I could smell the exhaust and the cigarette smoke every person seemed to blow my way. Coughing, I quickened my pace, feeling the sweat slide down my back.

By the time I reached the Peninsula again, the back of my shirt was damp. I entered the grand hotel, this time dressed like I belonged there, and strode to the elevators. There were two new hotel staff behind the reception desk, and though one lifted his head to glance at me, he didn't do more than that. I stepped inside the elevator and accessed the presidential suite floor with the card Lingyi had given me.

When I arrived at Jin's door, I pulled out the motion-sensing goggles from my briefcase and searched for movement in the other room. Seeing nothing, I used my key to enter the suite. The curtains in the luxurious sitting room were drawn aside. Airlimos glided over the river across the floor-to-ceiling windows' view.

The suite was silent. Daiyu and I had agreed that she needed a solid alibi when I showed up to steal the prototype, and this banquet luncheon she had to attend with her father was perfect. Jin would more likely suspect we had gotten our hands on some tech that could crack his safe rather than think his own daughter had betrayed him.

I headed straight to Jin's room, scanned for movement, then went in and flicked the lights on. Sensors turned on the lighting in the large walk-in-closet when I entered. I pulled down my mask and went directly to the safe. The tiny red light set at eye level seemed to wait for me to speak the combination aloud. I took out the recording device and depressed a hidden button on the underside. Jin's voice filled the room, crisp and clear. He spoke twelve digits, enunciating carefully. I had tested the recorder the night before, but it was more disconcerting to hear the man's voice fill the space in his own suite. I looked over my shoulder once, feeling the hairs on my arms stand on end. The recording stopped, and I waited, holding my breath. Three seconds later, the heavy safe door swung open soundlessly.

I pumped my fist into the air twice, refraining from shouting in triumph. The safe was empty except for the prototype placed on the lowest shelf. I eased it out, lifting it to test the weight—probably thirty pounds. It was cumbersome, but nothing I couldn't carry out of the hotel easily on my own. Working quickly, I removed the large duffel bag and motion detector from the briefcase, then carefully placed the filter and my detector in the duffel. I set the briefcase into Jin's safe; it was empty, except for one single note containing the number to a dummy device.

I had no doubt Jin would be in contact as soon as he discovered the prototype was missing. Shutting the safe, I hefted the duffel bag and left Jin's suite, not bothering to turn off the bedroom light. I wanted him to know something was wrong the instant he opened his door. I wanted him to feel alarmed, feel that unease climb down his spine and settle in his stomach, heavy, then turn into dread. The thought filled me with pleasure.

I cracked open the suite's heavy door to an empty hallway. After I stepped out, the door clicked firmly closed behind me. I lifted my head to where I knew the camera was and grinned. Jin would be going over the surveillance recordings, and this time, Lingyi wouldn't be deleting the files and replacing them with empty corridors. I knew the sight of my face would enrage him. I took pleasure in that as well.

For a moment, I considered taking the emergency stairs. But it wasn't even noon yet, so I took a risk and pressed the elevator button on Jin's floor instead. The down arrow lit up not a minute later, the elevator dinged, and the doors opened soundlessly.

Da Ge, Jin's main thug, stood inside.

Stunned, we both stared at each other for a heartbeat, before he lunged out of the elevator at me and I swung the heavy duffel toward him at the same time. The filter slammed against his shins, and the man grunted in pain. I dropped the duffel and palmed one of Daiyu's knives into my hand. He was reaching for his gun at his waistband

and I charged, thrusting the knife at him. Da Ge blocked me with one arm.

He shuffled back, still feeling the impact of the metal filter thudding into his shin bones, and I took advantage and continued to advance, giving him no leeway. Infuriated, he swung at me. I blocked with my left arm, feeling the impact in my teeth, then grabbed his wrist and made a swift upward slice along his bicep. He grunted again, an enraged sound.

He winced from the wound, but it was hardly enough to stop him. We circled each other, the large duffel between us. I knew he recognized me as the kid tied up in the basement the night Jin Corp was blown up—the kid Jin had instructed him to kill the next morning. Like Jin, Da Ge had assumed I had died in the explosion.

I grinned at him, only because I knew that'd piss him off.

It did.

Da Ge kicked at me, trying to dislodge my knife, leaving himself exposed again. Instead of dodging or deflecting, I spun into him. With my back to his torso, I stabbed him in his side, then twisted and slammed my blade into his other side. The momentum gave me enough power to plunge the knife in deep.

He stumbled from me, clutching one side with his hand. Blood seeped through it. "Fucking kid," he growled, and grabbed the gun strapped at his back. Anticipating this, I dodged just as he raised his arm and shot at me. His aim was crap, and his grip slippery from his own blood.

Not giving him a chance to shoot again, I kicked him hard in the shin, then knocked the gun out of his hand. Da Ge collapsed onto one knee, and I fought the urge to haul him up and pin him against the wall, my knife pressed against his throat. In a split-second decision, I hadn't depressed the button that would have had him thrashing on the ground right now in his final death throes from poison. Instead, I grabbed his gun from the floor and hefted the duffel up, then ran toward the emergency stairway.

Da Ge was too injured to follow me, but not too injured to call for backup. I ran down the stairs as fast as I could; Jin's suite was on the ninth floor, and that was nothing for me. But carrying a thirty-pound filter down the stairway was a different story. Winded, I didn't know what to expect when I emerged onto the main floor. Sirens blared outside.

Da Ge wouldn't have called the police. More likely someone had reported the sound of a gunshot or maybe found the injured thug out in the hallway. Grateful that the emergency stairway opened into a quiet corridor, I ran away from the lobby and increasing noise, as hotel patrons began to converge and speak excitedly, gossiping. I barged through a double swinging door marked EMPLOYEES ONLY and almost slammed into a man pushing a large cart filled with laundry.

He gaped at me, but I was already headed for the hotel's back exit.

I found it minutes later and pushed the bar, falling out into an alleyway. Nothing glamorous or beautiful here. It looked like all the dank and narrow alleyways I'd ever slinked through. I looked both ways, listening for anyone approaching, then placed the heavy duffel on the ground, flexing my palm before dropping Da Ge's gun into a metal garbage bin. I hated guns, and this one was still sticky with the man's blood.

In the end, I decided to walk the half mile to the Bank of China. I was conspicuous carrying a large duffel, assuming Jin's men had been informed to search for me. But I'd take to the side streets as much as I could. I put my face mask back on.

I stayed pressed against the shadows of the tall buildings, and the sound of sirens filled my ears. The police response seemed over-the-top, but this was the Peninsula Hotel, and the shooting had happened outside Jin's suite. The rich and powerful needed to be protected, I thought with a smirk.

Navigating through the backstreets, I still had to fend off a stream of pedestrians out in the early afternoon—wandering tourists and professionals headed for a late lunch. Once, I glimpsed a lean man dressed in black headed toward me, and my fingers grazed over my knife. He sidestepped when our paths crossed, and I used the duffel bag to keep him at arm's length. The man ambled on, never looking back; but my hand stayed poised over my knife for the rest of the journey.

When I reached the bank, I stopped in a shadowed corner, on the side street, out of view. During business hours, the Bank of China always had a security guard near the building's main entrance, and I had to make myself presentable. My arms and shoulders were sore from carrying the filter this far, and my dress shirt was soaked through with sweat. I had wanted to take off my jacket, but it helped me pass as an older professional. My palm was still smeared with Da Ge's dried blood from his gun. I wiped my hand against the back of my damp shirt and managed to get most of it off. I adjusted my tie, then noticed the scuff marks on my jacket. A few drops of Da Ge's blood had splattered onto my white shirt, too, as if I had suffered a nosebleed. I quickly buttoned my suit jacket to cover the stains.

Dusting off my jacket, I picked up the bag again and turned the corner, walking nonchalantly up the steps. As long as I'd played the rich kid, it still made me feel as uncomfortable as if I were donning a dinosaur suit. A young man wearing a black uniform and cap with a gun strapped very visibly at his side nodded at me. I nodded back, and seeing the large bag I carried, he walked toward the front entrance. My heartbeat picked up, thinking he was going to intercept and question me. Instead he simply pulled the door open.

"Thank you," I said.

"Of course, sir," he replied. "No face masks inside, please."

I murmured something inaudible and removed my mask.

The bank's cold air enveloped me immediately. A high-domed ceiling arched overhead, with ironwork sconces set in a neat line all the way through its deep interior. The bank was filled with customers, many of them sitting in single glass booths to my left, making their personal transactions. Open cubicles on the right allowed the bank's clients to sit with a banker to discuss their problems and needs. I stopped at the circular front desk, where a man dressed in a

211

navy suit greeted me. It was a different clerk than when Lingyi and I had visited earlier. "How can I help you, sir?"

"I'm here to use my safe-deposit box."

"Of course, sir. If I could just get your retina scan to verify access."

I stood still as the scanner adjusted to my height and took the data. The bank clerk glanced at the screen on his desk and nodded. "Feel free to take the elevator downstairs toward the back of the building, Mr. Zhou."

A soft hum filled the bank space, reverberating from its high arched ceilings. I tugged my tie loose. I despised wearing anything around my neck, and after this morning, the tie felt especially constricting. I took the wood-paneled elevator down one level to the basement floor, and the doors opened to another reception desk with a woman standing behind it. "Good afternoon, Mr. Zhou." She smiled at me. "You may access the vault with a retina scan." She indicated the scanner by the beautiful ironwork door of the vault.

"Thank you," I said. After another scan, the two-foot-thick door swung open.

I had never been in a bank vault before today, and it was as hushed as I imagined a tomb would be. The plush carpeting silenced my footsteps. Large sconces hung from the high ceiling, casting a golden light down on the long, narrow space, but I still felt claustrophobic. I quickly walked to the end of the vault, where the largest deposit boxes were located, and searched for our deposit box number. It required a thumbprint scan and a twelve-digit code to access. The door swung open; it was more like a small safe. I removed the prototype from the bag and carefully placed it inside and shut the door.

It was done.

Now we waited for Jin's next move.

CHAPTER FOURTEEN

DAIYU

Daiyu had been hosting the extravagant banquet with her father for over an hour. One hundred guests were gathered at the Empress's Chamber, an elegant and expensive restaurant in the Pudong District on the Huangpu River, looking across at the Bund. She made small talk and smiled graciously as dish after dish was set in front of the guests on gilded plates: ginger scallops, braised abalone with mushroom, tender stewed pork, and lobster. Daiyu watched as her father made the rounds, sealing business deals, grasping each investor's hand with warmth. She avoided looking at the time, for fear her nervousness would betray her.

Had Jason sneaked into their suite by now to steal the prototype?

Suddenly, her father glanced at his Vox, his unlined brow crinkling in puzzlement, before his dark eyebrows pulled down in displeasure. It was for a mere second, but she caught it before he turned with a smile, nodding at another guest who had approached to speak with him. But her father ended the conversation abruptly, excusing himself to send several messages via his Palm. He read the responses he received, stone-faced.

Her heartbeat quickened. Her father was always working hard to expand his networking and relationships in China—his guanxi—where he was still seen as an interloper in the business world. For him to cut off a potential investor or government official meant something was very wrong.

It had to do with Jason and his theft, she was certain of it.

Her father wrapped up the banquet brusquely soon after, barely giving his guests time to enjoy their dessert. His security ushered her and her father into his black airlimo, and it lifted into the sky, making a wide arc to glide back toward the Bund and their hotel. It'd be a short ride, but still felt too long in the car's stifling silence. Her father rarely spoke with her anyway; he was always conversing with some associate or reading the news on his Palm. Today, he only sat in silence, one hand clenched in a fist in his lap—a surprising tell. This silence was thick with tension.

Finally, he turned his attention to her, and Daiyu felt pinpricks dance across her scalp, seeing her father's leaden gaze. "You are not to leave the hotel today."

"Yes, Father," she said.

"In fact, you are not allowed to leave at all until the Jin Tower ceremony next Wednesday, unless I need you at a function."

"Yes, Father," she repeated. Nodding was not enough for him. Her father always demanded verbal affirmation, so he knew he had been heard and understood.

Their airlimo glided into the Peninsula's garage, and his security opened their car door, following them into the elevator to go down to their suite. The first thing Daiyu noticed was the stains in the corridor when the doors slid open—dark rust in the beige carpet. A knot rose to her throat and she felt light-headed for a moment. Was that Jason's blood? Had they caught him, and if so, was he still alive?

She knew her father had no mercy for anyone who stole from him.

Daiyu took so long that when she stepped out, the doors nearly closed on her. Her father didn't seem to notice any of these details, instead speaking quietly with the two men stationed outside their suite's door. He had been lax with security before, believing they were safe here in the hotel. That obviously had changed.

Her heart was racing now, and she refrained from sprinting to her room to check for any messages from Jason. She followed her father into the suite and was met with two more security members inside the large sitting room area. She turned to head toward her own bedroom, but her father stopped her with one word.

Her father was strict. Even at eighteen, she had been forbidden to date. Daiyu hadn't been certain if her father knew she had been seeing Jason, but her gut told her he knew now. "I saw him before I came to Shanghai." She murmured her response—a guilty daughter caught doing something she shouldn't have.

"You were seeing someone behind my back," her father said. "Not only that, someone who had stolen from me."

She raised her head then, eyes wide with shock, using her discomfort and fear of discovery in her reactions. "What?"

"He stole a large sum from me"—her father stared at her, still not revealing that she had been kidnapped last summer by Jason, still keeping her in the dark—"and he stole again from me this morning." He snatched both images back; a flash of anger. "This boy, this liar and thief, he's dating you to get to me, Daughter."

Daiyu blinked at him, knowing the color had drained from her face. "No."

Her father smiled. Maybe it was meant to be gentle. It looked mocking instead. Derisive. "Yes. He wanted access to Jin Corp, and what better way than to charm my daughter, the heir to the company?"

She jerked her head to the side, toward the large picture window. A tour boat drifted along the river; tourists clung to the rails on the top deck, clustered together.

"Whatever you thought you had between you was a lie," her father said. "He used you." His voice had turned to frost. "The boy's

"Daughter," he said. "You'll meet me in my office in half an hour."

Stupidly, she nodded, then replied, "Yes, Father."

In a daze, she tripped into her bedroom and tore off her high heels. She grabbed for the Vox sitting on her bedside table, checking for messages. Nothing. Desperate, she reached for her Palm, as if the results would be different somehow. She had left it on the round inlaid table set in front of her bedroom windows. It sat beneath the sprig of orchids in a clear vase. The flowers had been delivered to her late last night. She was surprised to see a woman she recognized from the reception desk standing there holding the small bouquet. "From Mr. Zhou," Ms. Chen said with a smile. "I was to deliver it directly to you."

Daiyu had been alone in the suite. She accepted the delivery, feeling herself blush. It was a reckless gesture, but also terribly romantic—which summed up Jason so perfectly in her mind.

Now she didn't know if he had been hurt, or was even alive.

She considered dictating a message to Jason's temporary number, hoping he might respond, but stopped herself. What if her father was tracking everything now, not only her movements, but also her communication? Daiyu couldn't risk it.

Instead, she peeled off her pale pink organza dress and stepped into the shower. She blasted hot water over herself, hoping this would calm her, make her more alert for the encounter she'd have with her father. Daiyu had no idea what to expect, but she had to have a clear head to deal with him, play him to her own best advantage. She chose a tan skirt and another floral blouse, before clasping her father's jade pendant around her neck again. Slipping some nude-colored pumps on, she made her way through the large sitting room, past the piano, toward the small library that also served as her father's office during their stay here.

Her father's security personnel stood like silent sentries in the sitting room.

The door was open, and her father was seated behind the large mahogany desk. He had been studying something on his MacFold, then shut the computer. He nodded at the leather seat across from the desk, and she slid into it, folding her hands in her lap. Despite the cool, regulated air circulated in their suite, Daiyu could feel the back of her neck dampen with sweat. She met her father's eyes and held his gaze. He couldn't suspect a thing—it'd put the entire plan at risk.

Her mind flashed to the dark stains on the carpet outside the suite, then to the beautiful light green orchids in her bedroom, and she quickly shoved both images aside.

Focus.

Her father leaned back in his desk chair. "Tell me, Daughter, what you know about Jason Zhou."

She stared at him, wondering how much *he* knew, how best to present this. If she were caught in a lie, everything would unravel. Her father hated being lied to as much as he hated being stolen from. "I met him in the new year." It was the previous year, at her father's

own party, but she was purposely vague. If her father didn['t] their history, he'd assume she meant this past new year, after left for China. "He's . . . he's American. From California." Sh[e] down at her hands, then looked back toward her father.

"And you are friends?" Jin asked, raising one dark brow.

"We were . . . friendly." She almost said much more to e[ ] this away. But stopped herself.

"I see." Her father pulled a piece of paper from a file and p[ut] it across the desktop toward her. It was the bad rendering of Jason one that had been captured when he had kidnapped her last sum[mer.]

"Do you recognize this?" he asked in a pleasant, conversati[onal] tone.

Daiyu controlled every inch of her being, even her breathing. [She] willed herself not to flush. Her father read tells as well as she di[d;] she probably learned the skill from him. "I . . ."—she played up [her] confusion—"No. He seems familiar?"

He pushed another image in front of her. This must have bee[n] captured today by the hotel surveillance. Jason was looking directly [at] the camera, a hint of a smile on his mouth. Cocky. He grasped a larg[e] duffel that obviously held the stolen filter, his bicep flexing from th[e] weight of it. She felt the blood drain from her face. She couldn't slow her heartbeat, no matter how much she tried. "That's him."

"Yes," her father said. "It is. When was the last time you saw this Jason Zhou, Daughter?"

She looked down again and felt her cheeks redden. This was fine.

"Daughter," he said. "You'll meet me in my office in half an hour."

Stupidly, she nodded, then replied, "Yes, Father."

In a daze, she tripped into her bedroom and tore off her high heels. She grabbed for the Vox sitting on her bedside table, checking for messages. Nothing. Desperate, she reached for her Palm, as if the results would be different somehow. She had left it on the round inlaid table set in front of her bedroom windows. It sat beneath the sprig of orchids in a clear vase. The flowers had been delivered to her late last night. She was surprised to see a woman she recognized from the reception desk standing there holding the small bouquet. "From Mr. Zhou," Ms. Chen said with a smile. "I was to deliver it directly to you."

Daiyu had been alone in the suite. She accepted the delivery, feeling herself blush. It was a reckless gesture, but also terribly romantic—which summed up Jason so perfectly in her mind.

Now she didn't know if he had been hurt, or was even alive.

She considered dictating a message to Jason's temporary number, hoping he might respond, but stopped herself. What if her father was tracking everything now, not only her movements, but also her communication? Daiyu couldn't risk it.

Instead, she peeled off her pale pink organza dress and stepped into the shower. She blasted hot water over herself, hoping this would calm her, make her more alert for the encounter she'd have with her father. Daiyu had no idea what to expect, but she had to have a clear head to deal with him, play him to her own best advantage. She chose a tan skirt and another floral blouse, before clasping her father's jade pendant around her neck again. Slipping some nude-colored pumps on, she made her way through the large sitting room, past the piano, toward the small library that also served as her father's office during their stay here.

Her father's security personnel stood like silent sentries in the sitting room.

The door was open, and her father was seated behind the large mahogany desk. He had been studying something on his MacFold, then shut the computer. He nodded at the leather seat across from the desk, and she slid into it, folding her hands in her lap. Despite the cool, regulated air circulated in their suite, Daiyu could feel the back of her neck dampen with sweat. She met her father's eyes and held his gaze. He couldn't suspect a thing—it'd put the entire plan at risk.

Her mind flashed to the dark stains on the carpet outside the suite, then to the beautiful light green orchids in her bedroom, and she quickly shoved both images aside.

Focus.

Her father leaned back in his desk chair. "Tell me, Daughter, what you know about Jason Zhou."

She stared at him, wondering how much *he* knew, how best to present this. If she were caught in a lie, everything would unravel. Her father hated being lied to as much as he hated being stolen from. "I met him in the new year." It was the previous year, at her father's own party, but she was purposely vague. If her father didn't know their history, he'd assume she meant this past new year, after he had left for China. "He's . . . he's American. From California." She stared down at her hands, then looked back toward her father.

"And you are friends?" Jin asked, raising one dark brow.

"We were . . . friendly." She almost said much more to explain this away. But stopped herself.

"I see." Her father pulled a piece of paper from a file and pushed it across the desktop toward her. It was the bad rendering of Jason, the one that had been captured when he had kidnapped her last summer.

"Do you recognize this?" he asked in a pleasant, conversational tone.

Daiyu controlled every inch of her being, even her breathing. She willed herself not to flush. Her father read tells as well as she did—she probably learned the skill from him. "I . . ."—she played up her confusion—"No. He seems familiar?"

He pushed another image in front of her. This must have been captured today by the hotel surveillance. Jason was looking directly at the camera, a hint of a smile on his mouth. Cocky. He grasped a large duffel that obviously held the stolen filter, his bicep flexing from the weight of it. She felt the blood drain from her face. She couldn't slow her heartbeat, no matter how much she tried. "That's him."

"Yes," her father said. "It is. When was the last time you saw this Jason Zhou, Daughter?"

She looked down again and felt her cheeks redden. This was fine.

Her father was strict. Even at eighteen, she had been forbidden to date. Daiyu hadn't been certain if her father knew she had been seeing Jason, but her gut told her he knew now. "I saw him before I came to Shanghai." She murmured her response—a guilty daughter caught doing something she shouldn't have.

"You were seeing someone behind my back," her father said. "Not only that, someone who had stolen from me."

She raised her head then, eyes wide with shock, using her discomfort and fear of discovery in her reactions. "What?"

"He stole a large sum from me"—her father stared at her, still not revealing that she had been kidnapped last summer by Jason, still keeping her in the dark—"and he stole again from me this morning." He snatched both images back; a flash of anger. "This boy, this liar and thief, he's dating you to get to me, Daughter."

Daiyu blinked at him, knowing the color had drained from her face. "No."

Her father smiled. Maybe it was meant to be gentle. It looked mocking instead. Derisive. "Yes. He wanted access to Jin Corp, and what better way than to charm my daughter, the heir to the company?"

She jerked her head to the side, toward the large picture window. A tour boat drifted along the river; tourists clung to the rails on the top deck, clustered together.

"Whatever you thought you had between you was a lie," her father said. "He used you." His voice had turned to frost. "The boy's clever, but you're smarter than that." He leaned forward and forced her to meet his steely gaze. "Aren't you?"

"Yes, Father." She acquiesced; she had been purposely submissive the entire time. Her father had always underestimated her, and she used this to her advantage. As long as she remained obedient and pliant, his eyes would always be turned in another direction. Away from her.

He nodded and settled back into his chair. She braced herself, waiting to hear him say that Jason had been caught, was seriously injured, or had been executed. Instead, she watched as her father stroked his chin, considering something. Then he took another piece of paper from the file and pushed it toward her. There was a single phone number typed onto the page. "Message him."

For a second, she didn't know who he meant by "him." Then she understood. Jason was still alive, then. He had succeeded. "What do you want me to say?" Jason would know this was coming from her device. She prayed he wouldn't give anything away.

"Give me back what you stole."

Daiyu typed the message, not trusting the strength of her own voice.

They waited a full minute. Then another. She watched the time change at the top of her Palm. A reply finally appeared: what i took isn't yours.

She read the message out loud, and her father barked a laugh, slamming his fist against the desk at the same time. Daiyu flinched despite herself.

"The fucking nerve," her father said. He drummed his fingertips against the desk. "What do you want?" He nodded once at her, and she typed in the message.

meet me at jin tower. 6 p.m. before the opening ceremony.

Jin Tower's opening ceremony celebration was set for seven p.m.

"Why?" her father asked.

to settle a score.

Her father laughed incredulously at that. "He acts as if he's the one who's been wronged. As if *he's* been stolen from."

Daiyu knew her father had stolen the filter from the clinic in the first place. But in his mind, he was *taking*. Everything was his right to take. Only *mei*s, young punks like Jason, were capable of stealing.

He tilted his head back, staring up at the ceiling, considering. Jason had made no mention of a trade for the prototype, but she was certain that her father thought he could corner him, beat him into submission if necessary. Jason would be on his turf; her father would feel he'd have the upper hand. What was there to lose?

He leaned forward and said conspiratorially to her, "Do you know what he's really after?" He didn't wait for an answer. "Money, just like last time." He straightened, seeming to have reached a decision. "The back entrance will be open. Take the elevator to the top floor."

She relayed the message.

done.

Her father rose from the desk, dusting off his suit sleeves and adjusting his tie. "You're finished."

He didn't just mean this exchange with Jason.

"Yes, Father," she said.

"And you'll come to meet him with me," he added. "You can see firsthand what desperate people are capable of, trying to grasp what they can never have, trying to take what will never belong to them."

Daiyu stared down at her hands.

"You made a grave error," he said, as he placed several files into his briefcase. "You won't do it again."

He grabbed the briefcase, obviously headed to another meeting. But he paused in front of her, waiting for a response.

"No, Father." He suspected nothing, believing she was still under his thumb, still within the fold. Daiyu had always thought that she could only ever make a difference constricted by her father's rules—she had never known anything else her entire life. But Jason had shown her otherwise, shown how his friends were fighting—risking their very lives—to do right. Daiyu thought she could only play on the game board her father had set down, and now she realized she could flip it.

It was a different game now, with a different set of rules.

Her father nodded in satisfaction, before leaving her alone in the library.

ZHOU

I knew I probably wouldn't have to wait long before Jin reached out. But my heart jumped into my throat when the message appeared from Daiyu's own Palm. Had she been found out somehow? Was using his daughter's phone to contact me a not-so-subtle threat?

Lingyi was by my side when it pinged with an incoming message. She rested a hand on my arm, sensing my agitation. My dummy device was using a Wi-Fi connection Lingyi had set up that was impossible to trace.

"Don't give it away," Lingyi said. "Jin's just playing his mind games."

"I've put her in danger by dragging her into this," I replied. After all that had happened today, this was the first time I felt sick to my stomach. "I should never have asked this of her."

Lingyi squeezed my arm. "Look at me."

But my dark thoughts had already spiraled away from me. Was Jin capable of killing his own daughter? Yes. I was certain of it, after he weighed the costs versus the benefits. My leg jittered and I stared at the single sentence on my dummy Palm: Give me back what you stole.

"Shit," I muttered. *"Shit."*

"Zhou," Lingyi said. "We have to respond."

what i took isn't yours. I typed in the reply as she looked over my shoulder.

The entire exchange was short. After, I sank into the chair beside Lingyi's bed, wiping my palms against my jeans. My hands were shaking.

"Wow." Lingyi touched my shoulder. "You're in deep."

I knew she wasn't referring to all this business with Jin. She was right.

But we had a meeting set up with Jin before the big opening ceremony, just like we wanted.

"All the details about the ceremony that Daiyu gave you were helpful," Lingyi said. "I still need to scope out the site before the event, buy and set up the necessary equipment."

"We need Iris and Arun's help," I replied. "We have to loop them in."

Lingyi nodded. "Iris won't like it."

It had taken only a few days to set the plan in motion. Yet so much of it relied on all my friends being invested in what we wanted to do, not to mention relying on the god of luck to smile down on us. Would Iris and Arun be on board?

And all of it hinged on Daiyu, whether she would be able to carry through for us to the very end, while deceiving her father the entire time.

It was a dangerous game to play, and she was risking everything.

DAIYU

Daiyu waited fifteen minutes after her father left their suite before calling for Xiao Wu to bring the airlimo around. She put large diamond studs into her earlobes and pulled an expensively carved jade bracelet onto her bare wrist. Giving herself a final once-over after powdering her face and applying a light lip gloss, she made her way to their suite's heavy door.

The two security guards followed her movements but let her open the door. She was stopped by the guards outside when she stepped through. "Ms. Jin," one muscular man said in a polite voice. His huge arms strained his suit's sleeves. "Your father gave explicit instructions that you are not to leave the suite."

"Yes," she replied coolly. "But I'm running an errand for him at his request."

"He made no mention—"

She had been ready for this and pulled out her Palm, showing a message from her father that she had manipulated to display on her device: This needs to be taken care of today, Daughter, as we discussed. The director will be expecting you. She had created the image to show that the message had been sent today, just ten minutes ago, after her father had left. The security guard squinted at her screen. She knew it all looked legit. Fooling these goons was nothing compared to dealing with her own father; still, she consciously controlled her nerves, exuded cool aloofness. If this didn't work, she would fail Jason and his friends.

Daiyu pulled the Palm to herself again. "I could call him if you want—but he's not going to like the interruption. He's in an important meeting now." She fiddled with her touch screen in the pretense of placing a call, mouth pulled down in displeasure. Daiyu had no issue using her status to act the imperious heir when she needed to. These men worked for her father, but they also technically worked for her.

The beefy man threw a nervous glance at his partner, then raised a hand. "That's all right, Ms. Jin. We wouldn't want to bother Mr. Jin with trivialities."

"You're free to come along if you want, but my car is waiting for me."

The man looked at his partner again, and the thinner guy shrugged. He might as well have thrown his hands up to indicate how much he, too, was at a loss. Daiyu kept her expression one of detached annoyance.

"Go with Ms. Jin," he suggested.

She turned and called the elevator, not bothering to see if the guard was following. When the doors opened, he stepped inside with her. She pressed the button for the rooftop garage.

When they slipped into her airlimo, Xiao Wu greeted her with a simple, "Good afternoon, Ms. Jin."

"The Bank of China on the Bund, please, Xiao Wu," she replied. "You can wait in the limo for me," Daiyu said to the guard, who had seated himself across from her. "The bank has its own security, and this matter is private."

She saw the man consider her proposal, uncertainty crinkling the corners of his eyes. "It's as my father wished," she said. She knew if she spoke assertively enough, he would never question her.

He blinked twice. "Yes, of course, Ms. Jin. I'll wait for you in the car. Message if you require assistance."

It was a short ride to the bank, but she hadn't wanted to deal with walking in the heat. Daiyu needed to do this with not one hair out of place. She nodded at the bank's security guard and stepped out of the limo when he opened the door for her. Murmuring a thank-you, she watched the man run up the steps to open that door for her as well.

She had never been inside this particular bank before, but they were all the same. And they all reacted the same way too, when they learned who she was. Daiyu touched her hair, which she had pulled back into a low bun, to better show off the giant diamonds in her earlobes. When she stepped up to the front desk, the clerk smiled at her. "Good afternoon. How can I help you?" he asked.

"I'm Jin Daiyu, the daughter of Jin Feiming. I need to speak with the director of your bank."

The clerk's eyes widened. "Yes, of course. I believe Vice President Ms. Yang is in her office today. Let me tell her you are here."

"Only the director, please," Daiyu replied firmly.

The clerk's mouth fell open, and it would have been comical if this wasn't so serious. He picked up a sleek in-house receiver and spoke quietly. It didn't take more than the mention of her name, and who she was, before he placed the receiver back on the glass counter, nodding at her. "We're in luck. Mr. Hong, our director, is available to see you. Let me take you to his office."

"Thank you," she replied.

She followed the man's straight back past the open wood-paneled cubicles for the average clients who needed to discuss their needs with a banker. But she had been deemed more than average. Instead, the clerk knocked on a wide redwood door gilded in gold, before opening it for her with a flourish. She walked into the large office, and the man disappeared before she was able to thank him.

A short man with thick black hair and silver-rimmed glasses rose from his leather chair. "Ms. Jin, to what do I owe this pleasure?" He thrust out a hand and she clasped it, before sitting down across from him.

Daiyu folded her arms in her lap. She had not changed her outfit since she'd met her father earlier, and she fingered the jade pendant at her throat. The character *Jin* was carved in the stone and inlaid with gold. "I'm here to discuss business. Thank you for meeting me on such short notice, Mr. Hong."

This far back in the building, there were no windows in the opulent office. Still, it had plenty of ambient light from sconces overhead, and the room was filled with orchids blooming on tables and set on tall stands. A large scroll of a landscape was hung on one of the walls.

"Do you come on behalf of your father?" Mr. Hong had sat back down and steepled his fingers, his round face shining with inquisitiveness.

"No. This is my own venture," Daiyu replied. "My father has taught me much and has encouraged me to have my own pursuits since I was a child."

Mr. Hong smiled. "Wonderful. Wonderful. Tell me, how old are you, Ms. Jin?"

"I'm eighteen."

"So young! And already an entrepreneur." He beamed in delight. Mr. Hong was obviously pleased that the heir to Jin Corp had chosen their bank to do business. "Tell me about your venture."

Daiyu proceeded to discuss Jany's invention with him, how the catalyst was the most powerful filtration system the market had yet to see, compact, energy efficient, and much cheaper to build. Jason had told her that Jany's family had agreed to take a royalty for every unit sold from the patent and leave the financing and production up to them. Daiyu was the only one in the position to bankroll this, and quickly, using her money and status.

"This sounds like an amazing venture." Mr. Hong nodded. "Your father must be so proud."

She smiled brightly at him, and the older man leaned forward over his desk. Daiyu had saved this smile for when they were about to seal the deal. "My father doesn't know yet. It's a surprise."

The man clapped his hands together. "Well, your secret is safe with me, Ms. Jin. And what a surprise it'll be!"

"I hope so, Mr. Hong." She tucked in a strand of hair that had escaped from her tight bun.

"And do you have a manufacturer lined up as well?" Mr. Hong asked. "Or will you be using Jin Corp for production?"

"Oh, no. But I do have a manufacturer in mind." Nothing had been signed yet, but Jason had told her they'd already contacted the manufacturer who'd helped to produce Jany's prototype, and the company was eager to enter into this lucrative collaboration. She also leaned forward, as if sharing a confidence. "We can begin production as soon as we have the financing."

Mr. Hong grinned and slammed a palm against the desktop. "It would be a pleasure to do business with you, Ms. Jin."

She smiled graciously. "I don't mean to rush, but I need to have the loan funded as soon as possible."

"How soon?"

"Tomorrow, if possible."

Mr. Hong's eyes widened, so they appeared huge behind his glasses. "That is highly unusual, Ms. Jin."

"I understand, Mr. Hong." She tapped a finger against his desktop. "That's why I came to *you*. I knew that if anyone could do this special favor for me, you could. There are many other banks in Shanghai"—she paused and gave him a nod—"but I chose yours."

The man straightened, and she swore he seemed to puff his chest out. "I'll need to pull some strings, but I am happy to make an exception. Everything will be ready to sign this evening. I can send the paperwork directly to you electronically." The older man reached for the receiver and spoke to someone on the other end, giving them specific instructions to expedite her loan.

In truth, Daiyu had chosen Mr. Hong because she had gone through her father's contacts in his Palm, and no one from the Bank of China was listed. She wanted to approach someone who had not previously worked with her father.

The director offered his hand across the desk. "The loan will be available by the end of the business day tomorrow, Ms. Jin." He smiled widely, the corners of his eyes crinkling.

She shook his hand. "Thank you, Mr. Hong." Daiyu glanced at her Palm. She needed to be back at the Peninsula before her father's own meeting was over, or all their plans could be ruined. "I truly appreciate it." At that moment, another clerk dressed in a navy suit entered the room, bearing a tray of tea and refreshments. He set it down on Mr. Hong's desk.

She had no appetite but forced herself to sip the fragrant jasmine tea and nibble on some candied persimmons out of politeness before she excused herself. Daiyu hoped that time—and luck—was on her side.

CHAPTER FIFTEEN

ZHOU

"You what?" Iris rarely raised her voice, but this was close. "You asked Daiyu to help fund Jany's invention? So she can hand it straight to Jin?"

"She's working *with* us," I said.

"*You* would think so," Iris spat out. "But I can't believe you bought into this too." She glared at Lingyi. "You've both jumped off the deep end. The longer we play Jin's game, the sooner another one of us will die."

I felt as if Iris had slapped me hard across the face. The sudden silence in our suite was eerie, too loud in my ears.

"Iris—" Lingyi said, her voice catching. "We're doing what's right."

"For the principle of it. For your ideals." Iris kneeled in front of Lingyi and grabbed her knees. "Why must it be us? Why does it have to be *you*?"

Color had risen to Lingyi's face, mottling her cheeks. "If not us, my heart, then who?"

Iris jumped to her feet and snarled in frustration.

"Tell us the rest of your plan," Arun said.

Iris scowled at him, and he gave an exaggerated shrug. "They've already set things in motion. I don't like it any more than you do, but I'm not about to let them flounder, either. Zhou somehow managed to steal the prototype back like some superhero—"

Iris snorted.

"So let's hear them out," Arun continued. "They *need* us."

"I didn't want to keep you in the dark, love—"

"But you *did*."

Lingyi let out a long breath. "I hated it." She followed Iris's angry stalking with bright eyes. "But there isn't a choice for me. I need to right this or . . ." She trailed off. Her face had paled, her expression pinched.

I sensed her suffering and remembered how useless I had been after witnessing her nightmare the other night. Too shocked and scared to comfort her. Not this time. I moved onto the sofa beside Lingyi and wrapped an arm around her. She rested her head against my shoulder, her body shaking with sobs. "It's going to be okay."

Lingyi made a choking noise through her crying. "I think it's too late for that. Sometimes life leaves you with nothing but shitty choices."

Arun passed over a tissue, and she swiped it over her eyes, then blew her nose noisily. "We're all here for you, Lingyi," Arun said.

"I've been a bad friend for months," I added. "I'm sorry."

She looked between Arun and me. "My heart isn't at peace. I *have* to finish this." She turned to Iris. "And you're right, what we're attempting is dangerous. And we're all still grieving . . . for Vic. For Dr. Nataraj. I shouldn't have kept anything from either of you. I'm sorry."

I glanced at Arun; he had paled at the mention of his mother. It'd been over a year, but that didn't matter. I knew from experience. When your mother died, it was a loss you lived with, like a hole in your heart, for a very long time. Maybe forever.

"I don't know if I can ever forgive myself for what happened to Jany—" Lingyi said.

"You did everything you could," Iris interjected. "There was no way you could have taken on Jin's thugs. You would have died too."

"Maybe," Lingyi replied. "But I was frozen in fear—I couldn't help her." She looked at each of us in turn.

"I can do something now," Lingyi finished. "We can do something to change the ending to this tragedy."

"We'll see this through," I replied. "We're here for you, boss."

I thought about Daiyu, and how we'd hurt each other,

intentionally or unintentionally. I had wanted to kiss her so badly in that hot closet in the ceramic shop; she'd stood close enough that I could smell her skin. But I had sensed her hesitancy, an uncertainty and tension that hadn't been there in months. That stopped me. It felt as if I were trapped in a Zhang Ailing novel: undelivered letters and missed phone calls, small misunderstandings that ultimately destroyed passionate romances.

We love each other, we hurt each other, we forgive or we move on.

Iris stalked toward us, coiled and lethal as ever, but her face was open, the emotions plain and raw upon her features. I rose, and she took my place.

"We'll take him down together." Iris grasped Lingyi's hand. "Then we'll be done with it."

Lingyi stroked Iris's cheek. "I won't keep anything from you again, my heart."

The afternoon light suddenly seemed overbright in our suite, illuminating my friends' features in sharp relief: the tenderness in Lingyi's dark eyes juxtaposed with the determined set of her jaw, Arun's black eyebrows drawn together in grief, but his shoulders thrown back, chin raised, as if he were ready to fight. Iris's head was bowed, and the sunlight glanced over her platinum hair in a way that reminded me of a silver flame. Her shoulders were relaxed as she drew Lingyi's hand closer, kissing her fingertips. But I knew she could be on her feet in an instant, poised to kill or protect, do whatever was necessary to survive.

I closed my eyes, capturing this moment, filing it away.

"Should we talk about how we'll destroy Jin, then?" Arun asked after a long pause. "For good?"

"It'll be public," Lingyi said. "So there's no denying his guilt."

"Our hope is to have my meeting with Jin broadcast in all-media news, in the biggest way possible." I grinned. "We'll use what Jin has created against him. Because what does he hate more than losing money?"

"Losing face," Lingyi replied. Her eyes were bright, and the color had returned to her face.

I knew this from everything Daiyu had told me about her father, from observing Jin's every action and decision made since Daiyu's kidnapping.

"I like it," Arun said.

Iris nodded.

I truly grinned then and sat down with my friends to go over our plans.

DAIYU

The entire meeting with Mr. Hong at the Bank of China had taken forty minutes. Daiyu returned to her airlimo, and the security guard who had accompanied her let out an audible sigh when she got in. Xiao Wu rolled down the street, then lifted into the air above the traffic at the first opportunity. The closer it got to the end of the workday, the more crowded it became along the Bund. Before she exited the airlimo, Xiao Wu handed her a brown package. She knew what it was and thanked him.

When they returned to the suite, the other security guard nodded at his colleague without saying anything. No news was good news. Daiyu retreated to her bedroom and opened the package Xiao Wu had passed to her. Inside was a cheap Palm knockoff, but it'd do its job. Best of all, it couldn't be tracked by her father.

An hour later, she heard her father enter the suite. His footsteps were brisk, and she trusted that his always urgent demeanor had deterred the security guards from saying anything to him. The fact that he was so busy and so intimidating worked in her favor. He was asking the butler, Mr. Han, to pour him a whiskey when his Palm chimed with an incoming call. He picked up immediately.

"You've found him?" her father asked.

A pause. "The hacker girl too?"

Daiyu slid toward her open door, straining to hear the rest of the conversation.

"So close?" he said. "Capture them."

She gripped her doorframe. She knew they were talking about Jason and his friend.

Another pause.

"No, not yet," her father replied. "Not until I get my hands on the prototype or that laptop." She heard ice clinking against glass as her father took a long gulp of whiskey. "I know this kid. He's not afraid of dying, but he won't like it when his friends do."

Another silence. Then her father said, "Let me know when you have them."

Daiyu switched on the dummy Palm with shaking hands. The cheap device took forever to power up. She continued to stay by the door, mentally preparing if her father decided to come down the hallway to see her, even though he'd never done so once since they'd stayed in the suite.

She continued to hear the sound of ice clinking against glass from the sitting room. The device finally powered on, and she searched for Jason's number in her own Palm, typing it in, messing up, then retyping the number. Were they already on their way to Jason? How much time would he have?

Finally she typed her warning, then double-checked the number to be sure it had gone to the right device. When the dummy indicated message delivered, she tucked it under her pillow. She didn't expect a response from Jason. She only hoped it reached him in time.

ZHOU

We had gone over our plans for almost two hours together, hashing out every small detail, making a list of the equipment Lingyi needed to acquire, when my dummy Palm pinged again. Besides my friends, only Daiyu and Jin had this number. But when I checked it, the message was from an unknown device.

239

My father's men are on their way to you.—D

"We have to clear out." I jumped to my feet, and my friends sat in shocked silence for a heartbeat before following my lead.

"Leave everything except what you need," Lingyi instructed, grabbing her MacFold.

I swept all my essentials into the leather duffel and checked the door monitor. The corridor, thankfully, was still empty. But when I opened the door noiselessly, I heard someone speaking in a low voice around the corner.

Too late.

I pressed a finger to my lips, then pointed at Iris; she was beside me before my arm dropped. Arun and Lingyi went into the bedroom nearest to the front door, hiding from view. Leaving the front door slightly ajar, Iris and I waited. Two thugs showed up on our door monitor. They glanced at each other when they saw our door wasn't closed, but didn't say a word. One man pulled a gun and the other a taser; the muscular guy with red spiked hair pushed the door cautiously open. Iris and I stayed hidden behind it as he walked in.

Once he cleared the threshold, Iris grabbed the red-haired guy in a choke hold from behind, jabbing a sleep spell into the side of his neck. He shouted, and his gun went off, shattering the glass table in our sitting room. At the same time, I slammed the door as hard as I could into the other thug and heard a sickening crunch. He groaned, then screamed obscenities and shoved his way inside. His partner dropped right then, and he tripped over him, falling to his knees. Iris grabbed the second thug by the collar and jammed a sleep spell into the back of his neck too. He struggled, trying to aim his taser, then slumped down ten seconds later, blood streaking from his broken nose.

I glanced at our door monitor, waiting to see if more thugs would show up. We stayed silent, listening for any other sounds. Only the second man's labored breathing could be heard, but a gunshot had gone off, and it'd be a miracle if a hotel guest hadn't reported it.

"Boss," I said.

Arun emerged with Lingyi, who was clutching a satchel to herself. Iris dropped down to search the men's pockets. She found a key fob and tossed it to Arun, then took their gun and taser. She passed redhead's Palm to Lingyi. Lingyi scanned through the messages, then left the device on the man's chest. "Let's go," she said simply. "Jin will send more men when we don't show up trussed like pigs."

Iris and I dragged the men clear of the door. I shifted the second thug's face so he wouldn't choke to death on his own blood, before we cleared out and walked cautiously down the corridor. "We should head to the garage," I said in a low voice.

Lingyi nodded in agreement, and Arun called the elevator. We stood on either side of it, out of sight until the doors opened. I'd learned my lesson from my encounter with Da Ge. But thank gods, the car was empty. When the doors slid open onto the garage's concrete space, we paused to listen for movement or sound but heard nothing.

Jin's thug's aircar headlights turned on when we neared, its engine humming to life, but Lingyi shook her head. "We can't take the sedan. Jin'll be tracking it. Let's get another ride."

We found a chauffeur asleep in a silver airlimo with a gray cap pulled over his eyes. He had the window down and snored so loudly, it wasn't hard to find him. I opened the car door and Iris hauled him out by twisting a handful of his crumpled shirt. The man snorted when roused from his nap. "We'll have to take the car," I said.

"What?" The man was instantly awake. "No!"

"You'll find it again," I replied.

Iris hit him with an injection in the back of his neck, and I caught him when he fell. We couldn't risk him giving any details if Jin questioned him. None of Jin's thugs would be able to tell him what had taken place either, thanks to the memory-wipes. I left the driver propped against the wall as my friends climbed inside the airlimo. Arun took the wheel. "I know somewhere we can go," he said.

The glass doors slid open as our car approached, then soared into the air. It was almost dusk, and the Bund was crowded with pedestrians. In that moment, Jin Tower's neon lights broadcasted the invitation to the opening ceremony next Wednesday across its glass panes. Daiyu appeared, shimmering into view like some pixelated goddess. She wore a pale blue dress and a silver necklace with dangling diamonds at her throat. *Don't miss the biggest celebration Shanghai has ever seen!*

She spoke, but as there was no sound, the characters scrolled across the building, above her head.

"We wouldn't miss it for the world," Lingyi said, her breath misting the dark window for a second.

That sense of unease returned, settling heavy in my stomach. We were taunting a powerful, angry lion in this game. But Daiyu lived right in his den.

▲▼▲

We didn't have to fly far. Arun parked the airlimo in a dingy side street near Yuyuan in the Old City of Shanghai, and we left it. The owner would be able to track it here. We followed Arun through the narrow side streets, passing a small storefront with steamed buns in bamboo baskets stacked high on its counter. Iris stopped to buy xiaolongbao, handing each of us a plastic bag stuffed with the soup dumplings. Mopeds zipped by, and bicyclists teetered on the side, their wheels kicking up dust.

"Where are we going?" I asked Arun.

He was checking his Palm for directions. "I'm trying to figure it out myself."

Lingyi appeared pale in the hazy sunlight. Iris touched her wrist. "Are you all right?"

Lingyi scanned our surroundings, then nodded. "This is near where Jany's apartment was."

Iris pulled Lingyi into herself, wrapping an arm protectively around her shoulder, and Lingyi leaned into the taller girl. "I'll be

243

fine. I'll feel better when we get to this place and are off the streets."

"I agree," Arun said. "This way."

We passed a convenience store with a wooden ladder propped against its entrance. Plastic toys dangled on a string in the open storefront window beside it, and a glass shelf was stacked high with cigarettes and lighters in all colors. A white cat with long silken hair perched on the store's front step, observing us silently with green eyes as we passed. A man with bushy gray hair stood outside another shop with a broken wooden door, cutting another man's hair with an electric razor. His client sat on a stool with a large red apron tied around his neck. No one paid attention to us, even though I kept looking over my shoulder, making certain we weren't being followed. The sun was slipping low on the horizon, but still the summer heat felt oppressive, and I coughed through my thin face mask. The pollution in Shanghai seemed even worse than Taipei; my throat felt scraped raw, breathing its air.

Arun turned down another side street, which narrowed even more than the one we had been on. This one was residential, with low concrete buildings. Old bicycles were propped against the walls beneath rusty air-conditioning units that jutted out from the homes. Laundry lines crisscrossed haphazardly overhead, and the clothes hung out to dry flapped in the hot summer breeze.

"Number 173," Arun said. "This is it." He had paused in front of a two-story building gray with grime. The home had a steel door and a touch pad installed for access. Arun punched in a series of numbers, once in a while glancing at his Palm. The door clicked open, and he entered cautiously. Then he turned back to us, waving, and said, "We're good. It's safe."

The dilapidated exterior belied the modern interior of the small home. It must have been renovated at some point, with warm recessed lighting, sleek furniture, and a new voice-commanded kitchen. Arun already had both tea and coffee brewing with a few verbal requests.

Lingyi slid onto a turquoise leather sofa. "This is perfect. But whose is it?"

"Ms. Wang's, the director of the clinic in Qibao," Arun replied. "The property was donated to the clinic, and she uses it to house doctors and specialists who might be volunteering their time at the children's clinic, giving them some extra days in this apartment as a perk." Arun filled a mug of tea for Lingyi and coffees for the rest of us as we sat down in the living room. I ate the rest of my xiaolongbao but could have done with two more bags of the soup dumplings. "She said we're free to use it for as long as we need." Arun set a mug of coffee in front of me, and I nodded in appreciation.

"I'll get started on gathering the things on our list," Arun said. "I'm sure I can pick up a lot of the stuff tonight."

"I'll look with you," Lingyi replied.

Arun slid onto the sofa beside Lingyi, placing a steaming mug on the titanium tea table beside her. Iris had gone upstairs to scout the joint, and I swiped through my dummy Palm. "Are you going to message her?" Lingyi asked.

I glanced up; the hardest part was not being in touch. "I don't want to risk it. We're only messaging if it's an emergency."

"That seems wise." Lingyi leaned forward. "I know you're worried, but Daiyu will follow through."

It meant a lot that Lingyi trusted Daiyu, because she believed in *my* trust. "I don't doubt her at all," I replied. "But what if something goes wrong?" Just thinking about the possibility made me feel queasy. "We both know how ruthless Jin is."

"If anyone could best him at his own game, I think Daiyu could," she replied. "Daiyu's smart."

Daiyu *was* smart, but so was Jin. If he discovered his own daughter had deceived and betrayed him, there was no telling what he'd do. The last thing he needed to know was how much I cared for his daughter.

I must have dozed off, when I woke to the chime of an incoming message on the dummy Palm. The one narrow window in the room showed night had fallen outside, and the sofa was empty. My friends were all settled at the round glass table near the kitchen, speaking in soft tones. I fumbled for my device. This, too, was from an unrecognizable number, but the message gave a clear indication as to who the sender was: You'll bring the prototype when we meet, or I'll exact a price from someone you care for.

Adrenaline rushed through me when I read Jin's threat. He had to mean Daiyu. Or had he gone to the room we abandoned at Les Suites and figured I had been working with friends this whole time? It was obvious there had been more than one person staying there.

It didn't matter. Jin got his point across. He knew I wasn't working alone, and he could hurt me through them. I could only pray that he didn't suspect Daiyu at all. Clenching my jaws, I wanted to pound my fist on the tea table. Instead, I drew a long breath and typed in my reply: I'll have the prototype.

There was no guarantee Jin wouldn't kill me on sight, once he got the catalyst in his hands. I sank back into the chair; it was exactly what Jin would do. It would put me in my place once and for all. My main goal was to survive this encounter and make certain my friends did too.

I tossed my butterfly knife, wishing I had a wall to climb instead to expend my energy. Suddenly, I had an idea.

I caught Arun's eye and waved him over. I hoped he would be able to make what I had in mind and do it in the five days before the actual ceremony.

My life depended on it.

▲▼▲

Later that evening, Arun and I set out to meet with various dealers who were able to sell us the equipment we needed fast, without us having to show up in a well-lit store during business hours to purchase them. Arun did all the talking. I simply stood beside him and looked threatening, which didn't mean much more than playing with my knife with a cap pulled low over my eyes.

The area in Yuyuan seemed to transform from a crowded tourist haven in the day and early evening into a warren of shadows and underhanded dealings late at night. Dark shapes pressed against the buildings and walls, sometimes peeling from them like ghosts. A few whispered in low voices, but more often, I merely saw a brief glint in their eyes when we walked past. Arun carried a taser, and I had enough knives on me to take down a small entourage. Still, I was hyperaware of our surroundings. Jin's men could be prowling these streets too, searching for us.

But other than the one lanky guy who doubled his price at the last minute, we had no trouble with our three meetings that night. And Arun paid the amount. We weren't there to haggle, but to get what we needed and head back.

The next morning, Saturday, Iris went with Lingyi to scope out Jin Tower and its surroundings. Lingyi wore a silver head wrap to cover her bright purple hair, then donned a black face mask and dark sunglasses over that. We decided it was safer if I steered clear of the area until the day of the opening ceremony. Instead, I went with Arun out on a few other late-night meet-ups with sellers until we had everything on his and Lingyi's list.

After canvassing the area with Iris, Lingyi drew up a detailed map for us, then went to work on Jin Tower's communication system. Arun spent all his time on putting together the device I had requested after getting the necessary parts, and researching, then experimenting for hours.

I was trying not to jump out of my own skin with every little sound, afraid it might be a chime from my Palm with another message from Jin or Daiyu, letting me know she had been found out. But my dummy device remained silent the entire time, and I caught up on my sleep, often waking with fragments of a nightmare clinging to the periphery of my consciousness.

On late Monday night, after two failed attempts, Arun was able to make a working device that I needed. He strapped it around my chest, and we gave each other excited high fives after it passed all his tests.

On Tuesday, after working nonstop, Lingyi let out a whoop of triumph in the morning. "It's done. I've hacked into Jin Tower's security cameras and display system! Soon the entire world will know what kind of man Jin is." She whirled on her chair at the dining table to face the rest of us sitting in the living room area, and her cheeks were flushed with excitement. "Now we just need to bypass security on-site to set up the necessary equipment."

She said it offhandedly, like it was only a small thing. But the city was expecting hundreds of thousands of people to show up along the Bund tomorrow for the extravagant opening ceremony. Security would be tight, with Jin's own hired guards along with Shanghai's police force. The hardest tasks were still before us.

But we whooped along with her, getting up to exchange high fives and bump fists. Our spirits were high, yet I was anxious in a way I had never felt before going into a job—because Daiyu was involved. I could only hope everything was going her way too.

Because at this point, it was do or die.

CHAPTER SIXTEEN

We all got a full night's sleep before the day of the ceremony. It was a beautiful, mild day for August, and the city began roping off areas near Jin Tower early in the morning. We watched news reports from on-site on our wall screen, keeping tabs. Iris had argued for Lingyi to stay behind and work everything remotely from the house, but Lingyi balked.

"I need to be there," she insisted. "It's too risky: if the equipment fails, our entire plan fails." She looked at each of us in turn, the way she always did when she needed to drive a point across. "Besides, I've stayed behind before. And I refuse to be separated from you again for this."

So it was decided that Lingyi, Iris, and Arun would leave earlier for Jin Tower to set up on the ground. I'd wait and head out near my agreed-upon time of six p.m. Before they left, Arun and Lingyi checked on the small but powerful cam and mic made to look like a simple silver buckle on my belt. He then checked the heart rate monitor strapped to my chest against the device we had installed within the prototype. "Everything is working great," he said, and we bumped fists.

My friends left a little after three p.m., their faces covered beneath masks and with hats and caps pulled over their heads. Lingyi's purple hair was tied up and tucked beneath a straw hat—the kind tourists wore to hide from the sun. It felt too quiet after they were gone. The minutes dragged miserably. I kept checking my dummy device, hoping for a message from Daiyu. Nothing.

By half past five, I couldn't wait to leave.

Arun had gotten a used airped for me. I carefully placed the prototype into the trunk that was attached to the back, making sure everything was secured in place. I was dressed in my favorite black jeans and a faded gray tee. I checked my knives, then the place where I had tucked three sleep spell injections at my waist. Arun had given them to me just in case. Drawing the thin mask over the lower part of my face, I started the airped and felt the thrum of the propulsion system come alive. The narrow alleyway was empty, and I sped down it, heart racing, before lifting into the sky, feeling that familiar surge in my chest. I grinned despite myself and turned the airped toward the Bund and Jin Tower, its silver spire gleaming prominently along the smog-polluted skyline.

Jin was waiting for me.

And I had a score to settle.

▲▼▲

More aircars and airpeds circled over the Bund than usual in antici-pation of Jin Tower's opening ceremony. I navigated the congested air traffic carefully. Seeing the crowds from above was different from on-screen. Even this high up, I could hear the low buzz of excited voices as people fought for a good spot to watch the festivities. Jin had provided free food and drink carts all along the Bund, and other carts gave away flickering toys and glowing tiaras and necklaces, all emblazoned with Jin's insignia. Tour boats were anchored along the river, with hundreds of people mingling on the open decks, having paid premium prices for the best views from the water. Jin had prom-ised Shanghai a fireworks display like the city had never seen.

I flew the airped over the river, its color as brown as Shanghai's skies, before veering toward Jin Tower. It glittered in the hazy late afternoon light, the tallest building in the world, a shining metal-lic feat of engineering. Air traffic appeared to be restricted near Jin Tower itself, but I met no resistance when I flew toward the back entrance, which was fenced off from the public. One of Jin's thugs stood waiting for me, his hands clasped behind him. I guided my airped smoothly into the enclosed area and turned the bike off, watching the man warily from the corner of my eye.

I knew Jin wouldn't try anything until he was certain he'd secured the actual prototype; then I was only someone else in his way he had to kill. Jin's man made no move toward me as I opened the trunk and lifted the air filter out. I nodded at him, indicating I was ready, and he made a move to check me for weapons. I stepped back with the duffel bag. "I go in on my own terms. Otherwise, the prototype is rigged to self-destruct. Nothing flashy. Its insides will just melt to nothing."

The guy stood still, obviously awaiting instruction from someone. After a pause, he nodded and indicated with a hand gesture that I should follow. The thick metal doors were gold, etched with Jin's logo set in a circle at their center. With a palm scan, the doors opened for the thug and he jerked his chin. I entered first and felt his looming presence at my back but resisted reaching for a knife. It was too early in the game for that. We walked through the immense building, our footsteps echoing; I pulled off my face mask, craning my neck, and couldn't help feeling awed by the grand scale of the building.

Sunlight filtered in through the tinted glass panels, and the building's center was open for as far as the eye could see. But I had read up on Jin Tower's design and knew that its thirtieth floor took up the entirety of the building as a full garden level, with its own aviary, multiple fountains, and a large pond. There was another full garden level on the sixtieth floor, and every thirty floors after that. The first twenty-nine floors were designed to be commercial and retail space, and everything above was slotted to be sold as private residences, with a few floors interspersed with markets, restaurants, gyms, and other amenities for Jin Tower's residents.

Jin's "vertical city" was designed to be self-contained, the idea being you never had to leave. Now, actually being inside the building, I saw firsthand how appealing that might be in a property where Jin had obviously thought of a *you*'s every need.

We passed the main foyer on our way to the elevators. It was elegant, featuring two oval jade consoles as reception areas. The tower was eerily quiet, built to house thousands, but with only me and Jin's henchman moving in the vast space. Neither of us spoke a word to each other. Instead, the other man called the elevator—touted as the fastest in the world—and we stepped inside. I stood in the back corner of the silver car and Jin's man stood in the other. He had no visible weapon that I could see, but I knew he was ready to kill me in an instant upon Jin's command.

I wasn't feeling nervous or scared. If anything, I was eager. Eager to finally face this man who'd lived and profited on the misfortune and deaths of *mei*s, who had gotten away with murder for so long. I wouldn't be tied to a chair like last time. It wasn't exactly on my terms, but this needed to be done on Jin's turf. He had to feel in control. I just needed to provoke him enough, get him to talk, and hopefully survive this. But truth be told, I'd never been afraid to die. As long as my friends were safe.

Jin's thug punched the button for the 188th floor and input a four-digit code on the security panel for access. My stomach dropped at the speed with which we climbed upward. My ears popped, and I swallowed, steeling myself for the encounter.

The elevator doors slid open noiselessly. I stepped out first, distancing myself from Jin's henchman. The first thing I caught were the astounding views of Shanghai sprawling below us in gray concrete tinged pink from the setting sun. The Huangpu River wove like a silver ribbon through the city, sleek and elegant from this far up. Ships and boats bobbed like toys on the water. The pollution that choked Shanghai was unmistakable, dirty and opaque; a looming monster. Yet it didn't diminish the beauty of this ancient city, jammed with buildings and people and history.

I only saw Jin standing to the side a moment later, dressed immaculately in an expensive black suit, his hands clasped casually in front of him. "It's stunning, isn't it?" he asked, but it was more a statement. "I saved this highest floor for myself." He swept one arm toward the expansive space. "I haven't decided on the exact design, but the possibilities are endless." Jin nodded at the duffel bag I carried. "And the possibilities for Ms. Tsai's invention are infinite as well." He extended a hand, as if I'd walk up and give the prototype to him like an offering.

"I don't think so," I replied. "What's my guarantee you won't kill me the moment you have what you want?" I jerked my chin toward the other two guards lurking in the background, threatening and silent.

"You have my word—"

I laughed. "Your word means nothing."

"I suppose because your own word carries no weight," Jin said in a cool voice. "But in the world of business, our words matter. Besides, I wouldn't kill you with my own daughter present."

I felt the blood drain from my face, and my hands went numb.

Daiyu.

She stepped out from behind a square column, and the sight of her was like a punch in the face. I wanted to throw up. Daiyu was dressed in a formfitting black gown with gold and silver accents. Her complexion was ashen, despite the heavier makeup she wore for the occasion, but her expression gave nothing away.

"What's she doing here?" I asked, never looking directly at her. Jin had to believe that Daiyu meant nothing to me, though I was trying hard to gain control over my tumult of emotions. All the bravado I had felt before vanished in a wink. Everything had changed now that Daiyu was here. How would Jin use her against me?

"I wanted my daughter, as the heir of Jin Corp, to see what happens to criminals who steal from me." Jin raised his hand, and a slight man stepped forward. He wasn't dressed like Jin's thugs, and his eyes darted from Jin to his goons to me. My hand tightened on the duffel bag straps. "Check to make sure he brought the actual prototype," Jin ordered.

The man hesitated, and Jin said, "Now." He jumped and scurried over, bowing apologetically when he took the bag from me. I relinquished it without a word.

"This prototype never belonged to you," I said. "*You* were the one who stole it from Jany Tsai. The invention belongs to her family, as she had wished."

Taking a few long strides, I drew closer to Jin and away from Daiyu. I could only hope that everything was working as Lingyi had wanted on the ground, that they were hearing this—broadcasting our image and conversation. Jin's face was as unreadable as his daughter's, but one eye twitched. That was enough to tell me he was angry. No one denied Jin anything. No one had ever dared. "I offered her a large sum of money," he said. "More than a fair sum."

"Money she didn't want from you," I replied. "Jany didn't agree with your vision, and you killed her for it."

I heard a soft noise from Daiyu's direction—an intake of breath—but I didn't glance her way.

"The poor woman killed herself." Jin raised an eyebrow. "She couldn't take the pressure of her studies as a doctoral student. Heart-breaking, really."

Jin seemed to believe his own lie, as if he could rewrite reality, obliterate the truth—always twisting things to his own advantage.

"Her family never released that information. It's a convenient story you created as a cover-up," I replied. "But I know the truth."

Jin smiled coldly. "It doesn't matter what you know, Jason Zhou. You're worthless." His gaze flicked to the nervous man who was scrutinizing the prototype. The man's brow was creased in confusion. "Well?" Jin asked.

"This is the prototype containing the catalyst for filtration, Mr. Jin," the man replied. "But there's something else embedded into the machine."

Jin nodded once, and one of his thugs stepped forward, his gun aimed at my chest.

I sensed Daiyu tensing; I could only will her to stay put, to stay safe.

"I wouldn't do that." I grinned, resorting to the cockiness that I had always relied on as a defense. "If you kill me, the prototype will melt from the inside out. It's rigged to self-destruct if my heartbeat is no longer detected."

Jin didn't look at me but rounded on the engineer instead. "Is that true?"

The man wiped the sweat from his forehead with a shaking hand. "A device has been embedded into the prototype, and it does seem to be monitoring a heartbeat," he croaked.

"Remove it," Jin demanded.

I shook my head and winked at Jin. "That'll initiate the device as well. Tamper with it or kill me, everything melts."

The color rose to Jin's face like a wave, and I saw his throat work as he gained control over his anger.

"We have proof you murdered Jany for her design," I said. "You won't get away with it."

Daiyu stepped forward, and there was a flurry of activity from my peripheral vision. I turned to find a lanky man pushing Iris toward us, her arms pinned behind her back. She was resisting, and the guard visibly struggled to contain her. I almost cursed out loud but swallowed instead, making a choking noise. This time, my hand did go to my side, and I palmed one of Daiyu's knives. Iris stared at me, jaws clenched, and gave a slight shake of her head. The guard who had brought me up stepped forward. As fast as I could take Jin's thugs down, one of them would still be able to kill my friend.

We were outnumbered.

LINGYI

Lingyi hated the crowds.

Reports by four p.m. already had the number of people along the Bund at half a million. She held hands with Iris and Arun so they wouldn't get separated. Even then, people crashed carelessly against them, breaking their grasps many times. Hundreds of police were already lined up in key areas, controlling the flow of traffic to avoid stampedes. Jin's security, wearing dark green uniforms bearing Jin's insignia, were concentrated closer to Jin Tower's enormous quad near the building's entrance, where the VIPs would converge.

Although it was a milder summer day, the surge of the crowds only made the air feel hotter. Sweat gathered at the nape of her neck. She tugged the straw hat covering her purple hair down lower. Most of the young people in the crowd had dyed hair, but she didn't need to give Jin's thugs an easier way to spot her.

Iris led them, her strong fingers pressed against Lingyi's palm.

They pushed their way toward Jin Tower's entrance. Every so often, loud pops punched the air; firecrackers set off by revelers not caring how dangerous they were in such crowds. Lingyi's heart sped up every time, and she'd cower instinctively. Loud, unexpected noises still often paralyzed her in fear. But Iris never paused, and Lingyi forced her feet to keep moving, while Arun brought up the back. Seeing her panic, he squeezed her hand each time in reassurance.

Right outside the roped-off quad area was a small wood-paneled hut selling cold drinks, snacks, lunch-box meals, sun hats, and other sundries. A huge mob pressed against the front of the modest shop, and Lingyi entered through the narrow door in the back. The owner, a round woman with a bright turquoise apron tied to her waist, half turned and gave Lingyi a slight nod before returning to the customers shouting for iced tea and candy.

Lingyi had found this perfect location when she'd scoped the area with Iris the other day and paid the woman a good sum to be able to work on her MacFold from this location. It provided the space and privacy she needed, out of sight from Jin's security nearby. She set up on a squat stool in the dark corner, next to a small curtained-off storage area. "It's safe to come in," she said into her earpiece.

Iris was the first to enter, carrying her duffel bag. She slipped behind the dark cloth curtain, then reemerged wearing one of Jin's security uniforms and pulled a matching dark green cap over her silver hair. She winked at Lingyi and snuck in a kiss before stepping back outside. Arun came in and changed as well. He had been able to confirm that Jin's security would be wearing their usual uniforms and had gotten hold of two replicas in his and Iris's sizes for today.

Lingyi logged into her MacFold. Jin had focused on the security within Jin Tower, setting up required palm scans to enter the building and digital codes to use the elevator, restricting certain floors, but his cameras and building display systems were newly installed with minimal security. It hadn't taken too long for Lingyi to hack in, accessing Jin Tower's cameras and display programming. A message popped up on her Palm, showing simultaneously on her MacFold screen.

Who is this?

The message had been sent from Detective Lu, the policewoman Lingyi had bumped into the morning Jany had been killed. Lingyi had sent an anonymous message to her this morning, detailing the murder of Jany Tsai on Jin Feiming's orders so he could steal her invention and sell it as his own. Jany's supposed suicide was only a ruse. Lingyi said she was a witness to the crime and would like to file an official report.

Lingyi quickly typed a response: We crossed paths that morning you went to investigate. I'm the one with the purple hair. Keep a close eye on the Jin Tower opening ceremony today.

She closed the message window, hoping Detective Lu would take the tip seriously. Lingyi had done her research, and by all reports, Lu had a reputation for being forthright and honest, taking her job seriously. If corrupt, she'd simply take a large bribe from Jin and work in his favor instead.

She checked in with Arun and Iris. "How is the installation going?"

"One speaker is done, boss," Arun replied. "One to go."

"Same, boss," Iris said into her earpiece.

"Great," Lingyi said. "Keep me updated."

Zhou had learned from Daiyu that the ceremony would be set up with a stage and speakers in the large quad near Jin Tower's entrance, with everything taking place in this VIP area broadcasted in all-media news by the reporters who had been invited. Arun and Iris were installing devices to the four speakers that would connect directly to the powerful mic Zhou wore for his encounter with Jin. Everything they said would also automatically be shown as live caption across Jin Tower.

Lingyi tested the connection again between the devices installed on the already connected speakers and Zhou's mic. Everything was working perfectly. Arun and Iris just needed to hook up the other two speakers so Lingyi could broadcast everything at the right moment. She then toggled through the dozens of camera feeds installed in Jin Tower. Movement caught her eye on the highest 188th floor. She saw a few security people, then a figure dressed in a suit moving in the background that appeared to be Jin. It didn't surprise her that Jin would do this on the highest floor of the tower. Lingyi went into the program that was set to show across Jin Tower before the ceremony. There was a brief intro by Jin himself. Daiyu spoke a few words, and then the program went into a loop of advertisements and a digital fireworks display.

It was programmed to broadcast across Jin Tower beginning at six thirty p.m. Lingyi disabled it and connected it to display a live feed from Zhou's body cam instead.

She checked the time, 5:40 p.m. Zhou was on his way to Jin Tower. The crowd made a low humming roar outside the wooden shop, the anticipation building. News reports indicated that the crowds had now increased to seven hundred thousand. Lingyi wiped the sweat from her hairline with the back of a hand.

She heard Zhou speak to someone, one of Jin's men, when he arrived. Lingyi watched his progress on the feed from his hidden cam. He was headed into the building. After eight minutes of silence upon entering, Jin's man called for the elevator. Lingyi watched as the thug punched in a four-digit access code.

When she saw Jin greet Zhou on the 188th floor, she initiated the program that broadcasted across Jin Tower's glass paneling, now connected to Zhou's cam and mic. She quickly flicked through various news feeds that were covering the ceremony and finally settled on a cambot that had panned to Jin Tower. Its windows were blank, reflecting the dusk surrounding the city. Lingyi swallowed, checking her work. Her heart thumped hard against her rib cage. She turned on the devices attached to the speakers on the ground.

This had to work.

A moment later, Jin appeared on the giant building, larger than life. The crowd gasped around her, then began speaking excitedly.

Someone at the stand waiting to buy a drink pointed. "Look, there's Jin on the building!"

"Is this part of the opening ceremony show?" someone else exclaimed.

Lingyi quickly went to the news cambots set up in the VIP area. Their broadcasts would be able to pick up and amplify the speakers near the stage, across all-media news. She could only pray that Detective Lu was watching.

The roped-off VIP area was a chaotic scene as everyone tried to figure out what was going on. "Mr. Jin is speaking from the highest floor of Jin Tower. He appears to be discussing new technology. Possibly something that will be put on the market soon?" The reporter smiled uncertainly into the camera. "We assume this preprogrammed content is part of the ceremony. A glimpse into Jin Feiming's life as the powerful CEO of Jin Corp."

"My second speaker is connected," Arun said into Lingyi's earpiece. "And broadcasting loudly." She could hear the grin in his voice.

"Great," Lingyi replied. Barely in time. The more speakers they had projecting Jin and Zhou speaking, the bigger the impact. In an era when any image or piece of news could be manipulated, there would be no denying Jin's true character broadcast live to millions. And if anyone could provoke Jin, it'd be Zhou. Zhou had made Jin lose face by stealing from him twice, and Jin wanted to make sure Zhou paid the price.

The thought made Lingyi nervous for her friend, but she took five long breaths and concentrated on the connections instead. The best thing she could do for Zhou was make certain everything was broadcast, seen and heard.

"Is this supposed to be playing? It's early," Lingyi heard a woman—presumably one of Jin's security guards—ask Arun through her earpiece.

"Yes," Arun lied. "Everything's preprogrammed, was what I was told."

The guard replied with a loud *huh*. "Da Ge isn't here to run the show, and Xiao Chen barely seems to know what's going on himself," the woman said. Da Ge was probably still in the hospital recovering from his stab wounds.

"Just following instructions," Arun said.

The guard must have left as Lingyi listened after a short silence. "Iris," she said. "Progress?"

Iris didn't respond, and Lingyi could only hear the noise from the crowd in her earpiece, amplifying the real hum surrounding her. Then a gruff voice shouted, "Hey! What are you doing there?"

"Guarding the speaker," Iris said. "Just as I was told."

There was a noise, like something knocking into Iris's earpiece.

"Let me scan your badge," the man's voice said. A moment later, the same man said, "Xiao Chen, I've got a girl here with silver hair skulking around the speaker. I scanned her badge—it's a fake."

Lingyi felt the blood drain from her face. Iris had been caught.

"Yeah, I thought so too. Just like the boss warned," the gruff voice replied after a pause. "I'll bring her up now." Then his tone turned nasty. "You're coming with me!"

Crap.

Lingyi sprinted out, ducking beneath the roped area. Because everyone was so caught up with the unexpected projection on Jin Tower, no one took notice of her. Then she heard Arun's voice in her earpiece. "Xiao Chen asked me to help with the girl."

She saw a flash of Iris's silver hair—that man must have knocked off her cap—as she was dragged away from the crowded quad, toward Jin Tower's main entrance. Two of Jin's security guards flanked her; one of them was Arun. Lingyi pushed her way through the VIP area, using her short stature to her advantage in the hubbub.

She hid behind a pillar when the trio stopped in front of Jin Tower's main entrance. It was set far back and roped off, away from the masses. "Do you have clearance?" the man with the gruff voice asked Arun.

"Of course," Arun lied.

Lingyi saw the guard nod at the palm scan at the entrance. "Let's see."

Her heart fell. Even if she were at her MacFold, there was nothing she could do to help. Continuing with his bluff, Arun placed his palm on the scanner. The machine must have indicated failure, because the guard said, "Doesn't look it. Stay down here. I've got the girl."

"Keep the door open, Arun," Lingyi said into her earpiece. "Keep it open however you can."

The only indication that Arun had heard her was a flick of his head to the side as he glanced toward the VIP area. The lanky guard used the palm scan, and the doors slid open a few seconds later. He roughly pushed Iris into the building. After they had entered, Arun lunged at the slowly closing doors. Lingyi ran toward him a minute later.

Arun was staring into Jin Tower, and she followed his gaze. Iris and the guard had already disappeared into its depths. "What are you doing out here?" he whispered.

"I've got to help Iris," she said. She had reacted viscerally when she ran out from where she had been safely hidden. All she could think was that Iris was in trouble. It was happening again—everything was going wrong—just like last time.

"I'll follow her," Arun said.

He had wedged the only thing he could use, his rectangular taser, between the doors. It probably wouldn't hold for much longer. "I'll go," Lingyi insisted. "Hopefully the police will be arriving soon. Look for a woman—Detective Lu. Take her to the highest floor."

Arun's mouth pressed into a hard line, but there was no time to argue. "Be careful, boss," he replied, and forced the doors open wider for her. She slipped through easily and considered picking up the taser, but when Arun let go, the device was crushed this time as the doors shut. They stared at each other through the clear glass for a moment, before Arun nodded once and she nodded back, then ran toward the elevator.

CHAPTER SEVENTEEN

ZHOU

"Didn't I say no interruptions?" Jin appeared calm but ready to punish the new guard who had appeared.

The guard bowed his head apologetically. "I found this girl impersonating security in the VIP area below. Xiao Chen thought it was best to bring her up to you directly as you had instructed us."

The man thrust Iris forward, wrenching her arms behind her back. She winced, and it was hard for me not to lunge at the thug. Jin's dark eyes lit with recognition. "You," he said. He nodded once at the guard, an indication of his approval. The man opened his mouth, as if he wanted to say more, but Jin lifted a hand, silencing him. "You aren't the hacker girl I wanted—but I believe you are someone she cares for."

At the mention of Lingyi, Iris doubled over, then slammed her head back, smashing the guard hard in the face.

"Fuck!" the man screamed. Blood streaked from his already swelling nose. His grip loosened on Iris, but before she twisted free, the guard who had brought me up clamped down on her.

She stilled and glared murderously at Jin.

"Yes, we found Ms. Tsai's wiped laptop in your suite, and I saw video of your group stealing out of your hotel." Jin smiled an indulgent smile; one you'd give to placate a difficult child. "But I know the design still exists somewhere. You and your friends have soft hearts. You wouldn't have destroyed it knowing the catalyst can help so many—and help Ms. Tsai's family, too." He turned to me, slanting his head. "It's your predictability that makes this so easy."

Jin didn't even look at Iris but nodded once at the guard who held her. The man pulled a gun and pressed it against her temple. My entire body tensed at the sight, pulse going on overdrive. I forced myself to focus, to think. I could throw my knife and hit the guard, but I couldn't trust that he wouldn't pull the trigger even with a knife in his chest.

Crap.

I lifted my shirt, pressing my thumbprint to the monitor connected to the prototype, then ripped it off. "I've deactivated it. Just take the prototype and let her go."

The two guards who had been here with Jin from the start both came forward. One lifted a gun and pointed it at me.

"That was rash," Jin said. "And foolish. Like you said, there really is no reason to keep you alive now."

Daiyu stepped in front of me. "Enough," she said in a cool voice, but I could sense her trembling.

"Move, Daughter," Jin replied. "You forget whose side you're on."

Daiyu raised her chin, and the diamond drop earrings in her lobes swayed with the motion. "I know which side I'm on—and it's not yours, Father." She enunciated the last word, said without warmth; something discarded.

No one noticed the guard with the broken nose drop to the floor. He had retreated into the shadows, clutching something to his face, trying not to whimper. Lingyi appeared from nowhere and slinked toward Jin, Iris, and the thugs' backs. I wanted to scream for her to turn around. Run!

"I have a very clear understanding of how you run your business now," Daiyu replied. "You resort to theft and intimidation. Is this what you wanted me to witness—what you wanted me to learn as your heir?"

"So you'd rather side with your thug boyfriend?" Jin's mouth curled in derision. "A thief and liar?"

"*You're* the thief and liar," Daiyu said. "You're a murderer."

Jin laughed, shaking his head. "You'll never pin anything on me. I'll disown you; you'll never have Jin Corp."

"I don't care," Daiyu said. "*I* was the one who helped them steal back the prototype."

Jin took a step toward Daiyu. His face had reddened in rage, and he lifted a fist without even seeming to realize it. "You?"

"Yes, I did it." Daiyu stared her father down. "Jany's catalyst is already in production. Thousands will be ready for the market within a week. I personally helped to fund it. Her design will never be yours. *Father.*"

"You lie," Jin said. His jaw muscles jumped, and I saw a vein pop at his throat. I flexed my arm, feeling the heft of my throwing knife, ready to push Daiyu out of the way if Jin was livid enough to hurt his own daughter. I couldn't see the expression on her face, but whatever Jin glimpsed there convinced him she was telling the truth.

He looked at the guard pressing a gun to Iris's temple and gave a slight nod.

A signal.

Instinctively, I stepped to the side, away from Daiyu, and threw my knife. A single shot rang out, and something slammed into my side. I reeled backward from the impact.

"Jason!" Daiyu screamed.

"Yes, I ordered Ms. Tsai killed. She was dispensable." Jin directed his words at Daiyu; he spoke slowly and evenly, but there was no mistaking the wrath beneath. "And so is he."

I felt wet warmth on my stomach and glanced down; the left side of my shirt was soaked in blood. I didn't feel pain, only like the wind had been knocked out of me. I drew another knife. My body buzzed with adrenaline. The man who shot me had doubled over, grasping a hilt in his chest, then collapsed to the floor, writhing. I guessed we were even. Iris stood alone, a sleep injection in each hand, physically blocking Lingyi from Jin.

Spots danced across my vision, and I clenched my knife, letting its cold hilt ground me. My thumb grazed over the hidden button that activated the blade's poison. Jin pivoted and, seeing Lingyi behind Iris, lunged at the girls. Jin was tall, and his reach was long. Iris dodged, keeping Lingyi behind her. Jin had missed grabbing Lingyi but was lunging again. I cocked my arm back and threw the knife.

"Stop! Police!" a woman's voice bellowed from the elevator. I heard the echo of feet running toward us.

"Jason," Daiyu said, her voice hoarse when she caught my arm's smooth motion.

The blade struck Jin in the upper back, and he stiffened, then jerked to face me, snarling in rage. Lingyi and Iris scrambled away from him even as the police surged toward us.

"Don't move!" shouted the policewoman. "Drop your weapons!" Her gun was pointed at Jin.

Jin swayed on his feet, his eyes never leaving me. "Arrest this boy. He stole from me!" he roared.

Daiyu stood beside me; I could feel her holding her breath. She had seen the hilt of the knife that hit her father—one of two she had gifted me not so long ago. But it felt like a lifetime.

"You're under arrest for the possible murder of Jany Tsai," the policewoman said as two of her colleagues came up and one grasped him by the arm.

"You can't arrest me," Jin said. "I know people in the police department."

"You can't bribe your way out of this," the woman replied. She held up a Palm Plus, showing a video of Jin displayed across Jin Tower's side. "Everything you said and did in here was broadcast live to millions. It's already gone viral."

Jin stared at the moving image of himself on the Palm, his words transcribed and scrolled vertically beside him, finally comprehending what had happened. His face leached of color, and his breathing became ragged. "I want to speak with my lawyer."

"I don't know how things work in Taiwan, Jin," the policewoman said. "But you can speak to your lawyer when we allow it."

They ushered him into the elevator in a wheelchair, swarmed by police.

I stumbled, and my vision blackened.

"Please, can someone call an ambulance?" Daiyu had wrapped an arm around me, holding me up. "He's bleeding out from a gunshot wound."

I leaned into Daiyu, breathing in her familiar perfume warmed against her skin. In the end, I hadn't activated the poison. I had told her long ago in a dark alleyway that things were never the same after you'd killed someone. I'd rather Jin rot in jail for as long as we could keep him there—knowing exactly what we'd taken away from him.

Lingyi ran up and pressed something against my wound. My knees buckled from the pain, and if it weren't for Daiyu, I would have fallen over. Suddenly, a squat policeman was holding me up from the other side. "Let's get him onto the stretcher," he said.

The next thing I knew, I was lying down, shaking uncontrollably. Paramedics bustled around me, applying pressure to the wound, which made me black out. I woke again and saw blearily that Daiyu was clutching my hand, but I couldn't feel it. Iris and Lingyi stood on the other side. Arun suddenly appeared. I blinked, wondering if I was hallucinating.

"Hang in there, man," he said. Arun looked like he was about to cry. "I'll follow you to the hospital."

I tried to nod.

"Jason," Daiyu said. My eyes had closed without my realizing, and I forced them open to look at her. There was a bright glow around her head, exactly like a halo. My vision was going. She was crying.

"Don't," I whispered. "I'll be all right."

I couldn't seem to draw enough breath to say more.

"I love you, Jason," she replied from somewhere far away.

I felt an oxygen mask pressed over my face and the rumble of wheels below me as they pushed the stretcher away.

I love you too.

▲▼▲

Bright lights seared my vision and loud voices pounded in my ears. Then people spoke in hushed and serious tones. I felt pain through a heavy fog that blanketed my body, robbing me of movement— robbing me of my thoughts and senses.

"You always said you weren't afraid to die, Zhou." Little demon me appeared on my bare shoulder. He had removed his tuxedo jacket, and a lock of hair fell into his eyes. His white shirt was drenched in blood. "Are you afraid now?"

DAIYU

There was so much blood.

Daiyu didn't realize until Jason swayed, and she wrapped an arm around him, then looked down; his shirt was soaked dark red. It seeped bigger, growing like an ink spill. His face had gone ashen, and a sheen of sweat gathered at his hairline. She watched in horror as his eyes slowly rolled upward. She was going to lose him; he would die right there in her arms.

For a second, she couldn't find her voice. The she screamed, "Please! Can someone call an ambulance?" She swallowed the sob erupting in her chest. "He's bleeding out from a gunshot wound."

Jason slumped against her, and inexplicably pressed his nose against her throat; it almost felt like a kiss. Lingyi ran up, the whites of her eyes standing out. Lingyi's terror hit Daiyu hard, resonating with her own. Lingyi put something against Jason's gunshot wound, and he doubled over in pain.

A stout paramedic appeared. "Let's get him onto the stretcher."

Suddenly, they were surrounded by people and a cacophony of noise. Multiple conversations buzzed in her ears, people shouted instructions, and voices crackled through in earpieces. Jason was lifted onto the stretcher, and although Daiyu tried to stay near him, she was repeatedly pushed aside as emergency paramedics worked to stabilize him. She and his friends managed to speak with Jason for a few seconds before they wheeled him away. "I love you, Jason," she shouted in desperation; she *needed* him to know. But she wasn't sure if he heard her.

Daiyu forced herself into the elevator with the stretcher. Lingyi and Iris stayed behind, stopped by a police detective who wanted to speak with them. She followed Jason closely when they were on the ground floor. Arun was by his side, talking in urgent tones with one of the paramedics. They emerged at the back exit, away from the crowds, and Jason was loaded into the airambulance. But when she tried to climb on, one of the paramedics blocked her. "There's no room."

Arun had gotten on, and he nodded at her. "Meet me at the hospital."

She was feeling frantic and trying hard not to panic. Every second counted, she knew. "I'll see you there," she managed to reply, before they pulled the doors shut in her face.

After the ambulance drove off, lifting into the air, Daiyu stood frozen, watching it grow smaller and smaller. She suddenly felt lost. She had to get to the hospital. Running back inside Jin Tower, she headed toward the front entrance, only to be confronted with a flurry of flashes, blinding her momentarily as the photographers took their photos. "Ms. Jin! Ms. Jin! Is it true about your father murdering a Ms. Jany Tsai?" It seemed hundreds of voices shouted at her. The crowd in the VIP area surged, and the only thing keeping them back were the few Jin security guards who had lingered in the quad.

But all attention shifted when a police car appeared from around the building. Her father sat in the backseat, his hands cuffed in front of him like a common criminal. But the most astounding thing was the knife still buried in his upper back, forcing him to hunch over. She learned later that when the airambulance arrived, they deemed Jason as the emergency, and her father was relegated to a police car instead for his ride to the hospital. A paramedic had determined he was stable, but it was safer to wait for a surgeon to extract the knife. Daiyu gaped along with everyone else, and the reporters all stampeded toward the police car, but were shoved back by police escorts.

The car lurched awkwardly, trying to maneuver its way through the mobs. Her father bowed his head; his hair was sticking up and his collar askew. She had never seen him look so disheveled. And that, inexplicably, broke Daiyu's heart. She mourned for something that had never been—a loving relationship between them. He had never truly been a father to her, but he was still her father. Then he raised his head to look out the window and met Daiyu's gaze. She flinched but didn't turn away. Instead, she fisted her hands and jerked her chin up in defiance, and his eyes slid from her, barely registering recognition.

When the car disappeared behind the throngs following it, a sob she had been holding back ever since Jason collapsed into her arms shuddered through her entire being. Again and again. She wiped the tears from her face and hugged her arms around herself, trying to still her body, trying to swallow down the sobs that threatened to rip from her throat.

Jason had said she did have the ability to choose, and now her father was being dragged to jail—thrust into the Chinese criminal justice system, which was probably corrupt itself. It'd likely be merciless.

The thought of Jason knocked Daiyu from her stupor. She messaged her chauffeur, Xiao Wu, who ignored the no-fly zone around Jin Tower amid the chaos and landed the airlimo just twenty feet away. She climbed inside and asked to be taken to the Shanghai University Hospital. He didn't ask any questions but simply soared upward after the handful of people who still remained in the VIP area scurried out of the limo's way.

As they headed away from the Bund, the loud whistling of fireworks filled the air, and a collective gasp rose from the crowds below. Daiyu turned and saw fiery red sparks explode in a plume right behind her, followed by gold and silver florets. Booms reverberated, then more colors splintered the darkened skies: blues, purples, and greens.

Daiyu watched for as long as she could from the airlimo's expansive windows.

It was a fireworks display like Shanghai had never seen—just as her father had promised.

ZHOU

I made it to the hospital alive.

Barely.

I had lost a lot of blood. The doctors took me straight to the operating room, administered blood transfusions, and opened my abdomen to assess the damage from the gunshot wound. The bullet had only hit me in the intestines, and they were able to remove the damaged portion and stitch me up again without complications.

It helped that I was young and healthy. It helped that I got damned lucky the bullet hadn't hit any vital organs or arteries or shattered bone. It helped that I got the best medical care available thanks to Arun's reputation and newly earned wealth. He told the hospital he would cover everything.

It helped that I *did* want to live.

"Daiyu never left the hospital once," Lingyi told me after I came to. "Arun had to force her to eat and sleep. Iris went to Daiyu's suite at the Peninsula and brought her changes of clothing and toiletries."

That surprised me. I knew that Iris had never been a fan of Daiyu, and I said as much to Lingyi. "We were all terrified for you,

Zhou," she replied, her eyes suddenly bright with tears. "And it was clear to everyone how much Daiyu cared for you—where her loyalties lay—especially after all she did to help us lock her own father in jail."

I learned all this from my friends in my days of recovery in the hospital after my operation.

But when I finally came to for the first time, it was Daiyu who was there by my side.

▲▼▲

I gained awareness again slowly after the operation, like rising through heavy darkness toward an obscure light. I had never felt so weighted in my own body, bound by pain and tubes and wires. But something familiar prickled the back of my consciousness, and I forced my heavy eyelids open. My eyes felt as if they had been sewn shut. Daiyu stood by the side of my bed, clutching my hand. Her face was wet with tears, and for a moment, I thought I was still in Jin Tower on a stretcher.

"Daiyu," I croaked, but couldn't manage to make it sound like her name.

"Jason!" Her face lit up, and she swept her free hand over her cheeks, wiping away the tears. "You're awake."

I tried to smile, and then nodded, unsure if my face was working. "How long have I been out?" This time, they actually sounded like words.

"A few days," she replied, her gaze never leaving me.

"Are you all right?" I asked.

Her brown eyes widened; then she let out a strained laugh. "*I didn't get shot at.*"

I glanced down at myself, tucked beneath white sheets and a blue blanket. Daiyu squeezed my hand, and I suddenly felt tingling in my fingers. "I'll be all right," I said.

"The doctors said you'll be back to normal in a few weeks." She stared at our hands. "But for hours"—she drew a shaking breath—"we didn't know anything. There was blood everywhere. Jason, I was so afraid." Her chin trembled.

I squeezed her hand this time. "Hey," I said. "I made it. I'm here."

She nodded, attempting a wavering smile.

"Come here." I shifted in the wide hospital bed. Machines beeped and equipment jangled.

"What are you doing?" Her dark eyebrows drew together.

I must have been in some luxury wing or somewhere with a private room. The large window showed a tree with bright green leaves outside. An armchair was pulled close to my bed. "Come up." I released her hand and patted the bed; there was enough space for her.

"I don't think that's a good idea. . . ."

I patted the bed again and gave her what I hoped was a pleading look. She shook her head in half reprimand but climbed onto the high bed. I raised my right arm, and she tucked herself gently against me, making sure she didn't jostle any equipment. We settled against each other, and despite how foreign my own body felt, her weight against me was familiar—comforting. I felt content.

Every part of Daiyu that touched me seemed to bring me more and more back into myself: my chest where she rested her hand, her hip against my hip, our thighs pressed together. She wore denim shorts, and I could feel her warmth even beneath the layers of hospital bedding. I had missed her so much. If it took a gunshot to get me back to this place, back to us being together again, it was worth it.

She swept her palm in a small circular motion across my chest, careful to avoid my lower left side, where the bullet had hit. "You didn't use the poison," she said in a quiet voice. "On my father."

"No," I answered after a long pause. *I was tempted,* I thought. Instead I asked, "Where is he?"

"Locked up still," she replied. "The police are gathering evidence against him. Detective Lu came by the hospital, and I'll be speaking with her again in a few days. She's already talked with your friends."

"How do you feel about that? Testifying against your own father?"

"I'm glad he's finally behind bars," she said in a low voice. "I knew what the consequences might be when I chose to help you and your friends." She seemed to struggle with what she wanted to say next. "I'm sorry, Jason. I didn't mean to lie to you about keeping in touch with him all those months. I knew it would upset you, after all he had done to you and your friends. But—"

"He's still your father," I finished. "I know. I'm sorry too." I drew her closer to me and kissed her temple, feeling more alert than when

I had first woken. She shimmied higher to press her lips against my throat, where my heartbeat pulsed. My face flushed, and I clasped the hand she had placed against my chest with my own. The machine in the hospital room seemed to be making more noise; not a minute later, a nurse poked her head in.

"Oh," she said; her eyes widened when she saw us. "I came to check on Mr. Zhou. You called for assistance?"

I glanced at the button on the side of the hospital bed that I might have pressed by accident in all our shifting around.

Embarrassed, Daiyu was attempting to slide off the bed, but I brushed my hand down her arm, cajoling her to stay. "I just woke," I said to the nurse. "And I feel great."

She stared at me for a moment, then laughed. "I don't think this"—she nodded at Daiyu still lying against me—"would be approved by Dr. Gao."

I grinned my most charming grin. "Then please don't tell?"

The nurse laughed again, shook her head, and closed the door behind her.

CHAPTER EIGHTEEN

I waited five weeks before trying my first climb on my apartment's rock wall. My wound had healed easily and fast, leaving a pale, four-inch scar on the lower left side of my abdomen. The doctor had warned against lifting heavy objects for six weeks, even if I was feeling back to normal.

But I don't play patient well and was jumping out of my skin unable to lift weights or climb. In the end, I convinced myself that climbing wasn't actually lifting anything heavy. The belaybot would be taking most of my weight on the rope.

The belaybot whirled over, lights blinking eagerly when I called for it. I voice-commanded the most basic configuration on the wall—something I hadn't done in a long time. I'd take it easy, just like the doctor ordered. My fingers felt thick and clumsy as I put on the equipment, then finally stretched my arms overhead to take the first grip. My muscles strained, unused to the exertion, but I found a foothold and reached for a higher grip, using my legs to push myself upward.

I wobbled against the wall as I continued to climb higher, the sweat already sliding down my face. By the time I reached the top of the wall, it felt as if I'd hit my limit. I hadn't been this bad since I had first started climbing years ago. Wiping my damp forehead against my bicep, I craned my neck to assess the overhangs, wondering if I could manage it. I'd have to swing my way across to get to the opposite wall for my descent—something I did without thought before I had been shot.

It was because I thought I couldn't do it that I swung myself toward the overhanging bar, wincing. But despite being out of practice, I managed to navigate across the bars, swinging as the belaybot followed my progress below, the ropes moving with me. By the time I scrambled down the opposite wall, my limbs felt like cooked noodles. Still, I couldn't wipe the grin off my face as I got out of my harness. The belaybot gave me two toots of congratulations, handed me a towel, then wheeled away.

I swept the towel across my face and chest and was wiping the back of my neck when the apartment door snicked open, and Daiyu came in carrying three boxes piled high for our Mid-Autumn Festival gathering tonight. Her eyes widened when she saw me. "You didn't," she said as she walked across the apartment to set the boxes on my small glass dining table.

"I didn't," I agreed, heading for the shower.

"Liar!" she shouted at my retreating back.

But she couldn't have been too angry with me, because I saw the shape of her beyond the steamed glass of my shower wall a few minutes later, slipping out of her dress.

Arun was the first to show up at my apartment. He had come straight from the clinic, as the Mid-Autumn Festival fell on a weekday on the lunar calendar this year. He had cut his hair short but still dyed the tips in orange, spiking it in the front. "I brought pan-fried vegetarian buns." I could smell their delicious aroma before he handed two boxes over as Daiyu swept past me to give him a hug.

"I feel underdressed," Arun said after taking in the flowing light blue dress Daiyu wore. He glanced down at his own black tee with a purple cartoon tyrannosaurus on it. The dinosaur was enjoying a giant bowl of dandan noodles.

"You look great," she replied.

I placed the fried buns on the table. Daiyu had draped a pale lavender cloth over the top and arranged an assortment of round and square mooncakes onto a jade ceramic platter. I had made sure to request my favorite: lotus paste with salted yolk.

Arun walked over to my wall of windows; it was dusk, the horizon swathed in a deep pink mingled with Taipei's brown smog. The neon signs were just beginning to flicker to life in the city sprawling below us. "I'd forgotten this amazing view you had, Zhou."

I joined my friend at the windows. I might have gotten more used to these views, but I never took them for granted. "Victor always arranged to acquire the best in everything—including apartments for his delinquent friend."

Arun gave me a sidelong glance, tilting his chin up in wordless agreement. The Mid-Autumn Festival was meant to be a gathering of loved ones, family, and friends. It was a thanksgiving, to take stock of everything we should be grateful for in our lives. But for us, it'd be remembrance, too. "Maybe we'll actually be able to see the mountains that surround us one day?" I said.

Arun turned to Daiyu then and asked, "Isn't the Legislative Yuan going to vote at the end of this month?"

Daiyu was arranging a bouquet of flowers I had surprised her with in the kitchen. She looked up from the large deep purple lily she was trimming. "Yes, I think it'll finally pass." She had been working hard ever since returning from Shanghai over a month ago, speaking on all the popular talk shows, throwing glamorous fund-raisers broadcasted in all-media news to help the cause. She used her name and image to bring attention again and again to our country's need for reform.

She was also the head of Jin Corp now, while her father was locked in jail. Jin had hired the best lawyers to help him, but his influence in China wasn't the same as it was in Taiwan. Although he got preferential treatment—he was kept in a private and more comfortable setting than the usual criminal—he was still locked up. And it didn't look like he'd be getting out anytime soon.

The Chinese police didn't allow him to have any business contacts or make any business decisions while imprisoned. Daiyu put an immediate stop to the work on suit production in the new Jin Corp located in Beijing, but Jin Tower still opened for business as Jin had planned. Despite the grand opening marred by Jin's arrest, the drama played worldwide in all-media news seemed to garner the building even more publicity. All the spaces sold, but Daiyu set aside several floors within the building for nonprofit organizations fighting for better environmental laws in China and access to education and medical care for the poor. I watched Daiyu make all these decisions for her father's company, knowing she knew full well what she was doing. Placing these organizations in one of the wealthiest and sought-after pieces of real estate in Shanghai gave them visibility as well as credibility. Jin's reputation might have been tarnished by the arrest, but his billionaire status held; and the public was casting an eye more and more toward Daiyu, Jin Corp's official heir, seeing what she was promoting or investing in.

The front door buzzed; I glimpsed Lingyi's bright purple hair and Iris standing behind her in our door monitor. I voice-commanded the door open and greeted them at the entrance. Lingyi hugged me awkwardly, as she was carrying two bags of groceries. She held them up after she hugged Arun, then Daiyu as well. "I'm making a mushroom and lotus roots dish." She threw a glance behind her. "Iris has the roasted duck we just picked up and lotus buns—still hot."

Iris headed to the small table and set her boxes down—it was almost entirely covered with food now. Iris wasn't a hugger, but she turned and made eye contact with each of us—her way of saying hi. Lingyi swept into my kitchen, and Arun followed to help her prepare the vegetarian dishes.

"I'll get a platter for the duck," Daiyu said.

"How's it going?" Iris asked after we were alone in the main room.

"Been feeling caged," I replied. "But I finally climbed today."

Iris arched one eyebrow. "That must have felt great, and you're not back in the hospital, so it probably went okay."

I laughed; I knew she was teasing. "It was a little rough, but it felt damned good."

Iris leaned over, and we bumped fists. She loved to climb too, and I'd barely ever seen her standing still. If anyone could empathize with how hard the recuperation process had been for me, it'd be Iris. The loud sound of food hitting a hot wok interrupted our conversation, and then the mouthwatering aroma of stir-fried garlic and chives wafted over to us.

Daiyu emerged from the kitchen with a square platter five minutes later; her hand glided across my lower back when she passed, sending a jolt through me. She put the platter down after rearranging the food. Iris opened the container with the duck, and Daiyu used chopsticks to put the pieces on the plate.

I brought out cold beers and iced teas when the vegetable dishes were done, and we pulled carved wooden stools toward the floor-to-ceiling windows to enjoy our meal together. The full moon hung low across the horizon, a nimbus of pollution tingeing its pale glow. Aircars flitted across the cityscape as *you*s made their way to fancy restaurants to celebrate the occasion.

We sat and ate in silence for a few minutes, enjoying the delicious food, but also one another's company—to be together in celebration instead of in hiding with our lives on the line, not knowing what might go wrong next.

Arun cleared his throat and raised his beer bottle. "To Zhou, for hosting this gathering, but also for surviving his first gunshot wound."

"First!" Daiyu exclaimed. "And last, I'd hope—"

"Yeah, what are you trying to imply?" I interjected.

Arun took a long swig of his beer and shrugged. "I'm not implying anything." He nodded at Daiyu. "I'm sorry, but your boyfriend is an assload of trouble."

Iris and Lingyi burst out laughing.

"Someone had to tell you." Arun grinned.

"I should have known better"—Daiyu gave me a sideways glance—"than to fall in love with a boy who plays with knives."

This elicited a loud *ha* from Arun, but Daiyu had slid her hand over to grasp my fingers during the exchange and gave them a squeeze when she replied to him. I had barely registered her joke, only hearing the *in love with a boy* part. I felt the heat rise from my neck to my face and took a long drink from my own beer to try and cover my rush of emotions. Daiyu had never been shy about sharing her feelings for me, but she had never declared it so boldly to my friends—to everyone I loved and who mattered to me in this world. And they accepted it, eyes glowing, their own cheeks pink from the food and company.

I lifted my own beer and said, "To Dr. Nataraj. Your mom was a mom to all of us, Arun. She loved us like we were her own kids." My friends grew quiet, but their eyes still shone. Each of them raised their drinks too.

"She always told us to do right," Lingyi said. "She *showed* us in everything that she did."

Arun lowered his head, overcome, and Lingyi put an arm across his shoulders, hugging him. He nodded, but directed his words toward his feet. "She did do that. It's all she ever taught me. Do right, Arun; you can't go wrong following that path. Help those who are in need. . . ."

"She'd be so proud of you," Lingyi replied.

Arun raised his face and wiped the tears from his eyes. "She'd be proud of all of us."

We sat in silence for some time, gazing out at the moon. Lingyi then leaned forward and cleared her throat, saying, "To Jany." We all lifted our glasses. "I was the only one who knew her, but she would have fit right in with us. I'm grateful her legacy lives on." Jany's catalyst had revolutionized the air filtration market overnight and made her family very wealthy very fast. They would never want for anything again. Lingyi clinked her glass with Daiyu's. "Thank you, especially, for securing the loan to make this happen. You took a huge risk—in everything that you did."

Daiyu smiled, appearing almost shy. "I was happy to help, in every way."

"How are *you* doing, boss?" I asked in a soft voice. Lingyi looked good, more like herself again. That eternal crease of worry between her eyebrows hadn't appeared all night.

"Yeah, how's it going, boss?" Arun asked.

"I'm doing better," Lingyi replied. "I've been seeing someone—talking through things—it's helping."

After a pause, Iris raised her glass filled with iced jasmine tea. "And to Victor—"

We clinked our glasses one more time.

"Charmer," I said.

"Suavest," Arun added.

"Most dapper person I ever heisted with," Iris said.

Lingyi clinked her glass with ours last, not bothering to wipe away her own tears. "Sweet talker," she murmured. "And the most loyal friend."

We all nodded, and Daiyu drew closer to brush her lips against my cheek. I didn't realize until then that my own face was wet. I got up and retreated into the kitchen, grabbing more drinks for everyone as an excuse to disappear briefly.

It should have been me.

The thought always came unbidden: accusatory, filled with sadness and rage. But they weren't Victor's words; it was something he'd never say to me. I understood that tonight, sharing this moment of remembrance with my friends. Victor forgave those he loved—it was what made him such a great friend. And I needed to learn to forgive myself.

I felt arms slide around my waist. Daiyu took care not to put pressure on where I had been shot, although the wound had healed already. "Hey." She hugged me from behind, and I felt her warmth against my back. "Do you need help?"

Shifting, I wrapped an arm around her and slipped my other hand behind the smooth nape of her neck. She shivered, then ran both palms up my back, drawing me closer. We kissed, taking our time, making unspoken promises with our hands and our mouths. Forgetting everything, we got to the point where we'd usually be stumbling toward my unmade bed as we clumsily undressed each other. Instead, Arun shouted from the other room, "What's a bro gotta do to get a drink around here?"

We broke apart, and Daiyu pressed the back of her hand against her lips, unable to hide her grin. She ran her fingers through her hair and straightened her dress. "Uh, we'll be right out"—she stuttered, sounding as guilty as we actually were—"with more drinks."

My friends did nothing to disguise their titters and guffaws as I grabbed more drinks from the refrigerator and Daiyu set them on a tray before she swept back into the main living area and I followed.

The night had grown full dark, and I was greeted with the image of my friends with their backs to us, leaning against one another, their attention caught by the shimmering lights below as our city came to life. The moon had risen, growing smaller but brighter—a goddess in the sky. No, I could never take this view for granted.

Shanghai had been a stunning city, but Taipei was ours.

We joined our friends on the short, carved stools and passed more drinks around, fielding both their chatter and teasing all the while.

I glanced out the window and drew in a breath, feeling the city take me by the heart.

It was good to be home again.

ACKNOWLEDGMENTS

Ruse is the completion of my third published duology, and a novel I'm proud of and love, but it's also probably one of the hardest books I've ever had to write. I lost my father this January, and it never felt like I recovered from that, scrambling my way through the entirety of 2018, trying to keep my head above water. I know for many of us, 2018 was a challenging and difficult year.

It's why I especially feel for my crew in *Ruse*. They are left to deal with hard choices they have made as they grieve, wondering if the path they are choosing now is the right one—if anything they are trying to do to make their world better *matters*. I believe we are all unique and special and everything that we do to effect change, no matter how big or small, truly does make a difference. I believe in holding on to hope. This is a theme that I kept returning to personally this year, and that also arises in *Ruse*, though these kids are much more badass than I'll ever be.

This book would not have made it into your hands if not for precious friends who helped me tremendously along the way with plotting, with hugs, by offering literal refuge, or by lending an ear. I adore you, and I'm thankful for you, Malinda Lo, Holly Black, Sarah Rees Brennan, Cassie Clare, Shveta Thakrar, Kate Elliott, and Leigh Bardugo.

Much gratitude to Shenwei Chang for their pinyin help in *Want*, but more so for being insightful, smart, and witty and always brightening my day when our paths cross in virtual or real space. I look forward to reading their stories in the future!

Thank you to Andrea Horbinski, Joseph C. Chen, Dr. Natalie Grunkemeier, and Dr. Marcus Doane for their help in research for this book.

Eternal /bootay shakes! for my purglets!

Hugs for writing friends near and far, some I have been lucky enough to meet, some I look forward to meeting. Thank you for the commiseration and also the plans for world domination, Zen, Tade, Mia, Aliette, Alessa, Vida, Victor, Nene, and Rochita.

I owe so very much to my amazing critique group: Mark McDonough, Amy Mair, Morgan Blythe, and John Atcheson. Thank you for seeing me through so much plotting that it almost broke my brain. Special shout-out to John, who always gives me great ideas and lends his knowledge to these titles!

I feel so very lucky to have worked on *Ruse* with my wonderful editor, Jennifer Ung, who is so encouraging, warm, and incisive. This book will always hold a special place in my heart, and you are part of that! Thank you to the amazing team at Simon Pulse. I am gobsmacked to have another stunning cover by Jason Chan. Thank you, Jason!

This year, 2018, marks my ten-year anniversary with my delightful agent, Bill Contardi. More anon, Bill!

As ever, love to my m, sweet pea, and munchkin. And to my best friend since junior high, Jany Tsai, who kindly let me murder her in this novel.

Finally, I wanted to thank all the readers, librarians, and booksellers who championed *Want*. I know for a fact that *Want* would never have had the reach it did if not for your enthusiasm, and I feel so lucky and heart-full for those who have connected with Zhou and his friends. *Ruse* is for you. <3

November 14, 2018
San Diego, CA